BOUND BY LAW

BOOK ONE
OF THE BOUND BY STARS TRILOGY

A BRAD MADRID STORY

GLYNN STEWART

TERRY MIXON

**FAOLAN'S PEN
PUBLISHING**
faolanspen.com

This edition published in 2018 by:

Faolan's Pen Publishing Inc.

22 King St. S, Suite 300

Waterloo, Ontario

N2J 1N8 Canada

ISBN-13: 978-1-988035-78-9 (print)

A record of this book is available from Library and Archives Canada.

Printed in the United States of America

1 2 3 4 5 6 7 8 9 10

First edition

First printing: June 2018

Illustration © 2018 Jeff Brown Graphics

Faolan's Pen Publishing logo is a trademark of Faolan's Pen Publishing Inc.

Read more books from Glynn Stewart at faolanspen.com

CHAPTER ONE

Serenade Station wasn't a source of happy memories for Commodore Brad Madrid of the Vikings Mercenary Company. He owed the doctors there more than even they seemed to realize—not only had they saved his arm in the aftermath of a vicious battle out at Saturn's orbitals, but his presence there had brought bounty hunters and assassins that had left far too many innocents there dead.

But the same events that had left him with unpleasant memories of the primary human habitation in Jupiter's leading trojan cluster also meant that when the Board of Directors of Serenade Station made contact with the Mercenary Guild and requested that one Commodore Madrid meet with them, Brad made the trip.

The station itself was a sprawling complex of hab sections, industrial sites, and a small shipyard, but the main driver of Serenade Station's economy and reputation was the medical school that occupied its own semi-detached space station.

Right now, a destroyer and two corvettes hung over that station while a second destroyer pulled back from the dock Brad had just boarded through. A massive observation window allowed him to check over the status of his little fleet, and the dark-haired officer smiled to himself.

"Was it really necessary to bring an entire battle fleet?" a familiarly sardonic voice asked, and he turned to salute the attractive auburn-haired form of Dr. Gina Duvall.

"Somehow, I doubt your Board asked me to come all this way to discuss my opinion of their fashion choices," he told her. "Since my 'battle fleet' is my stock-in-trade, I figured I'd best bring them along."

He gestured to his companions.

"You know Michelle and Saburo," he continued, introducing his executive officer—and wife—Commander Michelle Hunt and his ground forces commander, Colonel Saburo Kawa.

Gina had been in the background on the mission to rescue Michelle from the pirates known as the Cadre, and she embraced the other woman and traded a handshake with Brad's Asian ground commander.

"There's more ships out there than anyone was expecting," Duvall said. "Picked up some friends?"

Brad chuckled.

"Fleet is on, what, their third round of cuts in the last two years?" he asked his wife.

"Only the second," Michelle replied. "It just feels worse to those of us who expect to end up replacing Fleet at the sharp end."

"Okay, two rounds of cutbacks," Brad allowed. "But since their lords and masters on Earth have told them to cut their ship strength, Fleet is selling off their older light units—and if you happen to be, say, a reserve Fleet officer, they're selling them at pennies on the dollar."

He gestured out the window. "Hence the *Bard*-class corvette *Alan-a-dale* and the *Bound*-class destroyer *Bound by Law*. I may not *like* why they were on the auction block, but I can't argue with the price."

"That's probably for the best," Duvall allowed as she joined him in looking out the observation window. "The extra ships might make the Board happier, considering what they've got themselves into."

"Whatever that is, I owe Serenade Station a debt of gratitude I can't easily repay," Brad told the doctor. "And you, particularly, but I also owe the Station in general. I suspect they'll be pleasantly surprised by my rates."

Duvall snorted. "I know what platinum-rated mercenary companies sell their services for. I suspect even your *discounted* rate will give the Board a collective heart attack."

"Probably," he allowed with a grin. "What do they need us for?"

"It's not my place to say," she said with a shrug. "I'm just the greeter. If you three will come with me, I'll let the Board explain that themselves."

————

Most of the time Brad had spent in Serenade Station had been in the long-term rehabilitation ward—he had, after all, arrived in a medical coma with his arm missing.

After that, he'd fled the station in something of a rush to avoid assassins and hadn't had much of a chance to take in the sights. He didn't think that Duvall was intentionally taking them on the scenic route, but their destination apparently had an atrium park in front of the entrance.

It was one of the largest he'd ever seen on a station, too. The trees and plants made him feel almost unwelcome, a looming presence of life around spacers used to utterly sterile environments.

If they bothered Duvall, though, she gave no sign of it as she led them to a nondescript entrance tucked away in the park. There was no name on the door, just the paired-snake caduceus of the medical profession.

"I thought the Board of Serenade Station would be in a bit more obvious of a location," Michelle murmured.

"Serenade's Board has multiple locations throughout the Station," Duvall said. "They mainly operate out of Serenade Central, the old ring station that anchors the industrial site."

Brad noted that the doctor hadn't answered Michelle's implied question as the door slid open to admit them into a reception area. A pair of young women in nondescript uniforms most readily described as "black combat scrubs" but carrying mono-blades and pistols met them as they came in.

One of the guards ran a scanner over them. "Nothing unexpected, Dr. Duvall," she told the woman who'd brought them in. "All three are carrying mono-blades, and Colonel Saburo and Commodore Madrid are both carrying pistols."

The guard smiled. "Both the Colonel and the Commodore have several other monofilament weapons on them, but nothing sufficient to threaten the Board."

"And what exactly are you looking for?" Saburo asked with an arched eyebrow.

"Bombs," the guard said flatly. "Or fully automatic weapons. Even you or your Commodore would have a problem taking out the Board with a blade or a semi-automatic pistol before we could stop you."

Brad smiled coolly. "We'll have to agree to disagree on that, but we aren't here to pose a security threat to the Board."

His answer seemed to discomfit the guard. "If you'll follow me, Director Yamada is waiting."

———

Somehow, Brad was unsurprised to enter a small conference room, plain except for a gold caduceus on the back wall, and find only one person waiting for them. He wasn't familiar with Director Yamada, but he'd suspected Gina Duvall had picked up a bit more importance since the chaos of their adventures across the Solar System.

Being directly involved in bringing down the most notorious pirate in a century or two tended to do that. A seat on Serenade's Board would be entirely reasonable...though in that case, where was the rest of the Board?

"Director Yamada," he greeted the gaunt and aged Japanese man on the other side of the conference. "I understood we were meeting with the Board of Directors of Serenade Station?"

"A necessary deception, Commodore, for which I apologize," Yamada told him. "I am Dr. Masami Yamada, a geneticist by profession."

"The good doctor, of course, undersells himself," Duvall added. "Dr. Yamada was responsible for the counter-viral agent synthesized to contain the Red Plague thirty years ago."

That was well before Brad's time, but it was hard to avoid learning about. The Red Plague had been a mutation of the bubonic plague that targeted a specific set of characteristics common to humans raised in space and artificial gravity.

It had killed over a million people—and the speed with which Commonwealth geneticists had developed the counter-virus was credited with saving at least a hundred times that. It was one of the success stories the Commonwealth used to remind people of its value.

"Yes, well, my victories of late have been far smaller," Yamada said. "Saving a handful of children from a rare genetic disease rarely makes headlines, even if it was actually *more* difficult than my work on the Red Plague."

He smiled and gestured for Brad and his people to sit. "Director Duvall *does* sit on the Board of Directors of Serenade Station," he noted calmly, "and the Board is aware of this meeting and has approved our use of their name."

"I see," Brad allowed, carefully taking a seat. "I doubt it's news to Dr. Duvall that I am highly sensitive to being lied to."

"It was necessary," Yamada stressed. "Director Duvall and I represent a two-thirds quorum of a smaller and quieter Board of Directors than that of Serenade Station. We, Commodore Madrid, speak for the Doctors' Guild of Sol."

Brad blinked and slowly straightened. "I did not know there *was* such a thing," he said slowly.

"Like your Mercenary Guild, we provide a necessary service and unifying factor for humanity's stations and habitats beyond the true reach of Earth's Commonwealth," Yamada said. "Unlike the Mercenary Guild, few outside the ranks of our members need to know we exist.

"Any doctor you have visited off Earth, however, has been certified by us," he noted. "We operate every medical school outside the homeworld. We coordinate money, personnel, and other resources to try and make certain that every human has access to a certain minimum medical care."

He shrugged delicately. "It's hardly news to you, I'm sure, that we're far from successful. The influence of the Cadre and similar pirates has long been a thorn in our side. They wish to maintain control of the Outer System—or to at least prevent anyone *else* from controlling it. Honestly, we don't give a rat's ass who runs anywhere, so long as we're allowed to freely operate."

"And this brings us to me…how?" Brad asked carefully. "And why the deception? If the Mercenary Guild knows about you…"

"It is not your Guild we're hiding from," Duvall assured him. "The Cadre has been quiet since you killed the Terror, but eighteen months is long enough for them to reestablish chains of command, and there were leaders that were never caught."

"Doctor, there was a *cruiser* that we never caught," Brad admitted. So long as *Lioness* was at large, the Cadre wasn't—couldn't be—truly dead. Even if Brad Madrid had literally cut off its head.

"Indeed," Duvall agreed. "And there is…*something* going on in the Commonwealth government. The degree to which the death of the Terror is being used as grounds for disarmament is concerning to us… even if we are mostly bound by the Hippocratic Oath."

Mostly, Brad suspected, specifically excluded the black-clad young women at the front door.

"Again, then, what do you need from me?" he asked.

"You are familiar with Oberon," Duvall said. It wasn't a question and Brad shivered as memories flashed across his vision.

"I've…visited," he said mildly. Oberon was the outermost of Uranus's moons, well beyond what was regarded as "civilized space." It was a decently sized settlement, if something of an anarchic mess.

"Oberon has always played host to a small clinic run by members of our Guild," Duvall explained. "Every time we've attempted to set up a larger facility or organization there, 'accidents' have happened."

"We want you to make certain no such accidents happen this time," Yamada told him firmly. "We've assembled a convoy here at Serenade Station. Six freighters, carrying eighty-three of our people, and approximately four hundred million in medicine, equipment, and prefabricated facilities."

"We need *you* to make *sure* they make it to Oberon," Duvall concluded. "Once there, we'll make arrangements with a Gold company for long-term protection."

"I owe you a lot. I also owe Serenade Station and this Guild of yours almost as much. Still," he said with a grin, "I can't work for free. I have ships and troops to pay for. Let's get down to the haggling. Or does the Hippocratic Oath bar that kind of fighting, too?"

"Assuredly not," Duvall said with a smile. "It will even allow us to keep reminding you of that debt you keep mentioning to get the best deal we can realistically expect. Let's strike a bargain we can all live with."

CHAPTER TWO

RETURNING TO *OATH OF VENGEANCE*, **Brad** pulled his senior officers into an immediate videoconference in his office. The destroyer allowed for more space than his old corvette had, but his office remained a tiny, austere space organized around his desk and the conferencing screens.

Four warships was a small enough force to get moving quickly—but large enough that coordination was key to getting them all moving in the same direction.

Michelle joined him from *Oath*, sitting in as *Oath*'s "captain" as he was also the commodore of the flotilla. Saburo was also present in person.

Heart of Vengeance was the first ship Brad had ever commanded, an ex-pirate corvette that had fallen into his hands as payment for saving the liner the pirates had attacked. She'd been heavily refitted since, and he had faith that the little ship could easily take one of her Fleet counterparts. Especially under her new captain—formerly her tactical officer—Commander Jason Finley.

Bound by Law and *Alan-a-dale* were more standardized than Brad's older ships, both being essentially-unmodified Fleet surplus. The destroyer *Bound by Law* was commanded by Brenda Andre, a Fleet officer of Brad's acquaintance who'd found herself as surplus as the ship. The corvette *Alan-a-dale*'s CO was an old Mercenary Guild hand, Jace Olhouser, who'd come highly recommended.

Even with the platoon-strength combat teams aboard the two destroyers, the Vikings weren't in the top ten for most powerfully equipped mercenary companies in the Solar System. Still, they were definitely in the top twenty and only barely missed the top ten for warship strength.

Brad Madrid had come a long way since he been Brad Mantruso, a security officer ejected out the airlock by the Terror and picked up by a luckily placed Fleet cruiser.

"All right, people, I'm sure this is a grand shock, but we have a contract," he told them with a grin. "In about twenty-four hours, a convoy is going to be leaving Serenade Station for Oberon with the cargo and staff necessary to set up what may be the first true hospital outside Jupiter's orbit."

Andre whistled softly, the stocky woman looking surprised. "That's...quite the project. I'm surprised they don't have a Fleet escort for that."

"For various reasons, the principals involved are no longer prepared to trust the Commonwealth Fleet," he said gravely. "Like our own Guild, our employers are finding the speed of the drawdown in Fleet assets concerning.

"Also, that same drawdown means Fleet units aren't readily available...and we are. Previous attempts to set up this kind of project have drawn Cadre attention, and despite their recent quiet, nobody thinks the Cadre is done. And everyone knows we're the bogeyman where the Cadre is concerned," he concluded with a cold smile.

"Because we seem to *like* fighting what are effectively military-grade pirate ships on a regular basis," Olhouser quipped. "That sounds like fun."

"It pays well," Finley pointed out. "And, frankly, I *love* sticking it to pirates."

"The Cadre *may* show up on this run, but our expected opposition is more likely regular pirates," Brad said. "We're going to be escorting roughly half a billion in medicine and medical equipment. I doubt that managed to stay quiet enough to keep pirates from finding out about it."

"So, we expect to be using torpedoes and gatlings, not boots on the ground," Saburo said with a nod. "Nice to know we get to be passengers for once, boss."

"Once we get to Oberon, the ground troopers will be providing security until the long-term security contractors show up," Brad said. "Until then, you can be as lazy as you want."

"So, training and damage control drills, check," the Colonel confirmed with an approving nod.

"We have a list of the ships already," Brad continued. "None of them have more than popguns: a couple of six-barrel mass drivers for security. Keeping them all alive will be up to us. My current plan is to put *Bound by Law* in front, trail with *Oath of Vengeance*, and have the corvettes orbit the formation."

Thoughtful nods answered him. The biggest question was always going to be where to put *Bound by Law*. Unlike the rest of the company, *Law* was a gunship-type destroyer.

Most of the weapons manufacturers in the Solar System had standardized around the fifteen-millimeter, five-hundred-kilometer-per-second mass driver with varying numbers of barrels in a gatling arrangement. The only difference, really, between the popguns on the freighters and the guns on Brad's corvettes and *Oath of Vengeance* was the number of barrels. *Oath* and his corvettes had torpedo tubes as their main ship-killers.

Bound by Law didn't carry a single torpedo. Instead, she had dorsal and ventral turrets with paired fifteen-*centimeter* mass drivers firing a seven-hundred-kilometer-per-second round. In addition, she had sixteen standard eight-barrel mass driver gatlings for defense.

Their lack of active tracking meant that heavy mass driver turrets were normally a mid-tier armament on cruisers or battleships, but the *Bound* class had been an experiment. Brad had one of them, with a line on acquiring others as they were decommissioned.

The *Bound*-class ships hadn't really been considered obsolete so much as overly specialized, and in a Fleet that was cutting its hulls, a specialized ship-killer was less valuable than a ship that could do a dozen other jobs.

For the Viking Mercenary Company's mission, however, a specialized ship-killer was *exactly* what the doctor had ordered.

———

"So, did you confirm that this Doctors' Guild even exists?" Michelle asked Brad in their cabin later. Six months of marriage had put her influence all over the space, including a picture of her old diver ship from Saturn opposite his own complex nano-forged knotwork art.

She was even more used to austere spaces than he was, however, and the comfortable new furniture in the cabin had been installed by the ship's builder, Saburo's father, who had known Brad all too well by then.

One advantage of running a mercenary company was that no one particularly cared if the ship's captain was married to their XO. It wasn't particularly uncommon, to Brad's knowledge—especially in the Vikings, where Commander Finley was married to his coms officer, and *Bound by Law*'s combat team commander, Trista Doary, was engaged to *Law*'s tactical officer, Lisa Simon.

The scars across Michelle's back made Brad wince as she continued undressing. He'd done everything in his power to rescue her after the Cadre captured her, but they both knew she'd only lived long enough for him to do so because the Terror had wanted her as bait.

"It does," he replied. "It's actually in the files they give all of the platinum-rated commanders. It just hadn't ever come up for me before, oddly."

"It seems weird that a Guild as large and important as that is so secret," Michelle pointed out as she sat at the small built-in vanity and began brushing her hair.

"They don't need to be public," he said as his eyes drank her in. "People know where to look for a doctor. They don't necessarily need to know what kind of association or Guild is behind that doctor."

"And some people aren't willing to let others get proper care," his wife said grimly.

"Or are happier to make themselves a buck, covered in blood as it would be," he agreed. "I have no hesitation introducing anyone who decides to attack a medical convoy to the worst the Vikings can do."

Bound by Law's main guns had been fired in exactly one action for the Vikings so far, and the pirate corvettes that had tried to swarm the mercenary destroyer hadn't lasted long enough to complete their charge.

"It's been a weird couple of years," Michelle said. "But I'm okay with that." She shook her head. "Two years ago, I don't know if I'd have said that."

"I don't think Shelly thought I'd be *that* bad an influence when she introduced us," Brad replied, crossing the state room and wrapping her into his arms. They both had their regular therapist appointments, but theirs wasn't a life that leant itself to stable hearts and minds.

"My best friend was a mercenary and I was okay with that idea," Michelle reminded him. Shelly Weldon had been Brad's communication officer then. Now she was Finley's, keeping the married couple together aboard *Heart*.

"But I didn't expect to ever be the one giving the order to end lives. Now, though..." She shivered against him, and it wasn't from any chill.

"Vengeance is unhealthy," she concluded calmly, hugging him fiercely. "And everyone I'd want revenge on is already dead. That doesn't mean I can't make damn sure no one else ends up in the hands of similar assholes."

"It's a good life goal," he agreed. "And as a nice bonus, people *pay* us to do it."

CHAPTER THREE

BRAD KEPT an eye on the ships in the convoy as he sat on *Oath*'s bridge. The destroyer had been built from the ground up for the jobs it needed to do, which gave it a slightly different layout from Fleet ships. Brad's command chair with its repeater screens sat on a raised dais at the back of the space, with consoles for ship control in front of him.

All of that was identical to Fleet. The consoles to his left side, where Michelle and Brad could provide overwatch to Saburo's ground operations, would have been elsewhere on a Fleet ship, but the mercenary destroyer needed to be as capable in its attack-transport role as its warship role.

Six freighters with four warships in escort formation was one of the largest collections of ships Brad had ever seen away from the planetary systems or places like the trojan cluster that was home to Serenade Station. Only the Commonwealth Fleet usually had groups of ships moving around, and even that had been less and less of late.

Even regular pirates had been quieter in the eighteen months since Brad Madrid and his people had attacked the Cadre's main base with a nuclear door-knocker, but he knew that couldn't last. There was *somebody* behind the Cadre—the Terror had managed to produce an entire division of troops for the all-out assault on a Saturn refinery where Michelle had been captured, after all.

Until Brad had seen that "somebody" dragged out into the open and either shot or locked away, he knew that the Cadre would always be reborn.

"Boss, check this out," Konrad Bogdanov, *Oath*'s new tactical officer, said. The dark-haired man was actually from somewhere on Earth—Poland or Bulgaria or Russia or maybe Brazil; Brad's Earth geography was rusty at best—though the ex-Fleet officer never talked about why he hadn't gone back after Fleet declared him "redundant to requirements" and placed him in the reserves.

"What am I checking out?" Brad asked, crossing his bridge to lean over Bogdanov's shoulder.

"This here," the older man told his captain, pointing at his console. "It *could* be a sensor ghost, but…"

"But it could also be a frigate or corvette ghosting us outside what they think is our resolution range," Brad agreed, studying the data codes on the screen. Their shadow was on a ballistic course parallel to the convoy, but it was hard to hide your heat signature in space. "Can we get an optical on him?"

"*Alan-a-dale* is closest," Bogdanov replied. "She could be able to get a line on her, but I can't give Commander Olhouser orders."

Brad chuckled. "We're mercenaries, Konrad. Our chain of command is *much* more flexible than Fleet, especially if you ask nicely."

"If you say so, boss," the ex-Fleet officer said with a slight shrug. "She's out of torpedo range, but we could probably introduce her to some gatling fire—if we're smart about it, Captain Andre might be able to tag her with *Law*'s main guns."

It was tempting. There was no corvette or frigate built that could survive a direct hit from *Law*'s heavy mass drivers, but…

"We're mercenaries," Brad repeated. "That means we're still technically civilians and operate under something closer to police rules of engagement than Fleet." He shook his head. "We don't get to shoot first unless we're *very* sure. I'll talk to Jace. Let's see what our ghost really is."

————

"Yeah, that is not a ghost," Jace Olhouser agreed cheerfully. "It's an old *Barbados*-class frigate. It's a piece of junk with a single torpedo tube. What in the Everdark is she doing out here?"

"Scouting," Brad replied as he studied their unexpected companion in the data the other man was sending to him via laser. "You only need one torpedo to threaten merchant ships, so pirates are about the last people still using anything we'd call a frigate. That makes our friend a scout for a heavier force that hasn't revealed itself yet."

"What do we do about her?" Olhouser asked.

Brad shared a long look with Bogdanov. "If we warn her off, he knows we've spotted her and her friends will come in expecting trouble. That would make our life harder."

"*Alan-a-dale* could take her," the corvette captain volunteered.

"Guild and Commonwealth rules say we challenge before we open fire," Brad reminded Olhouser. This far out, Commonwealth authority was a polite fiction at best, but the Vikings had to go back to places where that authority was quite real, and breaking Guild rules was a rapid way to set the company on the road to bankruptcy.

"No, we'll pretend we don't see her," Brad decided. "If her captain thinks he's outside our useful resolution, then his friends will use that as part of their planning. So, if they're *wrong*…"

"Then we'll see them coming before they think we will," Olhouser agreed. "I'd *rather* blow the bastard out of the sky, though."

"And I'd prefer not to have to justify an unprovoked murder to the Guild," Brad said firmly. "We'll bring the flotilla to Ready Status Bravo and keep our eyes peeled. When this prick's friends show up, I want to introduce them to the Guild's *finest* hospitality."

————

The pirates at least *thought* they were being clever. Their second group of ships came swimming up out of the dark twelve hours after Bogdanov had picked up the initial scout, coming in at a relatively high velocity but keeping their acceleration down as they approached the convoy.

Unfortunately for them, stealth in space was difficult, expensive, and relatively ineffective…and they didn't have the heat sinks to even make it possible. "Sneaking up" on the convoy would have required Brad and his Vikings to not have been paying attention.

One didn't become a platinum-rated mercenary company by not paying attention.

"I make it two big boys that are either heavy corvettes or small destroyers, and six corvettes or frigates, including the initial *Barbados*," Bogdanov reported. "Range is about thirty thousand kilometers, and their overtake is about twenty kilometers per second. They've kept their acceleration under one meter per second squared, so they're going to be a while closing the distance."

"They're probably going to cut even that shortly," Brad replied as he considered the data on the screen. "Unless they've badly mis-assessed us, they have to realize that their only hope is to get to the powered range of their torpedoes and launch before we detect them."

"Are we assuming competence on the part of pirates?" his tactical officer asked suspiciously.

"In this case, yes," Brad said flatly. "I've seen too many Cadre flotillas in operation to expect amateur hour when it comes to the fight, though. Don't confuse a weakness in strategy with one in tactics once the torpedoes start flying."

"With that bunch of junk?" his wife asked from the pilot's station, her tone derisive. "I'm pretty sure this is amateur hour."

"*Heart* was a pirate ship once," he reminded her. "You can do a lot with imagination, time, and money. Nonetheless, I think we can safely assume these are hostile."

He slapped a key on his wrist-comp. "Vikings, battle stations." He turned to his communications officer. "Xan, get me a comms channel."

Xan Wong nodded once before pounding through a series of commands on her channel before she flipped her boss a thumbs-up.

Brad smiled thinly and faced his video pickup. "Unidentified vessels, this is Commodore Brad Madrid of the Vikings Mercenary Company," he told them. "We're out in the middle of nowhere, so you'll have to forgive me, but I can't trust your presence to be innocent. I have no choice but to order you to maintain a twenty-five-thousand-kilometer safety radius around my convoy. If you cross that line, I will regard your vessels as pirates and act to defend my clients. This is your only warning."

At the practical ranges where modern spaceships could interact, time delay wasn't really a factor. The pirate flotilla responded to his transmission almost instantly—but they didn't respond by communicating or trying to run.

"All eight ships have brought their engines up to full," Bogdanov reported. "They are now closing at twelve mps squared."

Brad's captains were linked in via videoconferencing to his command chair, and he shook his head at them. "I see no reason to get fancy or take risks. Captain Andre, the moment they cross the twenty-five-thousand-kilometer mark, you are to open fire with your heavy mass drivers. Anything that survives *Bound by Law*'s fire gets a full salvo of torpedoes from every ship as soon as they get into powered range.

"Keep your gatlings in defensive mode and set them to cover the convoy. We can all take a torpedo hit on the ablatives if we need to, but the freighters sure as Everlit can't."

Brenda Andre smiled evilly. "I don't think we're going to need to worry about that, boss."

———

Eight spaceships charged toward Brad's convoy and he watched them come with cold eyes. An amateur might look at the numbers—eight ships to four, equal numbers of destroyers—and think the Vikings were in trouble.

They'd be wrong. Oh so very wrong.

"*Law* has opened fire," Bogdanov reported.

It was hard to miss. The destroyer had to be careful how she fired her guns: the four fifteen-centimeter mass drivers had enough recoil to visibly move the ship, and the energy signature spiked across his screens.

The big slugs crossed the space to the incoming pirates in seconds and, to no one's surprise, missed the lead destroyer by about fifty kilometers.

The Vikings' Commodore counted down in his head. *Law*'s guns were vastly more powerful than the regular mass drivers in the rest of his ships' gatling drivers…but they also took a lot longer to fire.

Thirty-six seconds after the first salvo, *Bound by Law* lurched on his screens again, a second salvo of four rounds flashing across space.

Andre had the measure of her enemy now and had spread her fire perfectly. A multi-kilogram steel slug slammed into the second of the two destroyers. Armor could do a lot, especially the *right* kind of armor…but that was a four-kiloton impact.

And the pirate didn't have the right kind of armor. The hyper-sensitive ablative strips covering Brad's ships would allow them to survive a hit from one of *Bound by Law*'s heavy guns. Maybe even two hits.

The pirate destroyer didn't have ablative armor at all, and Andre's shot hit her about a quarter of the way back from her prow and proceeded to tear a hole through the rest of the ship.

"Second destroyer is down," Bogdanov superfluously reported. "Looks like Commander Hunt is correct: this *is* amateur hour. Second-rate ships, third-rate crews."

Something itched at the back of Brad's mind as he watched the pirates.

"Then why aren't they breaking off?" he asked slowly. "Pirates aren't death-or-glory types; they're here for profit and they know *our* mission is to protect the convoy. They can build enough of a side vector to stop us tagging them with anything except *Law*'s guns and extreme-range torpedo fire. So, why aren't they?"

Seconds ticked by in silence on his bridge, counting down to the third salvo from *Bound by Law*.

At this range, Brenda would still be taking measuring shots. Even that single hit on the second salvo was luck crossed with the fact that the enemy had no idea how to maneuver when dealing with heavy mass drivers.

As if to prove his thought, her third salvo went wide—but one round *barely* missed the surviving destroyer.

"They're amateurs, all right," his wife said softly. "So, either they somehow think they can still take us—unlikely—or they're more terrified of whoever sent them than they are of dying."

"Or they know something we don't," Brad pointed out. He looked at the link to *Bound by Law* and *Heart of Vengeance*'s commanding officers. "Brenda, Jason, hold this side of the convoy and keep these bastards occupied. They're out of their weight class and they know it, which means they're expecting a sucker punch. Jace, swing *Alan-a-dale* a thousand klicks out on the other side of the convoy and give me full active scanners. Assume you're hunting Fleet cruisers, Commander Olhouser, because I'm betting someone's got Fleet heat sinks."

His COs responded with a series of surprised affirmatives, setting to carrying out his orders immediately.

"What do we do?" Bogdanov asked.

Brad's expression might have been called a smile, if someone was being generous. "Michelle, swing us into the heat shadow of the biggest freighter in the convoy. Konrad—bring up *our* heat sinks."

CHAPTER FOUR

Two of the pirate corvettes disappeared from the scanners as Michelle sneaked *Oath of Vengeance* into the shadow of the convoy's freighters, the heavy slugs from *Bound by Law*'s guns obliterating the smaller vessels with crushing force.

Capacity charts flashed up on Brad's screens as his tactical officer activated their heat sinks and his wife cut their engines to a minimum. The heat sinks could contain *some* engine heat, but every second of firing the engines used up capacity that could absorb hours of regular operations.

"*Alan-a-dale* is in position for the sensor sweep; she's going live now," Bogdanov reported. "We're dark and quiet, drifting out of the convoy's trail, towards Commander Olhouser." The Slavic man paused. "If you're wrong, boss, we're leaving two ships to fight five on their own."

Brad snorted. "Look at them, Konrad. Those are the worst of the worst, useless amateurs even by pirate standards. They're not a unified force, they have no combined tactics—they're a bunch of fourth-tier solo ships unified by fear of somebody bigger than them. And they're getting more scared of Captain Andre by the second."

Three of the eight pirate ships were gone, and while the remainder continued toward the convoy, what little formation and organization they'd had was long gone. They were still moving together, but an experienced eye could pick out that they were in no position to cover one other against torpedoes.

"They'll break," Brad told his tac officer. "And whoever sent them knew they would. They're not the threat. They never were." He shook his head. "They're enough of one that we have to respect it, but the real problem is…"

"Bogies on the scopes!" Michelle barked. "Multiple bogies and one *massive* heat shield. What in Everlit?"

Brad looked at the data himself and echoed his executive officer's curse. "Clever fuckers. I don't know what that shield *is*, but it did a damn good job of hiding their heat signatures, and we *still* can't see past it."

The familiar cold smile returned to his face. He wasn't nearly as much of a berserker as he'd once edged toward being, but he wasn't going to turn up the chance to give some pirates—*especially* some competent pirates—a really bad day.

"Olhouser," he said to *Alan-a-dale*'s Captain. "That shield is going to block their weapons fire until they get rid of it. I'm assuming they have a plan for that, but let's make them accelerate it. Torpedoes down the center, if you please."

Alan-a-dale rotated from her position parallel to the convoy to point toward the oncoming pirate force. The heat shield made it impossible for Brad to distinguish numbers beyond "multiple," which meant the heat shield had to go.

Jace Olhouser's ship had the tools for that, and the paired torpedo launchers in *Alan-a-dale*'s nose flashed alive in response to Brad's orders. The kinetic weapons blasted toward the heat shield at an acceleration that would have killed any human crew.

The torpedoes wouldn't make it to the heat shield with their engines still firing, but the multi-kilometer-wide umbrella wasn't going to dodge very well, either. They'd have to accept the incoming fire or get rid of the shield. Personally, he had a strong suspicion which option they'd choose.

"And there we go," Brad said in satisfaction as the heat shield suddenly started to shrink, the thin material—probably aluminum or mylar or something similarly reflective and flexible—rolling back into whatever package it had sprung from.

"Everlit preserve us," Michelle half-whispered as the shield disappeared, revealing the Vikings' enemy.

"I make three destroyer-sized vessels, four corvette-sized ships, and thirty of…something else," Bogdanov reported. "Boss, I have no idea what those smaller ships are."

Brad nodded, studying them carefully. "They're going to be a problem," he said softly. "That much I'm sure of."

———

"Boss, something is *not* right."

Captain Brenda Andre sounded stressed. More stressed than her own part of the engagement could justify. *Bound by Law* had racked up four more kills in the fight so far and the pirates didn't look like they were going to live to reach firing range to strike back.

"There's a few things not right," Brad said calmly. "But I'm guessing you're talking about the pirate squadron on our Solward flank?"

"Yeah, except they *aren't* pirates. Have you IDed them yet?"

"Konrad's working on it."

"Run them against the Fleet listing," his ex-Fleet officer told him. "I see four *Invictus*-class heavy corvettes, a *Bound*-class destroyer, a *Corsair*-class destroyer, and thirty Javelin interceptor drones.

"Which means the big-ass 'destroyer' hanging back from the rest is a *Spearthrower*-class carrier, and there are only eight of those in the Everdarkened star system, Commodore. Fleet wasn't decommissioning any of them, I might add."

Before he'd been a mercenary commander, Brad had been a spaceship-obsessed engineer and security officer. He'd kept up that knowledge base since, but a Javelin interceptor was new to him. "Why haven't I heard of them?"

"Because the drones are semi-autonomous and Fleet doesn't like to advertise that there are computers out there fulfilling kill orders under their own auspices," Andre said grimly. "They weren't particularly efficient, all things considered, and require computer tech the pirates shouldn't have."

Brad considered what the woman was saying carefully. "Are you telling me that the squadron about to attack our convoy is *Fleet*?"

"I wish I could be certain they weren't," Andre told him desperately. "But every one of those ships is a current- or last-generation Fleet unit, and *nobody* else is supposed to have carriers. Whatever we do, we can't open fire on them without confirming one way or the other."

"I beg to differ," Commodore Brad Madrid told his Captain coldly. "If these people are attacking a convoy under my protection, Captain Andre, I don't care whose flag they're flying."

Andre paused, and he heard her swallow. "If they're attacking the convoy, they're in violation of their oaths," she finally agreed. "But you can't fight thirty Javelins and two modern destroyers with just *Oath* and *Alan-a-dale*."

"We'll have to see," Brad admitted. "I need you to cover the convoy from that first bunch. What am I looking at with these Javelins?"

"A single set of quad drivers and kinetic torps. They'll come at you hard and fast, using their own velocity to drop the torpedoes. They've only got one apiece, but those torps will come in faster than you're used to because the launch platforms are closing at speed too."

"Understood," he said. "Deal with those pirates and swing over to join us. We've got work to do. Either these bastards are rogue Fleet or they're Cadre." His cold smile didn't waver. "Either way, we are going to introduce them to the error of their ways."

Oath of Vengeance picked up speed now, still keeping her acceleration down as she flew away from the convoy, but now that Brad knew where his enemies were, they could radiate heat away from them.

The destroyer would still be visible to radar or optics, but thermal sensors were the fastest and easiest method to spot anything in space. The oncoming pirates "knew" where the Vikings were, and were approaching at speed.

The carrier was hanging back, her velocity low enough to allow an easy escape. The other six ships and their escorting drones weren't being nearly as cautious.

"The pirates in group one are breaking off," Bogdanov reported. "*Law* got a glancing hit on the second destroyer, and the whole lot just decided they're more scared of dying than they are of whoever organized this shitshow. Should Andre finish them?"

Normally, Brad would be tempted. Dead pirates ceased to be a problem, after all. This situation was far from normal, though.

"When the enemy has brought their own dedicated ship-killer, I want ours in play," he said. "Let the amateurs go. They were only ever a distraction."

"What about us?"

"Lay in your torps, Konrad," Brad ordered. "Hold your first salvo until they see us and then pound that gunship until she stops twitching. Keep half of the gatlings on her; use the other half to discourage the drones.

"Olhouser." He linked in to the corvette commander. "Use your torpedoes on the pirate *Bound* and cover yourself against the drones with all of your gatlings. Every Javelin we shoot down before she launches her torpedo is one less problem."

"Even with that, we have a lot of problems," Olhouser said. "Time to even the odds, yes?"

"We're going to try and sneak up on the gunship," Brad said. "But for the rest of the flotilla: fire at will."

Despite the steady growth of the Vikings Mercenary Company from Brad's single ex-pirate corvette to his current small fleet, this was his first time actually commanding a multi-ship action—and he was only starting to realize how little control he could actually exert.

The limitations of weaponry kept the battle at a scale where he could give near-real-time orders to his ship commanders, but they knew their ships and positioning better than he did. He'd hired competent people. Despite his urge to micromanage, he *knew* it was a bad idea.

That still didn't make it any easier for him to metaphorically sit on his hands and watch as *Alan-a-dale* opened fire and the other two ships flipped "over" the convoy toward the incoming pirate fleet.

Technically, Brad was required to summon any incoming force to stand off or surrender before firing, but he was counting this as the same force as the last one—and he knew the Guild would back him if someone harassed him over it.

The Mercenary Guild's two dozen platinum companies brought in a fifth of the Guild's revenue despite only being roughly a twentieth of their people.

The incoming force didn't pretend to be anything other than what they were, though. Almost at the same moment as *Alan-a-dale*'s torpedoes launched, *Oath of Vengeance*'s sensors picked up the energy spike of the pirate's *Bound*-class destroyer firing.

"Everlit keep them from hitting the convoy by accident," Michelle breathed. "Even one hit…"

"Get us closer," Brad ordered.

"How close do you *want?*" his wife demanded. "We're in extreme torpedo range."

As she asked, six of the drones dropped out of their attack formation. Their new vectors took a second to settle down—and they opened fire with their gatling mass drivers before *Oath*'s computers had dialed them in. *Alan-a-dale*'s lonely pair of torpedoes disintegrated under their fire.

"As close as they'll let us get," Brad ordered. *Alan-a-dale*'s mass drivers were opening fire on the closing drones now. Brad wasn't a huge fan of Fleet's general standard of the eight-barrel mass driver, but he had to admit that the *Bard* class had a *lot* of the things.

Olhouser's command probably wasn't going to be killing destroyers today, but she was a solid counter to the fragile and expendable drones.

A second flash of fire from the enemy gunship destroyer warned him of the corollary: *Alan-a-dale* had to *survive* to counter the drones—and the drones, in turn, weren't coming after the corvette.

With *Oath* still in stealth and *Bound by Law* on the other side of the freighters still, the drones were going for the convoy.

———

Brad watched *Alan-a-dale* charge into the teeth of the interceptors, gatling drivers blazing as Olhouser did his damnedest to protect the convoy. Thirty drones, however remote-controlled and stupid, versus one corvette was not a winning equation.

Two of the drones blew apart, and four dove directly *at* the corvette to intercept the second salvo of torpedoes. For a few seconds, it looked like they were going to successfully ram the corvette, something Brad wasn't sure the ex-Fleet ship could survive.

Then all four vanished in matched balls of fire as *Bound by Law* cleared the convoy and demonstrated why flying in a straight line around a gunship was an extremely bad idea. Four heavy mass-driver rounds hit four separate drones and the enemy was down a fifth of their force.

But not before two of them fired, and even desperate last-ditch gatling fire couldn't stop the weapons at that close a range. Ablative armor detonated, pushing the torpedoes away and reducing the impact, but *Alan-a-dale* still took both torpedo hits.

The mercenary corvette spun away from the impacts, mostly intact but clearly no longer properly under control. Brad sent the Everlit a silent prayer for his crew as he tried to assess the situation, feeling as if his failure to keep on top of things was getting people killed.

The second wave of drones collided with *Law* and *Heart*, gatling fire flickering between the two mercenary warships and the smaller robots. The drones seemed to be saving their torpedoes for the freighters, but their gatlings were enough to strip armor and external sensors away from the warships.

And then a salvo from the pirate gunship caught *Bound by Law*. Two of the fifteen-centimeter rounds missed completely. A third scored a glancing blow that the ablatives flicked off into space.

The last slammed dead-center into *Bound by Law*'s dorsal turret, ripping the structure apart and scattering debris and bodies into space.

"There goes hiding," Brad snapped, even though *Oath of Vengeance* was being more successful at the stealthy approach than they had any right to expect in this mess. "Konrad, engage the pirate *Bound*."

He didn't need to give any more orders; he'd already told the tactical officer how he wanted to engage. *Oath* shivered as the destroyer's weapons spoke, her heat sinks venting as well as torpedoes and gatling rounds were flung into space.

They took the pirates by surprise. They shouldn't have, and that was the first confirmation Brad really had that whatever ships they might be flying, his opponents weren't Fleet. Fleet wouldn't have lost track of a destroyer in the fight.

Mass-driver rounds hammered into the hostile gunship, slamming her off course as she tried to redirect her heavy guns toward *Oath*. Her defensive fire was late and off course—and then the dazzler rounds in *Oath*'s salvo lit up.

Two of the torpedoes disintegrated, spending themselves in sparkling bursts of chaff and energy that covered the rest of the salvo. The pirate ship hadn't been ready for that—hadn't been ready for *Oath of Vengeance* to enter the fight at all.

Four torpedoes slammed into the *Bound*-class destroyer, punching through her ablative armor and sending her careening away from the fight in a dozen pieces.

"*Yes!*" Brad hissed. "Well done, Konrad. Now hit that *Corsair* and let's clean up this mess!"

———

In Brad's experience, one of the best ways to tell the difference between serious pirates and their amateur cousins was to watch how they reacted when the battle turned against them. The first wave of pirates, the distraction, had pushed harder and longer than they should have, but had lost all coherency and organization along the way.

Whoever was in command of this new squadron—and unlike the first group, Brad was certain someone *was* in command, probably aboard the carrier—clearly wasn't prepared to throw good money after bad. They'd lost a destroyer and half a dozen drones, none of which could be easily replaced.

As *Oath* lunged toward the *Corsair* and her *Invictus* companions, they all launched torpedoes at her. That was a *lot* of torpedoes, but

Brad's flagship was within range to be covered by the rest of his flotilla now, and it was still extreme range for the torpedoes. He had better than even odds of surviving the salvo.

His opponent clearly agreed, because all five ships turned as soon as they'd fired and went to emergency acceleration. They flung themselves away from him at over thirty meters per second squared, falling back on the carrier that was already vectoring away.

Most of the Javelins followed, but ten of the drones followed the torpedoes in. Brad closed up his vac-suit helmet and strapped himself in. This was going to be rough.

"Any orders?" Bogdanov asked quietly.

"You know your job, Konrad. Link your systems to *Heart* and *Law*, and coordinate your fire. The priority remains the convoy. If it's between letting *Oath* take a hit and letting a freighter take a hit, you know what to do."

His tactical officer nodded silently, turning his attention back to his screens and focusing on the gatlings. With a few keystrokes, Brad assumed direct control of the destroyer's torpedoes.

Michelle was dodging them around on their original vector, confusing the incoming fire as best she could. The torpedoes were smart but not that smart. Between the gatlings, the electronic countermeasures, the supporting fire from the rest of the flotilla, and the fact that Brad's wife was one Everlit star of a pilot, the incoming fire wasn't the big threat.

The ten Javelins closing the distance with their own torpedoes aboard were. They were receiving orders from their mothership, *and* their onboard computers were a lot smarter than a torpedo's.

How much smarter, Brad hoped not to find out.

He re-sequenced his loading queues, the first salvo blasting into space almost as an afterthought. He needed to clear his tubes for the specialty munitions he was loading, so he flung eight torpedoes at the drones.

It bought his people time if nothing else, forcing the Javelin drones to evade and shoot down the incoming fire. To his surprise, he actually *hit* one, the remote-controlled space fighter vanishing in a brief fireball.

Two more died under the guns of his flotilla and then his salvo was ready. Eight of the stupidly expensive dazzler ECM torpedoes blazed into space, charging toward an enemy that he hoped wasn't bright enough to work out what Brad was doing.

"Drones are launching!" Michelle snapped. "Seven more torps incoming and they are moving fast."

"And now they're blind," Brad replied calmly as he triggered the dazzlers. The drone fighters had better sensors than their torpedoes, but he'd flung the anti-sensor weapons directly into their faces, disrupting their sensors and their coms.

Heavy mass-driver slugs from *Bound by Law*'s remaining turret smashed half of the survivors to pieces, and then *Heart of Vengeance* slashed into the middle of the drones' formation. Brad's old ship obliterated the remaining drones in a single pass.

"Are we clear?" he asked after a moment.

"We're clear," Michelle confirmed a few seconds later. "Enemy force is out of range, opening the distance fast." She shook her head. "We'll have them on thermal for a while, but there's no way we can catch them."

"We can't chase them in any case," Brad said regretfully, checking *Oath*'s damage reports. The ablative armor had dealt with most of the fire they'd taken, but that only meant that he had a lot of ablative strips to replace. *Bound by Law* and *Alan-a-dale* were much less lucky.

"We need to watch the convoy and we need to watch *Law* and *Alan*," he continued. "Let's get an S&R team in motion. I want to know if *Alan-a-dale* is an evac or a tow."

CHAPTER FIVE

IT TOOK over an hour to get *Alan-a-dale* stabilized and a team aboard. The corvette had spun off on a chaotic course that left her getting farther away from the convoy by the second.

Thankfully, once they'd managed to link up to the little ship, the shuttle crew was able to connect Brad with Jace Olhouser.

"Commander, it's good to see you alive," Brad told the other mercenary. Today was a victory, but if they'd lost *Alan-a-dale*, it would have been a victory with more casualties than his entire previous career.

He'd still lost as many of his people today as in any other single mission he'd led. That stung.

"It's good to *be* alive," Olhouser told him. "The impact knocked out our coms—and most of the crew, including myself."

The dark-skinned mercenary had a large white bandage wrapped around his shaven head, and the screens visible behind him were dark.

"I didn't actually lose anyone," Olhouser continued. "Damn miracle, so far as I can tell, but it's true. What I *did* lose was my power core. Emergency systems scrammed the pebble bed when we were hit."

Brad nodded his understanding. In the middle of the battle, *Oath's* sensors wouldn't have been able to distinguish between the debris from the hit and the debris from the safety protocol blasting *Alan-a-dale*'s radioactive uranium pebbles into space.

"Can you get it back up?" he asked. Even *Heart of Vengeance* ran a primary fusion plant and could restart her reactor from her fuel tanks, needing only a power boost from another ship in the worst-case scenario. *Alan-a-dale* was his only fission-powered ship, and even his own experience as an engineer and spaceship nerd left him only vaguely aware of a modern pebble-bed nuclear reactor's emergency protocols.

"Scramming only blows about ten percent of the pebble bed into space," the junior man explained. "The rest is just split up to make sure we don't have an unintentional critical mass." Olhouser shook his head. "Of course, I don't have a power core to put them back *into*," he quipped. "I have a wrecked mess of debris and cables that used to be a power core."

"Is *Alan-a-dale* salvageable?" Brad asked bluntly. Fissionable uranium was relatively straightforward to come by, even out there. The skills and material necessary to rebuild a micro-pebble reactor core… Brad wasn't so sure.

"We can rebuild the plant ourselves," Olhouser told him. "The value of something like this is that it's basically just pipes and water, boss. It's not a fast process, but we can rebuild the plant."

"All right. Do you have life support if we take you in tow?" the Commodore said. He'd salvage the corvette if he could, but he wasn't going to risk his people. He'd lost enough of them today.

"I wouldn't turn down a power cable along with the tow lines," *Alan-a-dale*'s commander answered. "The environmentals are intact, but everyone over here will be happier if we're not running them off the batteries!"

Brad chuckled, an honest if drained laugh.

"All right, Commander. I think we can make that happen."

———

"Is there any assistance we can provide, Commodore?" Captain Garibaldi asked. The tall woman with the shaved head and the pale white skin was the senior captain of the Doctors' Guild convoy, an employee of the Guild though not a doctor herself.

"I doubt it's a surprise that we have medical supplies and doctors available if you need them," she noted with a smile.

"We have medical staff aboard all of my ships and, frankly, space battle doesn't leave a lot of wounded behind," Brad admitted to her image on the screen. "That said, if you've got a medical team to spare to check out *Alan-a-dale*'s crew and make sure any of my stubborn idiots who *should* be resting actually do so, I'd appreciate it."

"We can do that," Garibaldi promised. "Do we need to delay the convoy any further?"

"No," Brad told her. "*Oath of Vengeance* has *Alan-a-dale* in tow; we'll be fine to get everyone to Oberon. A little late, but not too badly."

He'd pass on the location of the wreckage of the pirate fleet to the Commonwealth Intelligence Agency once they were at Oberon. They had the resources to try and identify the source of the ships—and didn't have a convoy to escort, either.

"We can afford to be late," Garibaldi pointed out. "We can afford it better than we can afford losing your ships."

"Further delay won't make any difference," he admitted. "*Bound by Law* needs serious shipyard time, and even *Oath* could use a few days with access to a decent repair slip. There's a limit to what we can do in deep space."

They'd continued coasting toward Oberon while the Vikings were sorting out the fate of their damaged companion, but bringing the convoy's engines online would still cut over a day off their trip—and they could only go a few more days before they had to decelerate anyway.

"Of course," Garibaldi allowed. "I'll admit I'm out of touch around the refit-and-repair requirements of warships; I'm just a merchant captain."

Brad glanced at the screen showing Garibaldi's six-ship convoy, the vessels alone worth more than many well-populated stations' annual GDP.

"So I see," he said dryly. "I'll warn you, Captain, that your employers may be less than happy with the 'expenses covered' clause in my contract when we're done."

The Guild captain shook her head sadly.

"Commodore, the only thing my employers are going to be unhappy with is that any of your people had to die," she told him. "We can always make more money, but even we can't bring back the dead."

———

In the end, one of *Alan-a-dale*'s crew of fourteen didn't make it. *Bound by Law* had lost twenty of a crew of sixty. *Oath of Vengeance* had lost three.

Twenty-four dead. For a "victory," that left the taste of ashes in Brad's mouth. They'd saved the new hospital for Oberon, but the enemy they'd faced was terrifying. Navy surplus in the hands of the Mercenary Guild was one thing.

Navy surplus in the hands of pirates was another—and of the ships that had attacked the convoy, only the two destroyers were of classes that were supposed to be undergoing decommissioning.

"They're not going to magically come back to life if you keep staring at the names," Michelle told him as she entered their quarters. His wife hadn't even bothered to look at the screen to see what he was looking at.

Brad sighed.

"Would it help to admit I'm *also* studying the ships that came after us?" he asked. "This whole thing stinks."

His XO dropped her uniform jacket with its blazon of a large Viking warrior over a chair, which she pulled over to him before strad-dling it.

"Yes," she agreed calmly. "You're not from out here, Brad. I am. We don't *see* Fleet capital ships. Corvettes? Sure. But the only destroyers we see out here are either Guild or pirate."

"When the Cadre attacked Saturn, there was a Fleet cruiser force nearby," Brad pointed out. "It's not like Fleet doesn't get out here."

"They're out here, yes," she agreed. "But they're not *seen* out here. Odd distinction, but an important one. Plus, well..." Michelle shrugged. "Saturn isn't really 'out here' as I mean it, love. Jupiter and the Belt are still civilization as the Outer System sees it. Saturn's more of a gray zone—but the real Outer System starts at Saturn's trojan clusters and Uranus's moons.

"There's six million people out here in the dark, same population as the Jupiter planetary system, but spread out to the Everdark and back again. Fleet might come out here, but even a dozen ships are a drop in the bucket against this much of the Everdark."

Brad shivered. He'd been raised on a freighter that mostly did the Mars–Belt run and had never been farther out than Jupiter until he'd become a mercenary commander.

"So, two last-generation destroyers and a carrier is not exactly a normal sight out here," he noted.

"Fuck, did anyone except Brenda even know the carriers *existed*?" Michelle demanded. "I sure as Everlit didn't.

"Neither did I," he admitted. "That's the scary part. Almost scarier, though, are those *Invictuses*."

"What's one corvette versus another?" his wife asked.

"Not much. Except that the *Invictus* design is only six years old and Fleet is hanging on to every one of them that they built with both hands," Brad told her. "Which makes five ships out here that shouldn't have been outside of Fleet hands—and that's ignoring the fact that Fleet is being *damn* careful about who they sell the surplus *Bound*-class ships to."

Only Guild companies with long reputations and Fleet Reserve officers were supposed to be getting the *Bound* ships. As a Fleet Reserve officer, Brad wasn't complaining—and he could see the problem with selling even reputable mercenary companies a ship designed to kill cruisers.

Michelle sighed.

"You know who needs to know about this," she told him. "Falcone."

He paused thoughtfully. His wife had been occasionally quite sharp about Kate Falcone, mostly since he'd spent a *lot* of time with the Commonwealth spy while trying to rescue her. Michelle wasn't particularly jealous, but Agent Falcone had been an area he'd decided to step lightly around to be safe.

Which meant he hadn't even thought of sending the Commonwealth Intelligence Agency operative the information on what appeared to be rogue modern Fleet units in pirate hands.

"You're right," he agreed. "I'll make the call."

"Of course I'm right," Michelle told him. "Now, if you're not going to sleep *anyway*, we need to discuss the guard rotation for…"

He threw a pillow at her. Things progressed quite satisfactorily after that, as he was sure had been her plan.

CHAPTER SIX

Oberon had not improved in the year and a half since Brad Madrid had last been there. Still the most populated and wealthiest colony outside of the orbit of Saturn. Still a disorganized hole with fourteen different "cities" that depended on domes and caves to survive.

That wasn't to say it didn't hold some surprises. He's been in such a bad mental space on his last visit that he'd mistaken Oberon City as the largest of the settlements. Boy, had he missed the mark on that one.

First Oberon, the actual main settlement, was home to just over fifty thousand people, a quarter of Oberon's population. It was still just as run-down as Oberon City, though.

The government was a joke. There was, technically, an elected Governor on Oberon supported by the Commonwealth. The elections were even, so far as Brad knew, relatively honest.

That was because nobody *cared*. The Governor wasn't even a figure-head. Outside of a tiny detachment of Commonwealth Marines and a few beleaguered bureaucrats, no one even paid attention to her.

Authority in First Oberon belonged to the Council of Speakers, a glorified "city council" made up of representatives from whoever could justify having a seat to the current Council. There were merchants and industrialists on the council, along with a representative of the non-Guild mercenary that ran the largest private security enterprise on the planet, and at least one person the Agency was convinced represented the local pirates.

The First Oberon Council of Speakers ruled Oberon. The arrival of the Doctors' Guild's planned hospital was *probably* welcome, Brad assumed, but it was also a change in the balance of power.

Which was probably why the entire convoy had sat in orbit for twelve hours while Garibaldi argued with the Oberon Security Enterprise and Brad ran tactical simulations.

OSE's defenses probably looked formidable on paper. Six combat frigates and two dozen manned interceptor fighters hung above the planet, supported by a trio of immobile gun platforms.

Of course, with the frigates weighing in at barely two thousand tons apiece, *Oath of Vengeance* outmassed Oberon's "fleet" all by herself, and the interceptor fighters were worse than useless. Unlike the Javelin drones, these had people aboard, which meant they couldn't accelerate any faster than a regular spaceship.

And they were small enough that a single round from a gatling driver would end any threat they represented. The tactical simulations Brad was running suggested the fighters wouldn't survive the first six seconds after his people opened fire.

The immobile gun platforms were dead meat to his torpedoes, trapped in fixed orbits and unable to dodge. The combat frigates were actually worth their mass, relatively decent little ships, but even *Heart of Vengeance* was double the mass of any of them.

"You know, boss, I'm sure there are ways we could be *more* obvious about the fact that we'll blow their little squadron to Everdark if Garibaldi gives the order," Bogdanov snarked. "Bring up active targeting radar, flush the air from the torpedo tubes, that kind of thing. Gunports open, so to speak."

Brad chuckled and eyed the frigates.

"Don't tempt me," he told his subordinate. "We all know those are, at best, ex-pirates. This isn't a place that normally sees multi-ship convoys, let alone multi-ship Mercenary Guild companies. I suspect we make OSE nervous."

"Garibaldi's calling," Xan Wong reported. "I guess she's either made them see sense or she is very done."

From the exhausted expression on the Doctors' Guild Captain's face, either could be true.

"Commodore, I think I've *finally* cleared us to land, but the locals are being twitchy about your fleet," she admitted.

"Do you need me to blast my way through?" Brad offered brightly. "From what I know of the OSE…"

"We need to work with these people," Garibaldi replied. "The facility is already sorted out and these ships are designed to land, but…"

"Yes, Captain?"

"They don't want either of your destroyers coming any closer to Oberon," she admitted. "I know *Alan-a-dale* can't fly yet, which leaves us—"

"With *Heart of Vengeance*," Brad finished for her. "I know my job, Captain Garibaldi. *Heart* will accompany your ships in and provide overhead cover until you're all down and clear. Our ground troops, however, will go in first.

"Your people don't get within shouting distance of the landing pad until Colonel Kawa has cleared it, understood? Until our replacements arrive, we're responsible for your security…and I am *not* trusting it to the Oberon Security Enterprise for even one second."

"I can live with that," Garibaldi replied. "Believe me, Commodore Madrid, I can live with that."

———

Saburo Kawa was in command of the ground contingent—that was a lesson Brad had learned the hard way—but Brad was still on *Oath*'s third shuttle as his troops went down. Saburo would be in command, but Brad was *responsible*.

He was also just as good a shot as most of his troopers and a better swordsman. He could hold his own in a ground fight, and he'd at least been to Oberon. As Michelle had carefully *not* pointed out, however, he'd never been to the city of First Oberon.

As he arrived, however, he realized his presence was a better idea than he'd thought. The black-jacketed Viking troopers were setting up a perimeter around the landing site picked out for the Guild freighters, but there was a squad of red-uniformed locals getting in the way.

"I'm going to guess the locals are trouble?" he murmured over the command net.

"I could probably convince them to back off if the twit in charge would stop staring at my tits and *listen* to me," Lieutenant Trista Doary snapped. She commanded *Bound by Law*'s trooper detachment and had been with Brad and Saburo from the beginning.

"Though he might just be an idiot," she added in a considering tone. "Rules of engagement?"

"*Polite*," Brad told her. The ROE under their contract didn't call for them to fight the local rent-a-cops. "I'll be there in three. Keep your guns and blades sheathed."

"Can I gouge his eyes out with my thumbs?" Doary asked sweetly.

Brad suspected that being aboard a spaceship that had taken some serious hits had been bad for Doary's calm.

"That would be impolite," he replied, accelerating his pace. If the local was managing to stare at Doary's chest—despite combat armor! —that noticeably, there was a risk of serious stupidity.

And not on *Brad*'s people's part.

———

"The site was authorized for the freighters, no one else," the red-uniformed man was repeating as Brad arrived. "There are additional docking charges and oxygen costs for your shuttles and personnel.

"Right, this is Oberon, land of the outstretched palm," Brad observed as he stepped into the conversation. "Lieutenant Doary, meet up with Colonel Kawa and get our perimeter organized."

He "graced" the local with a cold smile.

"I don't want anyone who isn't ours within line of sight of the site," he continued. "We wouldn't want any accidents, after all."

"Who in Everdark are you?" the local officer demanded.

"I am Commodore Brad Madrid, commanding officer of the

Vikings Mercenary Guild Company and the man responsible for the safety of the convoy that's coming in," Brad told him. "Which means you and your people need to get clear of this site, officer…"

"I am Command Constable Athanasius Stanislav Daskalov," the man reeled off with the ease of long practice. "You have no authority to give me orders."

"Are you Commonwealth?" Brad snapped. "Because the Guild acknowledges the authority of the Commonwealth government of Oberon, not…whoever you are."

"I am a Command Constable of the Oberon Security Enterprise and represent the First Oberon Council of Speakers," Daskalov snapped. "I have the authority here, whatever games you want to play. It is my responsibility to see that all docking charges and oxygen fees are collected and that no…accidents happen."

"So, you run the local protection racket," Brad said calmly. "We aren't playing, Constable. All charges and fees were negotiated directly between the convoy's owners and the Council of Speakers. Anything *additional* would be a violation of that agreement, an agreement I am charged to enforce."

An alert siren echoed across the landing dome as the first freighter began its descent.

"Now, I have no basis on which to trust your people, and I *do* trust mine," he continued. "My people have vac-gear on them and will be fine when the dome opens. Will yours?"

"We're not *stupid*; this is our job," Daskalov told him. "This is our responsibility. Your mercs are unnecessary and unwelcome; their presence increases the potential risks to the convoy."

"Oh, I was *hoping* you'd say something like that," Brad purred—and then *moved*, the silver cylinder from his gun-belt in his hand and extended in an instant, electromagnets flaring to life to send the meter-long monofilament blade flashing toward Daskalov.

"You can threaten me and my people and bluster, and the Guild says I have to take it," he told the local. "You threaten my *client*, however, and my contract says I am authorized to use 'all necessary force' to protect them."

The impossibly thin blade glowed azure in its magnetic field, humming slightly from the power source in the cylinder in Brad's hand. Daskalov had a similar weapon at his own waist, but he didn't go for it, staring at the tip mere centimeters from his face.

"I suggest you go talk to your bosses, Command Constable," Brad said softly. "They went to a lot of effort to get my client here. Don't fuck it up for them."

CHAPTER SEVEN

ONCE THE OSE panhandlers had been ushered on their way, Brad's people quickly got the landing site under control. The dome was large enough for all six of the freighters to touch down and had been completely empty.

"Kind of surprising they even had a landing site big enough for all of this, given how little traffic Oberon must get," he noted to Saburo on the command channel, watching the third freighter transition through the immense airlock toward the ground.

"They've got two more that I spotted on the way in," the older Asian man replied. "Three big landing sites, each as big as the spaceport at Ceres." He shook his head. "There's more going on out here than I thought there was, or there's no point in having those ports."

"Six million people in the Outer System," Brad said quietly. "They may not have the tech or the automation or the rest of what we take for granted inside the Belt or at Jupiter, but…that's still six million people in artificial environments and flitting around on spaceships.

"There almost *has* to be more out here than we give it credit for."

His ground forces commander was a Jovian native, and he snorted.

"It seems like every layer of the system thinks the layers out from them are barbarians in pigpens pretending to be starships," Saburo noted. "The Belt thinks Jupiter is a dystopic Everdarkened-hole, Mars thinks the Belt is a dystopic Dark-hole, Earth thinks *everywhere* is lacking in basic amenities...."

"No human is ever going to realize that their prejudices against everyone else are just as ill-founded as the prejudices against them," Brad said with a chuckle. "How's our actual job going, Colonel?"

"Doary is working on some actual *official* channels with Oberon Security Enterprise," Saburo told him. "Those seem to involve much less fishing for bribes and staring at her chest."

"No offense to your subordinate, but even Trista doesn't have much to stare at when she's wearing combat armor," the Commodore said dryly. "I get the feeling someone was as much testing us as anything else."

"This is that kind of place," Saburo agreed. "If you let people push you around, you *get* pushed. You made the right call, I think."

"Our job is to make sure our clients are safe. If I can do that by threatening someone instead of killing them, I will," Brad concluded. "Of course, if I can do it *without* threatening someone, that's even better."

Saburo laughed at him.

"You, Commodore, would be *disappointed* if you hadn't been able to threaten someone. I don't get the impression that you like Oberon."

Brad shook his head.

"I don't," he admitted. "This whole contract seems to be a reunion tour of places where shitty things happened—though at least on this moon, *I* was what happened."

And if anyone wanted to raise trouble over that, well, he wished them luck. They'd need it.

———

Most of the Doctors' Guild personnel were being intelligent and staying inside the ships as the remainder of the convoy made their landing approaches. Brad and his people were well away from the landing pad and, in theory at least, didn't need to worry about the dome losing air pressure. That was what the massive airlock was for.

Of course, the mercenaries weren't going to trust the airlock, which was why they all had vac-gear built into their combat armor. It took Brad a moment to realize that the three people walking across the dome toward him were not only not his, they also weren't wearing any kind of vacuum safety gear.

"Can I assist you?" he asked the broad-shouldered tall woman leading the trio.

"I hope so, Commodore," she told him with a smile down at him. He wasn't a small man, but she towered over him. "I am Dr. Leonhardt, the head administrator for the new hospital. I need to go check out the build site while we bring our people and supplies down, and I was hoping I could impose on you for an escort."

Brad scoped out her companions. Both had the universal look of bureaucrats, even if Leonhardt herself looked like a rogue Amazon from a recruiting poster. None of them were wearing proper safety gear for the landing dome, and he sighed.

"I'll take you myself," he told her. "That will get you and your colleagues somewhere where you're not at risk of getting trapped in vacuum."

She blinked in surprise, then looked up at the massive airlock door above them and sighed.

"Specialties, Commodore," she told him lightly. "I now understand why Captain Garibaldi was looking so pained when she spoke to me as I was leaving."

"You *can* wander around a landing dome during descent operations," Brad replied. "But you want an emergency automatic helmet." He tapped the collar he wore. "Let's get you into the main colony."

He turned to Saburo.

"Saburo, can I borrow a squad?" he asked. "Let's get our client safely to her new building and check it ourselves."

They'd need to go over the building with a fine-toothed comb before they let the doctors set up. The sooner they found it, the better off everyone was.

"Take Vaughn and his people," Saburo told him. "They can do the security sweep for you while you're there."

"Security sweep?" Leonhardt asked.

"Bombs, bugs, squatters," Brad reeled off instantly. "We want to make sure you have no unexpected surprises."

She wrinkled her nose.

"Is that likely?"

"This is Oberon, Dr. Leonhardt," he told her. "I am not being paid to assume your safety. Quite the opposite."

———

First Oberon didn't have much in terms of streets or transportation, with the entire city being made up of interlinked domes and underground tunnels. Similar cities farther in toward Earth would use small corridor runabouts, but First Oberon was a foot-traffic-and-subway city.

There were probably vehicles somewhere in the colony, for the Council of Speakers if no one else, but as Brad led his client through the tunnels, all he was seeing were pedestrians and the occasional subway entrance.

The address Leonhardt gave them was close enough that they didn't need to risk the subway, and the exercise was good for them. Oberon kept the colony gravity mostly around the half-standard-gravity most human settlements used, though at least one spot they passed through had no artificial gravity at all.

The moon was large enough to have gravity of its own, but it was almost nonexistent—just enough to make sure that nobody fell off the surface.

"I'm guessing your people brought ambulances?" Brad asked Leonhardt as they carefully made the transition from one of the low-g zones back to the artificial gravity of the colony "streets."

"We have a few specialized corridor cars, yes," she confirmed. "I think they're even designed to handle gravity transitions like this."

"The address you gave us is just down here," Brad told her as he gestured down the tunnel. "What should I be looking for?"

"It's a trio of old warehouses we bought up over the last year or two," Leonhardt told him. "Workers should have been blasting out walls and linking them all into one building for us. We'll want to see what kind of job they've done and what the new floorplan looks like."

That made sense at least. The Guild had brought a lot of gear and people.

"What about residences for your folks?" he asked.

Leonhardt sighed.

"While I regarded it as an excess of paranoia, the decision was made to have everyone live inside the hospital and its security perimeter for at least the first year or so," she told him. "From what you've been telling me, I guess that wasn't so paranoid after all."

"It might be," Brad admitted. "I don't believe Oberon is *quite* as barbarous as my Belt-born self wants to think, but you're still probably wise to keep everyone safe."

It was hard to tell the difference between a warehouse, a hotel, or an office from the tunnel "street." Some had signs, but many just had numbers to look at. Brad found the ones he was looking for and scoped out the entrances carefully from across the street.

To his surprise, Leonhardt proved quite cooperative with his paranoia, quietly stopping with his squad as he surveyed the space.

"There's a cargo entrance as well, I'm guessing?" he murmured to her. From this side, all he could see were sets of double doors with discreet numbers. "And a plan for signage."

"Yes, and yes," Leonhardt confirmed. "This is the main public entrance; the cargo access actually requires authorization codes to get to. What we bring in and in which order will depend on the layout."

"Vaughn?" Brad asked. "Anything pinging your scanner?"

The NCO had a concealed array of sensors layered through his armor and linking back to his wrist-comp and helmet.

"Nothing flashing red warning lights," Vaughn told him. "A couple of odd things. I'll definitely want to sweep the building before we let any of the civilians inside."

"Really?" Leonhardt asked incredulously. "What are you expecting? Killer robots? Assassins? Bombs?"

The squad leader coughed delicately.

"Bombs, ma'am," he admitted. "A few pings of radio transmissions that could be bugs or detonators, some chemical signatures that might be left over from the workers blasting the space open."

He shook his head.

"Like I said, no flashing red warning lights, but a few things that don't look right. I don't think we can let the clients in just yet."

"Agreed," Brad said instantly. Leonhardt might be looking rebellious, but even if Brad didn't agree with Vaughn's assessment from what he had been told, no good commander *ever* overrode their troops in front of the client.

"Doctor, if you and your people can wait here? Corporal Achmed, keep your fire team with them," he ordered. "Sergeant Vaughn, let's go take a look!"

For a few seconds, Leonhardt looked like she was going to object, but she finally sighed and nodded.

"This is your area, Commodore," she admitted. "We've already seen a million times more trouble than I actually expected for this trip."

"I know," Brad told her. "But that, after all, is why your Guild hired us."

Brad Madrid was in command of the Vikings. There was no question that the Commodore was in charge: he signed the paychecks, signed the contracts, gave the orders.

But when Sergeant Vaughn gestured for him to wait outside as the first fire team went into the building, Brad followed orders. A sergeant who knows what's going on outranks *everybody*.

Three armored troops, led by Vaughn himself, went in first. Brad went in with the second fire team, keeping well back and letting his specialists do their jobs.

The hospital-to-be definitely showed its warehouse heritage. They came in through a closed-off set of offices that would act as a reception for the new operation, and then entered into a vast open space.

The walls on either side still showed the signs of fresh demolition, with scaffolding and rough floor layouts installed. It was...well short of what Brad had been expecting from Leonhardt's description, almost as if the work had stopped at some point along the way.

There was enough space in the three warehouses for a hospital, easily, but while the space was five stories high, there'd been only the beginnings of an effort to turn it into separate floors.

"Sergeant, does this smell off to you?" Brad asked.

"I'm still picking up radio signatures and chemical explosives, so I'm going with yes," the non-com replied. "What are you thinking, sir?"

"This was supposed to have a full five-story floor plan the doctors could slot their equipment and beds into," Brad told his subordinate. "This does not look remotely close to being complete…and I don't see workers."

The space was silent, in fact. It looked like the worksite had just… stopped. Everyone had put down their tools and walked away, well before the work was done.

"Vaughn, have your people get Leonhardt and the rest well away from here," Brad ordered, looking around and letting the reality sink in. "Everdark, contact OSE and the Marines—they need to evac the area. I'm guessing gas and bombs, someone has rigged this whole thing to go up in fire and death."

"Yeah," the Sergeant confirmed after a moment. "Son of a bitch."

"Sergeant?"

"Motion-activated infrared tripwire across the exit. That was *not* there before."

A chill ran down Brad's spine.

"Linked to what?" he asked.

There was a long pause.

"I'm going to guess to the new traces of VX-65 that the scanners are picking up," Vaughn told him very, very slowly. "It's a binary neurotoxin, wouldn't have started mixing until the activation code was sent."

"Someone set this up to trap the first responders and gas them," Brad concluded grimly. "There is *definitely* a bomb around here, too."

"We'll find it," Vaughn promised. "Achmed is dragging Leonhardt back to the landing site, but he doesn't have the manpower to evacuate the area."

"You find the bomb and see if you can disarm the gas," Brad ordered. "I'll see if I can coordinate with the OSE. Even if we can find a way out of here, this entire sector is at risk!"

Their vacuum gear wouldn't protect from VX-65. It could dissolve gas masks and clothing and was lethal on contact. Whoever had rigged this trap wanted to make *damn* sure the first people to visit died.

Along with everyone else in the sector. VX-65 wasn't exactly containable once mixed.

"This is Commodore Madrid," he barked as he broke into the Oberon Security Enterprise's emergency channels. "We are in the target site for the new hospital, and someone has rigged this space with explosives and VX-65 canisters.

"We need a full evacuation of Sector LD-73 before it's too late. I'm not certain that we are going to be able to disarm the bomb *or* the gas."

There had been conversation on the channel when he linked in. Now there was only the silence of shocked cops.

Then a familiar voice cut in.

"This is Command Constable Daskalov," the man who'd tried to extort Brad for money at the landing pad stated. "My section is in LD-76; we can be there in under five minutes to commence the evacuation if no one is closer.

"How much time can you buy us, Commodore?"

"I don't know," Brad admitted. "It seems to be set up to trigger when we leave, so I think we can try and stay in here until you've evacuated the area."

"Fuck." The curse hung in the official channels for several long seconds.

"We will clear the area, Commodore, if you can find a way to disarm the active bombs. We..." Daskalov swallowed loudly enough to be heard. "I don't believe we have the counteragents for VX-65. We don't generally see WMD-grade chemical weapons out here!"

"You don't generally see them anywhere," Brad said. "Get the area clear, people. The Vikings will deal with the damn bombs."

Brad dropped the channel and brought up his helmet. Scanning the space, his combat optics could pick up the infrared beams blocking the exit. It was a full mesh; there was no way they were getting through it without shutting it down.

"So, we have a problem," Vaughn said in a calmly conversational tone.

"I knew that," Brad told him.

"No, you knew we had bombs and nerve gas," the NCO told him, his voice still perfectly calm. "I think we should have guessed the level of the bombs once we knew they'd put VX-65 in here."

"Sergeant…" Brad swallowed. "Are we talking nukes here?"

"No. Just hyper-compressed thermobarics." Vaughn paused. "If this bomb goes up, this entire sector is going to get blasted into orbit."

"Can we stop that from happening, Sergeant?"

"I'm not sure yet."

CHAPTER EIGHT

"We have the immediate vicinity of your location evacuated, but the sector is home to thirty-five hundred people," Daskalov told Brad grimly. "I've pulled barely twenty OSE people into the region and there's more on the way, but I'm not sure we can evacuate all of LD-73 in time, Commodore."

"We're doing everything we can," Brad promised the OSE Command Constable. Their first encounter had been hostile, but the man seemed to genuinely care about the people under his protection.

Strangers probably weren't so lucky, but that was par for the course for small communities on the back end of nowhere.

"Keep me advised," he continued. "What's our current safe radius, just in case?"

Daskalov snorted.

"We've cleared the industrial sector, so if you could keep it to the warehouses, that would be great," he said dryly. "Of course, that nerve gas isn't exactly known for being stopped by much of anything. I had my HQ research into it. The only way we're going to stop its spread is by flushing the air from the entire sector."

"I'm not planning on letting it get that far, Constable," Brad promised. "I'll let you know."

Leaving Daskalov to his thankless task, the Commodore found Vaughn approaching him. The Sergeant still looked as unflappably calm as ever, which Brad was starting to realize meant the man was potentially scared out of his wits.

"Okay, boss," Vaughn greeted him quietly. "I've got good news, bad news, and 'I can't believe I'm suggesting this' news."

That didn't sound promising.

"Lay it out," Brad ordered.

"Good news: we disabled the tripwire grid at the exits and we think we can disarm the thermobaric bombs."

Brad wanted to sigh in relief, but somehow he knew he wasn't going to like the other shoe that was coming.

"The bad news is that the people who put this together were sick fucking bastards who knew their chemical weapons," Vaughn said bluntly. "Once the VX-65 was assembled, it started eating through its container. We've got *maybe* thirty minutes before we've got lethal levels loose in here…and about an hour before it eats its way into the main concourse despite anything we can do. Assuming there's no lovely extra holes we don't know about."

"So, we can run…if we're prepared to write off everything OSE can't evacuate," Brad concluded. "Which means we aren't running."

"I could make an argument for it, but…yeah," Vaughn agreed. "I'm not sure First Oberon's people would manage to contain it to one sector. They'd lose this one at least and potentially the ones next door as well. Five, maybe six thousand dead, depending on how quickly they evacuated."

"I don't like that option. What's your suggestion?" Brad asked.

"VX-65 dissociates *back* into harmless components at sufficient temperature in an anoxic environment," his Sergeant told him. "Such as the conditions in the immediate aftermath of a high-compression thermobaric bomb."

"So, their own weapons would undo each other?" Brad said. That seemed unusually incompetent.

"The bomb and the VX are quite handily separated," Vaugh explained. "The bomb would mostly only kill everyone in the hospital site and blast the wreckage into orbit. The gas is designed to screw the people who come in to disable the bomb—we were *supposed* to find and disarm the bomb."

"But you can use the bombs to disable the VX?"

"Yeah…but I'm going to need *all* of them."

Brad winced.

"How bad?"

"If I'm careful, I think I can *only* wreck the hospital site itself," Vaughn said quietly.

"The only part of this place we're actually contracted to protect." Brad sighed. "Set it up, Sergeant. I need to talk to our employer."

The NCO coughed delicately.

"If we don't do this, boss, well…five, maybe six thousand dead," he repeated.

"I know," Brad snapped. "I'm not going to let the good doctor tell me no, but I'd like to at least *tell* my client before I blow their facility to kingdom come!"

———

"Commodore, please tell me that your people are all right!"

"We're fine," Brad told Leonhardt. "We identified everything before it become a threat, but we have a new problem."

"Can you get out? I'm more concerned about preserving lives than anything else right now," she said rapidly.

"So am I," he said grimly. "There is a stockpile of VX-65 rigged to blow inside your hospital site, Dr. Leonhardt. Enough to gas about three sectors and probably kill over five thousand people—and that's *if* OSE evacuates promptly."

Leonhardt was silent.

"We did *not* order that," she said carefully.

Brad couldn't help himself. He laughed.

"Doctor, I'm pretty sure everyone realizes the bombs and nerve gas were here to destroy your attempt to build a hospital and kill you. No one thinks the stockpile of WMDs had been on layaway for you."

"What do we do?" she asked.

"We've deactivated most of the triggering mechanisms and we can evac, but…are you familiar with VX-65 at all, Dr. Leonhardt?"

"If it was a bioweapon, I'd know something, but chemical WMDs are far outside my area of expertise," she told him. "If you can get out, get out!"

"Doctor…the nerve gas is going to destroy its containers in the next hour," he said quietly. "If we don't do something to counteract it, it will kill thousands. I can't stand by and let that happen."

She was silent again.

"What can you do?"

"To destroy VX requires super-high temperatures and a lack of oxygen," Brad told him. "It'll help get rid of anything left if we blast the remnants into space, too."

"That sounds destructive."

"It is. I can save this colony, Dr. Leonhardt, but I have to destroy your hospital to do it."

There was a different tone to the silence this time, and it ended in a soft chuckle.

"No, you don't, Commodore Madrid. My hospital is the people and equipment on the freighters you delivered. The space you have to destroy is just that: a space. An empty void.

"Do what you must."

———

"Make it happen," Brad ordered Vaughn. "How many people do you need?"

"One fire team," the Sergeant replied instantly. "One fire team to help move and set the bombs, one fire team to make sure my *commanding officer* is outside the Everdarkened *blast radius*. Move, Commodore. The tripwire is down and this is not your place anymore."

Brad shook his head.

"This was never my place, Sergeant; it was just where I happened to end up." He offered his hand to the NCO. "You can do it?"

Vaughn took his grip and shook firmly.

"I can do it."

"Don't lose anyone," Brad told him. "No suicidal heroics. We don't get paid for that."

The Sergeant laughed.

"Boss, I don't believe we're getting paid for this bit at all."

"I'll worry about that later. Let's save the colony."

———

There was an earth-shattering kaboom.

Watching from the landing dome, Brad felt the tremors even through the artificial gravity keeping his feet to the ground. A spike of fire blasted out through the surface, opening a hole through almost a hundred meters of solid stone as the refitted bombs overpressurized and shattered the surface above what had been supposed to become the Guild hospital.

With the artificial gravity plates in that section vaporized, there was nothing to stop the debris clearing orbital velocity. Thousands—potentially tens of thousands—of tons of rock and other wreckage were flung into the air.

"Konrad, are you tracking this?" Brad asked his channel to *Oath of Vengeance*. "I'm sure we've got a traffic hazard here. Flag the biggest chunks and see if we can do anything about them."

"On it, Commodore." His tac officer paused. "That's one impressive explosion."

"Vaughn shaped the charges for effect," the Commodore replied, shaking his head. "If we hadn't...well, there'd be a *lot* of funerals going on instead of no funerals."

From the height the spike of flame had reached before running out of oxygen, Brad had badly underestimated the scale of the bombs, even with the NCO's warning. Three sectors was probably lowballing the likely damage.

"I'm impressed with your enemies, Commodore," Daskalov told him, the Command Constable stepping into the surveillance room with a haggard impression. "And with your people's skill. I apologize for how we met. Outsiders are considered...um..."

"Fresh meat?" Brad suggested. "I know what kind of colony Oberon is, Command Constable. I wasn't exactly surprised."

Daskalov shook his head.

"I wouldn't use those words," he said primly, "but you're not wrong. And I apologize for it. We owe you, Commodore Madrid. A lot. Our own scans show that LD-73 maintained overall integrity despite the blast. We'll do a survey before we let anyone back into the sector, but it looks like the damage was contained."

"To my hospital site," Dr. Leonhardt interjected. "I would hope that the Oberon Council of Speakers will see some way to recompense us for that sacrifice. Insurance certainly won't cover the intentional demolition of the space, regardless of how noble the intent."

Daskalov winced.

"That, Doctor, is entirely out of my purview," he admitted. "I intend to suggest to my own superiors at OSE that some form of reward be paid out to Commodore Madrid's people. You prevented a major disaster here, Commodore. The Vikings will never be outsiders in First Oberon again."

That was more meaningful than it might have sounded to many, but Brad understood.

"Thank you, Command Constable."

With a crisp salute that Brad knew he wouldn't have got from the man before, the OSE officer stepped out, and Brad turned back to Leonhardt.

"What now, Doctor?" he asked. "This is your operation, and we may have blown your original plan to pieces."

The tall woman grinned at him.

"I and my staff have been going over that with Captain Garibaldi while you were so kindly dealing with the *weapons of mass destruction* someone tried to short-circuit our plans with," she said. "The Guild has purchased Captain Garibaldi's ship and two of the other freighters. We will be operating our hospital temporarily out of this landing site while we have the original space rebuilt. Since we now have a larger space to work with and a blank slate, the possibilities are nearly infinite."

Dr. Leonhardt, it seemed, was able to find the silver lining in anything.

"We are under contract until the Pythons arrive," Brad told her. The follow-up mercenary company was still several days out. "Our ground forces will maintain security of wherever you choose to operate, and our space forces will do the same by virtue of, well"—he grinned at the medical administrator—"protecting the moon you happen to be standing on."

CHAPTER NINE

At this point, the Vikings were mostly a space fleet that happened to have a landing contingent. The Pythons, however, were an entirely ground force that needed to have ships to carry them around.

The two *Fidelis*-class heavy corvettes escorting the Pythons' transport were almost a formality, older ships built on the same base hull as *Heart of Vengeance* but significantly less upgraded than Brad's original ship.

The Pythons' ships slotted into orbit alongside the Vikings' vessels. They'd probably sort out a permanent placement with the OSE defenders like the Vikings had, but for the moment, their job was to make sure the transport got there safely.

With half of the convoy scattered to the winds of space and the remaining three ships moved together to form an approximation of a single "building," there was plenty of space for *Python's Voice* to settle down in the landing site.

Before the ground had even cooled, armored vehicles designed for just that environment rolled off the transport's landing ramps. This part of the landing was the only use anyone in the Solar System *had* for anything resembling a tank at this point, but the turreted and treaded vehicles were capable of surviving the heat of a landing.

They couldn't maneuver around a colony like Oberon, but that wasn't their purpose. The intimidating three-point perimeter they formed around *Voice*'s exit was their purpose. Brad's people had, at his count, five different ways to eliminate the light tanks—but the Vikings were *very* well equipped.

Ten minutes after landing, the rest of the company began deploying. The Pythons had almost three times the Vikings' listed strength, and the kind of long-term ground protection detail the Doctors' Guild needed was exactly their forte.

Brad and Saburo stepped forward as the Pythons' commander emerged, trading salutes with the tall Middle Eastern woman.

"Colonel Bathsheba Ahmed," she greeted them. "It sounds like you've had quite the contract, Commodore Madrid."

"I've had quieter," he agreed with a chuckle. "I've had louder, too, though I'd prefer to *avoid* getting pigeonholed as the Guild's WMD expert."

One of the reasons for Brad's Fleet Reserve commission, after all, had been a legal fig leaf to cover the fact that he'd taken on the Terror with a wave of nuclear warheads. Something that was very, *very* illegal.

But results earned forgiveness even when you would have been denied permission.

"According to my reading of the contract, you have now completely fulfilled your portion of the terms," Ahmed told him formally. "I so record and authenticate. The Pythons relieve the Vikings, Commodore Madrid."

"We stand relieved," Brad said formally. "In more sense than one," he continued with a smile. "Though I hope you don't find any chemical surprises waiting for you."

"The Pythons, Commodore, have far fewer enemies than you do," she reminded him. "Though it appears you have friends we don't as well. There's someone waiting for you aboard *Voice*. I was asked not to tell you more."

From Ahmed's expression, she hadn't been *told* much more…which reduced the number of people it could be to a small handful.

There weren't that many people who could commandeer their way onto a Guild Mercenary transport for a ride without explaining themselves to the company commander.

What was scariest, Brad realized, was that still left him with multiple possibilities.

———

One of the Pythons escorted him through their transport, a very different type of ship from most he'd been on. Brad had seen everything from warships to bulk freighters to passenger liners, but a troop transport required different layouts from all of those.

He had enough experience with every other type of spaceship that he was sure he could find his way around eventually, but he was glad for the guide that led him to the guest staterooms and knocked politely on the door.

"Miss? Commodore Madrid here to see you."

Well, *that* narrowed the list down enough, and Brad smiled at the tall blonde woman rising from the chair as he stepped into the room.

"Kate Falcone," he greeted her. "You know, you *can* reply to my messages with messages instead of just showing up."

Falcone's smile was briefer, and she surprised him with a brief hug.

"I could, but the Cadre is still my file and everything is going to *shit*," she told him. "Have a seat. I need to brief you."

"Have you been filled in on the mess here?" Brad asked.

"Yeah. Hence being glad to see you alive," Falcone replied. She shook her head. "So far as we can tell, the attack on the convoy was primarily an attempt to stop the hospital being built—but the bombs were primarily an attempt to kill *you*."

Brad took the offered seat as that thought took his breath away.

"You can't be serious."

"The Cadre doesn't want a major presence of any of the Guilds out here, whatever that ends up costing the locals, and really, *really* wants you dead," she said bluntly. "So, you escorting the Doctors' Guild's convoy let several factions line up in the same direction with a lot of resources."

"You're sure it was the Cadre?" he asked.

"Unfortunately, yes," Falcone confirmed. "The attack on your convoy was the first salvo in a new campaign by the bastards. We've seen a dozen attacks over the weeks since, ranging from stealing starships to wrecking the support infrastructure for station-colonies.

"Plus, well…"

She tapped a command and gestured him to a screen.

At the center of the screen was the distinctive bulk of a trio of Fleet cruisers, the preeminent warship type in the Solar System. Fleet battleships existed, but they were guard ships. The cruisers were Fleet's actual hammer.

This division was standing guard over what looked like a fuel depot, a task group of destroyers and corvettes spread out around it. A small note in the corner of the screen informed him the video was playing at an accelerated time rate.

"This was the Augustus Logistics Facility, Fleet's fuel depot in Jupiter's opposing trojan cluster," she told him. "Augustus was kept relatively quiet, we didn't like to draw attention to its presence, but it provided us with major refueling facilities on the opposite side of the Solar System from Jupiter."

Was. Provided. Past tense. Past tense referring to a facility with a cruiser division guarding it.

Brad held his peace and watched the video. He was one of the few people in the system who could instantly recognize the explosions when they happened. Someone had sent nuclear-tipped ballistic missiles into the depot. One of the cruisers ate at least four of the weapons and died with an ignominy Brad didn't expect Fleet to forget soon.

The depot itself was ripped apart, the major fuel tanks erupting into massive fireballs, the cruisers moving to shield their lesser sisters with their own bulk. They could take the debris hits that the corvettes and destroyers couldn't…but only at the cost of weakening their own defenses.

Brad wasn't surprised when the Cadre heat shields collapsed, revealing the destroyer divisions sweeping down on the depot. Four heat shields had concealed twelve destroyers and twenty-four heavy corvettes—where had the Cadre *got* that many ships?

Even he, however, was surprised when the cruiser dropped her heat sinks and opened fire. *Lioness* plunged into the heart of the battle, her heavy mass drivers and massed torpedo banks hammering her former sisters with brutal force.

From the time-compression note, the entire battle had lasted less than thirty minutes from the arrival of the ballistic torpedoes to *Lioness* positioning herself to use her heavy mass drivers to wreck what was left of the depot.

The video ended, and he turned his gaze back to Falcone.

"How bad?"

"There were no survivors," she said flatly. "Three cruisers, eight destroyers, thirteen corvettes—and our largest fueling facility not attached to a major settlement. Just over twenty thousand dead."

"I knew *Lioness* was going to be a problem," Brad admitted. "I was hoping they hadn't been able to fuel her, though."

"Apparently, they fixed that. And the Cadre has a new leader, a name we've been hearing a lot: they call him the Phoenix."

"Does he have a giant bird tattooed on his face?" Brad asked. The Terror had gone in for a skull and crossbones, after all.

"We don't know. We're not sure who he—or she!—is," Kate admitted. "That's why I'm here, Brad. I have my own tasks out here in Oberon, and the Pythons were going my way."

"Good to know we're incidental," he said lightly.

"If you weren't, your wife might hate me more," the Agent pointed out. "And part of what I need to do is interview your officers."

"Michelle doesn't hate you," he corrected. "She just thinks you want to drag me into full-time Agency work instead of glorified mole and reserve. Even she realizes that if you were a threat to our relationship, something would have happened before I met her."

Falcone chuckled.

"No offense, but you're *still* too young for me," she said. "But Michelle's not wrong that I think the Agency could use you. For now, however..." She sighed.

"If I could get you to hang out here for about three more days, I could use a ride back to Jupiter once I'm done. There's only a limited chance that this is going to blow up in my face, but I need to get home quickly—and you need to get your ships repaired."

"We were paid enough for this job that we can take some extra time," Brad allowed carefully. "But why do you care how quickly we get fixed?"

"I'm still collating data," she told him. "But once I've put the pieces together, I'm going to go hunting.

"And right now, Fleet is understrength, undersupplied...and I don't know if I can trust them.

"So, while I know keeping your Agency connection secret is pretty high-priority, we can bloody well hire your company for our secret sword."

CHAPTER TEN

Brad's expectation of quietly spending the next three days on board *Oath* lasted exactly two hours. That's how long it took for a representative from First Oberon's Council of Speakers to come looking for him.

The young woman they'd sent might delicately have been called short. Tiny, even. If she topped 150 centimeters, he'd be astonished.

Oath's assistant combat team leader, Kyoko Phan, escorted their delicate visitor to his office just off the bridge on *Oath of Vengeance*. The visual contrast between the two women was striking.

Kyoko was almost as short as their visitor but seemed about twice as wide and deep. The compact former Commonwealth Marine could probably break the envoy over her knee without any trouble whatsoever.

One couldn't tell that from Lieutenant Phan's posture, though. She stood two steps behind their visitor with her right hand hovering close to the butt of her holstered pistol. His officer's sharp eyes never left their visitor's back.

Brad had no doubt that if the envoy made any move that could be construed as hostile, the woman would end up with several large holes in her back. So, it was probably good that the Council's envoy appeared blissfully unaware of how suspicious her guardian was.

"Thank you, Kyoko," Brad said with a smile. "I've got it from here."

His assistant combat team leader's expression didn't change, but she still managed to get her disapproval across. She inclined her head slightly. "Yes, sir. I'll be right outside the hatch in the corridor. Just call out if you have any trouble. Any trouble at all."

Amused, he made a brief shooing motion with his hand. Once his officer had stepped out into the corridor and closed the hatch behind her, Brad focused his attention on his visitor.

"Welcome aboard *Oath of Vengeance*. As you've probably already guessed, I'm Brad Madrid. What can I do for you and the Council of Speakers?"

The woman bowed deeply at the waist and held that pose for two heartbeats before straightening. "My name is Jewell Lathrop, and the Council of Speakers wishes me to convey their deep gratitude for your actions. The loss of life had you not mitigated this shocking and despicable attack would have been inconceivable."

He allowed himself a small smile. "I like to think that anyone in a similar position would've done the same thing. Still, on behalf of my people, I thank you and the Council. Was that the primary purpose of your visit?"

The woman shook her head slightly. "Merely the introductory remarks, Commodore. I've been instructed to escort you to an emergency gathering of the Council of Speakers to discuss the attack. As you might imagine, everyone is quite worried that this is not an isolated incident."

"That doesn't exactly sound like an invitation," he said thoughtfully, tapping his index finger on the desk. "I'm as disturbed as anyone at what happened today, but what makes them think I have any additional information to offer? I only just arrived on Oberon, after all."

Lathrop shrugged eloquently. "I was instructed to perform a task. That doesn't obligate you to cooperate, though I do hope you will. If you decline to appear before the Council, I will return to them with your decision. Allow me to stress, however, that working with the Council would improve future relations between your clients and the Council of Speakers."

"Former clients," he corrected. "Frankly, I can't imagine why the Council of Speakers wouldn't want to have the very best relationship they could with the people who they are going to be relying on for superior medical care, no matter what I do. It doesn't pay to annoy the person who may one day save your life.

"And let me be honest: the Council of Speakers really let them down. This was no small operation. Someone waltzed in right under their noses, sent all the workers packing, smuggled contraband nerve agents into your city, and planted bombs inside a soon-to-be hospital complex. How exactly could *anyone* miss that?"

Her eyes turned cold. "I assure you that those events are being examined in exquisite detail. Certain powerful members of the Council are raving about the failures, and OSE operatives are searching for the workers even as we speak. They'll also be examining every mode of entry the smugglers might have used to get the weapons of mass destruction onto Oberon and into our city."

She took one small step forward. "And when we find whoever did this, I assure you that they *will* pay. That's one of the reasons the Council needs you to come discuss precisely what you found, what you suspect, and what you believe. When they extract their revenge, they want to be very certain it falls upon the right people as quickly as possible."

Lathrop considered him for a moment longer. "It seems to me, Commodore, that the attack might have been levied against both you or your company and the doctors. That's a personal opinion, of course, but one that I suspect that many members of the Council will eventually come to share.

"If so, it may well be that we have information that could allow you to find *your* enemies. You do have a certain reputation, after all. Perhaps you should look at this meeting as more of a sharing of data on potential suspects than a questioning."

He tipped his chair back and presented the appearance of considering her words. He'd already decided he'd attend the meeting. Pretty much for the reasons she'd just stated.

"That's insightful," he confessed. "What exactly does an envoy to the Council of Speakers do? Excuse my forwardness, but you don't come across as a simple messenger."

She smiled and inclined her head. "Allow me to compliment your insight as well, Commodore. An envoy of the Council of Speakers is tasked with carrying out the will of the Council. Whatever that will happens to be.

"It often involves delivering messages and fetching people, whether they wish to be fetched or not. Occasionally, it means delivering summary justice in one form or another. Thankfully, it most often falls between those two extremes. Bluntly stated, envoys are the voice and strong right arm of the Council of Speakers."

Brad had a difficult time imagining Jewell Lathrop being the heavy for anyone. That said, many of his own people were strong women, so he wouldn't dismiss the concept out of hand, no matter how harmless she seemed.

"You're very persuasive, Envoy Lathrop. I assume that the meeting is taking place now." At her nod, he rose to his feet. "Then I'd best grab what I need and we can leave immediately. As you say, it serves both our interests if I cooperate. No matter who these people were after, I want to see them taken down."

Lathrop's smile turned arctic. "Oh, they *will* go down. If I have to travel across the system to find them and slit their throats while they sleep, they *will* pay for what they've done."

"I think we're going to get along just fine, Envoy Lathrop. Just fine."

———

Kyoko wasn't pleased by his decision, but she knew him well enough by now not to argue. In fact, she'd anticipated his decision, and a fire team stood ready to escort him to the meeting.

He certainly could argue with her caution. There was ample reason to believe that someone on Oberon wanted him dead. The real question was whether they were still there or not. The prudent response was to assume they were, so he wouldn't argue.

Just to play it safe, he stopped off at his cabin to put a concealable armored vest underneath his uniform. He was still strapping on his weapons belt when his wife came in.

Michelle raised an eyebrow. "This doesn't look promising. What craziness are you planning now?"

"I'd hesitate to call it craziness," he said with a smile. "The Council of Speakers would like to discuss the events with me so that we can sort out exactly who our mutual enemies are."

"And what makes you think your enemies aren't going to be sitting on that Council?" she asked, putting her hands on her hips. "If I had to put money on it, I'd wager someone in a position of power in this city either ordered the attack or provided material assistance to make it possible."

"That wouldn't surprise me in the slightest, but if I don't see them face-to-face, I won't know that. Everdark, I might not be able to tell even if I do meet the person or persons behind this, but I've got to try."

She considered him for a moment longer, her eyes narrowed. "What kind of security detail are you taking with you?"

"Lieutenant Phan and a fire team will be accompanying me."

Michelle laughed. "She obviously hasn't considered the sheer amount of trouble you've gotten into in the past. A fire team isn't going to be enough to contain the type of enemy strikes you tend to attract.

"Allow me to suggest that Saburo have a much larger team shadowing you. That way, when trouble strikes, there's at least the possibility you can get out without being shot. Again."

There was an element of truth in that.

"I'm not certain how happy they'd be to have all our troopers wandering through their tunnels armed to the gills. And potentially blowing big holes in everything around them."

"Considering that these people are the ones that allowed weapons of mass destruction to be levied against us, I don't think they've got a leg to stand on."

"That hasn't stopped the people in charge anywhere else. I suppose we'll see how they feel about it when we get there."

He found Saburo Kawa with a significantly larger group of troops already gathered outside for his escort. They were armed and armored for heavy combat. A cluster of red-uniformed OSE men and women watched from a short distance away.

Brad raised an eyebrow as he stepped over to Saburo. "Going somewhere?"

The Asian man grinned. "Just a little stroll through the city. I figure we'll hang around while you meet with the Council of Speakers and then head back to the ship with you. No muss. No fuss. Unless they make a fuss, of course."

"And exactly how do you think the OSE is going to react to your sightseeing trip?"

"Under the circumstances, we'll just tag along and make sure everybody stays peaceful," Command Constable Daskalov said as he walked over from a group of his own people.

"Understand, this isn't normally how we do business, but the Council has instructed me to grant you a little extra leeway."

Brad allowed his eyes to meaningfully wander across all the firepower arrayed around him. "A little? You have quite the gift for understatement."

The man smiled ruefully. "At this point, I wouldn't object if you brought along a polka band. Okay, strike that. I *would* object, but I'd allow it. Regretfully."

"I think we can avoid polka music or any other crimes against humanity," Brad said dryly.

Envoy Lathrop cleared her throat. "If the two of you are finished discussing our escort, may I suggest you that we get moving? The Council is waiting."

———

The trip to the chambers used by the Council of Speakers was blissfully free of incident. In spite of Brad's relative certainty that they wouldn't be harassed, he had to admit that the crumbling tunnels and disused side spaces easily converted in his mind to ambush locations and potential choke points.

He considered asking Lathrop and Daskalov why they allowed their city to deteriorate like this, but decided it was none of his business.

The quality of the stonework improved markedly as they neared their destination, and trash no longer littered the corridors. The people they passed seemed more prosperous, too. Well-to-do, even.

More OSE guards stood watch outside one of the most ornate sets of corridor doors Brad had ever seen. Made of burnished bronze almost four meters tall, someone had cast each of them as a single piece with a number of men and women in heroic poses.

It didn't look like any historic scene he was familiar with. Based on some of the homelier individuals, he suspected he was looking at the people who had commissioned the doors. The Council of Speakers had made certain to leave their mark on the city.

Envoy Lathrop noted his gaze and smiled. "A bit ostentatious, I agree. Still, if you knew the Council as well as I did, you wouldn't think it at all out of place."

He gave her a sideways glance and smiled. "Won't they mind you being critical of them?"

She laughed and shook her head. "People in positions of authority will always find fault with something, no matter how you choose to behave. That said, I fulfill a certain need for them, and so they allow me a bit more space to do so. After all, I *am* the person they'd have to send to show me the error of my ways."

Brad laughed. "I have no idea how to react to you. I suppose I'll just be glad that we aren't enemies."

"We are absolutely *not* enemies. In fact, I suspect that we'll become allies. So, before you go in, I'll give you one final piece of advice. The Council is angry. Both the attack on the doctors and the use of a nerve agent have galvanized many of them to demand action, but not all on the Council are your friends.

"There are some there who had no desire for the doctors to be on Oberon in the first place. Those same voices were none too pleased to see a platinum-rated mercenary company escorting them. Those people will be hostile to you."

He allowed his smile to become cold. "Over the last few years, I've developed skills at dealing with people that are hostile to me. Not all of them involve killing. Trust me when I say that I can take care of myself."

She nodded, a satisfied expression on her face. "Good. I don't particularly care for those individuals and wouldn't mind seeing them taken down a peg or two. Shall we proceed?"

CHAPTER ELEVEN

THE HUGE BRONZE doors began opening slowly when Envoy Lathrop pounded her small fist on one. The designer's no-doubt-majestic intentions were ruined by an annoying, high-pitched whine from one of the hidden motors.

On reflection, that seemed perfectly fitting.

With Command Constable Daskalov right behind them and Brad's security team bringing up the rear, he and Envoy Lathrop walked inside.

The entryway was more ostentatious than the doors. Marble floors that looked imported stretched deep into the foyer. The wide, tall room hosted alcoves containing what appeared to be bronzed busts.

He turned to Envoy Lathrop as they crossed the expansive chamber. "Seriously?"

She nodded. "As serious as it gets. One thing you have to remember about the Council of Speakers is that the only thing bigger than their greed is their ego. I've often wondered if things worked the same in other parts of the system. Does everyone with wealth and power think exclusively about themselves and how to get even more wealth and power?"

Brad chuckled. "Not always, but I'm pretty sure those few are the exceptions that prove the rule."

Half a dozen large men in black uniforms and holding automatic weapons stood guard at a second pair of bronze doors that seemingly matched the exterior set.

One of those men took two steps forward and casually raised his hand for Brad's party to stop. "Who comes before the Council of Speakers of First Oberon to seek justice?"

Envoy Lathrop rolled her eyes and shook her head. "You know damned well who I am, Wiley Goodlett. I got you this job. Not only that, I told you who I was going to go get when I left. An hour ago."

The man looked uncomfortable. "Sorry, Jewell. They told me I had to say that even after I told them it sounded idiotic. You and Commodore Madrid can go in. Everyone else stays outside."

Brad nodded. "Well, this has been a nice visit, Envoy. You can rest assured that I'll be telling stories about it for the next couple of years. Come on, Saburo. If we hurry, we can get back to *Oath* before they get dinner ready."

"Do we really have to do this?" Lathrop asked with a sigh. "Why don't I go ahead and cut through all the posturing and provide a solution that doesn't induce testosterone poisoning in every onlooker within 300 meters?

"Commodore Madrid, the Council is obviously concerned about their security. On the other side of the equation, so are you. I suggest Lieutenant Phan and her fire team escort you into the Council chambers and take a position near the entrance for your personal security."

She held up a finger before the guard in black could object. "And when I say *suggest*, I really mean *insist*. At least so far as the Council Guard is concerned."

The large man shrugged. "Far be it from me to tell an Envoy what to do. If the Council doesn't like it, they can tell you themselves."

Lathrop raised an eyebrow as she turned toward Brad. "Will that be acceptable? Colonel Saburo can remain here in the grand foyer. I'm certain that he won't have any difficulty finding you if there's any disturbance."

The Vikings' combat team leader grinned at the Council Guard. "I won't have any trouble at all."

Once again, Lathrop rolled her eyes. "Jesus. It's like riding herd on a bunch of twelve-year-olds. Let's get inside before I have to put anyone in time-out."

This set of doors, unlike the previous pair, opened silently when Goodlett pressed his comlink. With Lieutenant Phan behind him, Brad followed Lathrop into the Council chamber.

A wide horseshoe-shaped table dominated the chamber. If he thought the foyer was gaudy, he was now forced to reassess his judgment. In comparison to the inside, the foyer was bland.

He mentally floundered while searching for the appropriate description. After a few seconds, he decided the room had the feel of a bordello that catered to men with no sense of taste.

Garish reds and washed-out blues dominated the walls. Unless he was mistaken, the fabric was velvet. He could just imagine how skin-crawling it would feel to run his hands across the slick surface. He barely managed to repress a shudder.

In addition, seven massive oil paintings hung evenly spaced around the room. Following the theme so far, they were of the seven people sitting at the table.

Unless he was gravely mistaken, the wide, polished table was made of genuine wood. The expense of importing something that size could have probably refurbished an entire tunnel in the city outside. Maybe two.

A dozen guards similar to those in the foyer stood arrayed against the rear wall, each rigidly at attention with an automatic rifle held at port arms. Brad suppressed his amusement. Positioning the guards in that manner made it extremely unlikely that they'd be able to respond in a timely fashion to any threats. His fire team could take them out before they got their feet in the right posture to return fire.

Brad focused his attention on the Council of Speakers. Six men and one woman. The woman, seated at the middle of the left-hand wing of the table, was older than any of the men around her.

That didn't necessarily make her weaker, though. Experience with his own crew proved that, and Brad could tell from the glint in the woman's eyes that she was a hawk.

Lathrop stepped forward and stopped in the middle of the chamber, executed a bow similar to the one she'd graced him with in his office aboard *Oath*, and then placed her hands behind her back.

"Councilors, I present to you Commodore Brad Madrid of the Vikings Mercenary Company."

Without any further fanfare, she walked to the right side of the room and leaned somewhat insolently against the wall.

The man seated at the center of the table, a somewhat corpulent individual, leaned back in his chair and considered Brad. The man's motion caused an ominous creak somewhere in his seat.

"So, this is the man who saved so much of First Oberon? I somehow suspected you'd be much taller, Commodore Madrid."

"Appearances can be deceiving, Councilor…"

"Warner Killian, Grand Councilor of First Oberon. Seated to my right are Councilors Booker Santistevan, Lynda Eden, and Stefan Bernier. To my left are Councilors Dewitt Nakamura, Jeromy Maez, and Zackary Schrum. Together we rule First Oberon."

Brad took a moment to examine everyone at the table. Only one of them appeared on the bronze doors: Lynda Eden. That was probably important.

Something even more critical was the fact that he recognized one of the other Councilors. Brad had met the man identified as Zackary Schrum before, though under a different name.

He knew him as a shady merchant in Oberon City named Ferarre. Back when he'd worked with the Cadre.

———

Brad was surprised to see the man again. He'd expected the Cadre to hunt Ferarre down and murder him for leaking information that led directly to the destruction of the Terror's base.

Oh, Brad hadn't exactly left the man a choice when he confronted him in his dingy office in Oberon City. He expected the man's long sleeves covered the two gashes Brad had cut into him with his vibro-blade two years earlier.

Ferarre's face certainly still bore the scars of their meeting. Brad had struck him there with both the hilt of his vibro-blade and his pistol during their brief meeting. Hard enough to knock the man unconscious in the end. And he'd obviously broken the man's nose, because it hadn't healed correctly.

Brad was grateful that he'd been wearing a face wrap during the interrogation. While Ferarre—or should he think of him as Schrum?—was scowling, Brad didn't believe it was because the man knew who stood in front of him now.

No. If Ferarre suspected that Brad was the man who'd beaten and cut him, he'd already be on his feet, shouting.

Falcone would be pleased to get her hands on Ferarre. And, Brad admitted, it was exceptionally convenient that she was on Oberon right now. He wasn't precisely sure what she was doing today, but he'd be able to get hold of her once this meeting finished.

Finding Ferarre opened up several new lines of investigation that might very well lead them to the people they wanted. In fact, since the man was in a position of power there, it was almost a certainty that he'd been responsible for smuggling in the nerve agent and explosives.

Of course, the fact that he was a person with power there made seizing him directly a chancy thing. They'd have to be somewhat delicate.

The man hadn't been that wealthy or powerful in Oberon City. How had he accumulated the juice to become one of the seven ruling members of a much larger city in only two years? The answer, Brad suspected, was the Cadre.

Ferarre must still be working for them.

Brad decided to roll with it. If he played his cards right, he might get a direct line to the Cadre's new base. First, however, he needed to make certain the Council of Speakers respected him.

He spread his hands, emphasizing the empty space in which he stood, and then meaningfully looked at each of them behind their wide table. "I was under the impression that the Council of Speakers wished to discuss today's events and find solutions. This, however, looks more like you intend to call me on the carpet. If this is how you intend to play things, I'll just leave now."

Killian scowled. "The Council of Speakers isn't used to being spoken to in that tone of voice, Commodore. I suggest that you remember who you're dealing with. We control this city and our guards control the exits to this room."

Brad laughed. Moreover, he made certain that he laughed deep and long.

Finally, wiping fake tears from his eyes, he smiled widely at the Grand Councilor. "That's good. I didn't expect you to go for farce, but this show is *very* entertaining."

He waved a hand across his face and put on his most deadly serious expression. "A number of people have found to their sorrow that they can't push me around. I strongly suggest that you don't become one of them.

"We can either discuss things in a civilized manner or I'm going back to my ship. If you try to stop me, my troops are more than capable of killing anyone in our way. And that includes the people you think are going to protect you. With the exception of Envoy Lathrop, I should add."

Brad allowed the silence to drag out for a few seconds so they could consider the seriousness of the situation.

"If you want to fight, we'll fight. If you want to find the people that tried to kill thousands of your citizens, we'll do that. Personally, I'd much rather find the bad guys and make them pay, but in the end, the decision is really up to you. Make the call, Grand Councilor."

The silence that pervaded the room for the next few seconds ended abruptly when Envoy Lathrop began slow-clapping. Every single member of the Council of Speakers, no matter how shocked or angry they were, shifted their glares to their employee.

Rather than deterring the woman, it seemed to only make her clap harder.

She winked—she actually winked!—at Brad. "Twelve-year-olds. Didn't I tell you?"

The woman ceased clapping and strode out to stand beside Brad. She faced the Council of Speakers with her hands on her hips.

"If you can stop this idiocy, we have would-be mass murderers to find. The Commodore was right to use the word *farce*. You're behaving like spoiled children. If you want revenge on the people that tried to overturn everything that we built here, you need to set your petty egos aside and start talking rather than posturing."

For the first time, Lynda Eden spoke. "Insolently put, but correct. On behalf of the Council of Speakers—whether they want me to speak for them or not—I apologize. If you will allow it, Commodore, I believe that we should adjourn to a more private location where we can discuss these serious matters."

From the corner of his eye, Brad saw that Ferarre strongly disapproved.

The other councilors were also displeased, but none of them spoke out against their colleague. That had to be a true sign of her influence.

Brad inclined his head. "Nothing would please me more, Councilor Eden."

CHAPTER TWELVE

As the councilors rose to file out through the door at the back of the chamber, Brad stepped close to Lieutenant Phan. "Call *Oath* and see if they can get a message to our guest. Let her know that I've met an old acquaintance of ours from Oberon City. He's moonlighting with the Council of Speakers."

"Which one?" the officer asked softly. "I'll make sure the Colonel knows as well."

"Schrum, but don't use his name on an open channel. I'm pretty sure they can't tap into our equipment, but we can't take the risk."

"I'll send a runner," she said with a nod. "I need to let Saburo know we're going to a different room, in any case. He'll send someone back to the ship. What do you want him to do?"

"Nothing for the moment," Brad said after a moment's consideration. "Trying to directly take this guy into custody might cause us all kinds of unintended complications. Now that we know he's here, we should be able to take steps against him once he's away from this building."

"Copy that. I'll send my man out now. Once he comes back, we'll escort you to wherever they're taking us."

As soon as Lieutenant Phan walked away, Envoy Lathrop stepped over to Brad. "You handled them better than most. I've seen plenty of people come and go, and rolling over for the Council never works. They sense weakness and they can't seem to stop themselves from trying to exploit it, even when it's not in their best interests."

Brad nodded minutely, having already grasped that. "I noticed that Councilor Eden is the only one of them pictured on the doors. I assume that means she's the only holdover from the Council of Speakers that dedicated the doors. If so, I wonder why she doesn't hold the central leadership position. Is that by choice?"

"Turnover in her line of work is, as they say, high," the envoy said with a small smile. "Infighting on the Council tends to have drastic consequences for the losers. The biggest target is always the Grand Councilor.

"In my considered opinion, trying to run this city is a death sentence in slow motion. Somewhere, somehow, the holder of that office always ends up with a knife or two in his back."

Lathrop inclined her head toward the door the Council had departed through. "Councilor Eden is no one's fool. Her longevity on the Council of Speakers comes from her patiently laying the groundwork to exercise her power and guarantee her safety. She doesn't need to sit at the center of the table to exercise that control."

"Good to know. I have another question, if you don't mind. Councilor Schrum looks somewhat familiar to me. Is he a new arrival? I feel certain that I've seen him somewhere else in the system."

Lathrop shrugged. "He's relatively new here in First Oberon. I became aware of him two years ago, but he's only been on the Council for about nine months.

"I'd watch out for him if I were you. He was one of the strongest voices against allowing the doctors to take up residence here. Strident, one might say. He's not your friend."

Lieutenant Phan's trooper came back through the foyer entrance, and Brad nodded toward the rear exit. "Well, it's time to go see if anyone on the Council is friendly."

———

The room behind the main chamber was a normal conference room. A standard table filled the center of the room, surrounded by comfortable office chairs. Even the wall decorations would have fit inside almost any business center.

This was probably where normal business was conducted. Why the Council felt the need for the drama in the other room was a mystery to him.

There were enough seats on one side of the table for all seven councilors to sit facing him. Once again, Lathrop found a handy wall to hold up.

Lieutenant Phan and her troops spread out along the wall holding the door they had just come through, opposite the Council guards that arrayed themselves along the far wall.

Brad took the hint and sat opposite the Grand Councilor. "Shall we get down to business?"

Ferarre chose that moment to lean forward and scowled. "I want to know why you smuggled those bombs and the nerve agent into our city. What kind of game are you really playing?"

"Excuse me?" Brad asked softly as he raised an eyebrow. "What would make you think I would ever do such a thing, Councilor Schrum?"

The man pointed an accusing finger at Brad. "No one else in this city has anything to gain, and your reputation for destruction proceeds you, Commodore. For reasons unknown to me and the rest of the Council, you smuggled a weapon of mass destruction into First Oberon.

"Or did you? Perhaps you only planted explosives and told the OSE that there was a nerve agent. We have no proof of that, either. Just your unsupported word."

"Actually," Command Constable Daskalov said from where he'd taken up station beside Envoy Lathrop, "the Commodore was kind enough to turn over all of the recorded video and audio from his combat team. I'm afraid the proof is incontrovertible. Not only were there explosives—that they had not brought along, I might add—but there was definitely nerve agent in that building."

"As if he'd give you data that hadn't already been tampered with,"

Ferarre said with a sneer. "OSE is already in plenty of trouble, and you're just looking for a way out of it. Not only did you allow an unauthorized military force to land here, you stood by like an idiot when they blew up half the damn city."

From Daskalov's dark expression, Brad was certain this wasn't the first run-in these two had had. He considered keeping his mouth shut and letting the Command Constable tear a strip off the Councilor, but decided that he needed to take control of the situation.

"You've got a pretty big mouth, Councilor," Brad said judiciously. "There's only one problem with your paranoid delusion. OSE technicians tested our combat suits and they were positive for VX-65. The doctors can confirm that with their own testing.

"As for the bombs, I'm sure you have quite a lot of video of us leaving the port. None of us could have been hiding that amount of explosive on our persons. So, Councilor, when exactly are we supposed to have planted the bombs?"

The man half-rose from his seat. "I'm not the one needing to explain his actions. If you're not going to answer my questions, I believe that we'll have to provide some negative inducements to get the answers we want."

"You mean, to get the answers that you want," Councilor Eden said dryly. "I believe we've allowed this to play out long enough. You've had an ax to grind about the doctors being on Oberon for as long as I've known you.

"I can't say that I personally understand it, but perhaps it has something to do with what happened to your face. Did you get bad medical care at some point? I suppose the answer to that is obvious, but just for the record, I thought I'd ask the question."

"How dare you?" Ferarre said as he stood slowly. "I don't care who you are, you have no right to speak to me that way."

Eden laughed as though he'd just told her the most delicious joke. "Don't be any more of a fool than you must be, Schrum. The Council already decided that the doctors were staying. Perhaps you'll recall the vote, five to two. You and Grand Councilor Killian have made your dissenting views plain, but you lost. Get. Over. It."

With a dismissive wave of her hand, Councilor Eden turned her attention to Brad, ignoring the sputtering man she'd just sparred with.

"Rest assured, Commodore, that the majority of the Council does not believe what you just heard. We allowed it to play out so that you could see for yourself who your friends are in this body."

That almost made Brad laugh. He had no friends in this body. Potentially, he might find temporary allies, but this nest of vipers was incapable of friendship.

"I appreciate that," he said, hoping the lie rolled effortlessly off his tongue. "Now that we've settled that matter, shall we see if we can discover how a weapon of mass destruction made its way into First Oberon?"

Councilor Eden turned her attention to Command Constable Daskalov. "Let's see what our security service has been able to determine. Athanasius?"

Surprised in spite of himself, Brad followed her gaze. Perhaps he'd been too hasty in saying that no one in this body had friends.

The OSE man nodded. "We figured the easiest place to start looking was the work crew assigned to renovate the buildings. We found plenty of basic construction workers, and they all had the same story.

"Their management team told them that there'd been some kind of regulatory hold-up. They told them that the doctors were continuing to pay the workers' salary while this was cleared up, so no one made a fuss. They were getting paid to stay home and do whatever they wanted."

Eden frowned. "I've been keeping an eye on the bureaucracy where it concerns this project. There was no hold-up on our side."

"No, there wasn't," Daskalov agreed. "We figure that was a lie so that they could get the workers out of the building while they rigged their trap. We haven't been able to confirm that, because none of the construction managers seems to still be here."

"What?" Grand Councilor Killian asked. "Where did they go?"

"Various places over the last month. They and their families slipped away on vacations and other pretexts. Not one of them is still here to be asked pointed questions. Someone went to great lengths to make absolutely certain no one was talking out of school."

Brad was willing to give a lot of credit where it was due, but he felt the need to clear his throat. "Forgive me, Command Constable, but it seems to me that whoever was doing the investigation missed some significant details. What about building inspectors? Port inspectors? Someone must have seen something."

"I'm sure they did," the OSE man said agreeably. "The challenge is going to be to find them and get them to admit it. Within broad limits, one can get anything they want for the right amount of money here on Oberon.

"Let's take the building inspectors, for example. So long as the building will safely hold pressure, just about anything else can be overlooked for an appropriate bribe. I've got people out speaking to the man assigned to inspect the new hospital complex. Or I suppose I should say the *former hospital complex*.

"I can virtually guarantee what he'll tell us. That once he was notified by the contractors that they were pausing work, he stopped going to the site. They probably paid him a little extra to be absolutely certain he didn't stop in for an unexpected visit, but the man had no reason to expect high explosives and nerve agents. Those aren't exactly the kind of thing any building inspector would be looking for."

"So, you're telling me that we're never going to find out who did this?" Grand Councilor Killian objected. "That's preposterous! This was obviously a very large operation. Someone must know something and I expect you to find them."

The red-uniformed man nodded. "I and my people are doing everything humanly possible to find a lead, Grand Councilor. It's clear this attack was meticulously planned and executed over a period of months.

"It's likely that the nerve agent entered through the port in an innocuous container that no one could have spotted. We don't have testing machines looking for that sort of thing. Why would we? I mean really, who can get their hands on military-grade nerve agents? Frankly, I thought they'd been outlawed decades or centuries ago."

Brad cleared his throat. "Why don't I run you through everything that I know. Truthfully, that's all I can contribute to your investigation. The ambush was planned and put in action before I even landed.

Whether I was the target, the doctors were, or we both were, that's probably only going to be determined long after I've departed Oberon."

When he'd left *Oath* to come to this meeting, that was exactly how Brad had felt. Now that he knew someone on the Council was likely in the pay of the Cadre, what he'd just told the Council was a polite fiction. It was very likely he'd have answers within the next day or two.

He focused his attention subtly on Ferarre. The man's sour expression told Brad that he wasn't pleased his ploy had failed. With three days until Brad's ships were scheduled to depart, it was going to be a race to see which of them struck first.

Brad suppressed a cold grin. With Agent Falcone at his side, he knew where he'd be putting his money. *Let the games begin.*

CHAPTER THIRTEEN

AFTER WHAT FELT like going over the same dreary details a thousand times, Brad returned to *Oath* without incident. As he'd expected, the meeting had been a complete waste of time. With the exception, of course, of coming face-to-face with Ferarre.

That was an unadulterated stroke of luck. One he hoped they could leverage into a solid lead on the people behind the attack. He felt confident that if they tugged the threads hard enough, they'd lead back to the Cadre. And the mysterious Phoenix.

Xan had carried out Brad's instructions and Falcone was waiting with Michelle in the wardroom.

Over the years, they'd spruced up the wardroom to the point that it actually felt homey. They'd paneled the serviceable metal cabinets with thin sheets of dark wood and hung pictures taken from the scanner records of their various battles. Their victories.

Those reminded him of Sara Kernsky's office on Ganymede. The Mercenary Guild factor had just such an image over her desk to commemorate the hard-fought victory over the Cadre that had cost her so many friends and comrades all those years before. This was similar, though with a thoroughly Vikings feel.

The two women were huddled at one end of the wardroom table, chatting over coffee. They looked up as he walked through the hatch, and smiled.

"I was beginning to wonder if we'd have to come pry you out of their hands," Michelle said. "I heard they were being asses."

"Self-important asses," he agreed. "I don't think I was directly in danger this time. It was more a matter of them trying to show me who was boss. It didn't quite work out the way they'd planned."

"What was this other matter?" Falcone asked. "The message was somewhat garbled. Something about someone we knew from somewhere. I hope it was important enough for me to break off my investigation and rush back here. Not that having some time to get to know your wife wasn't fun and useful."

Michelle nodded. "We've been talking about you, of course."

Of course they had.

He poured the last of the coffee into a cup, turned off the burner, and sat across from them. "We've met one of the people on the Council of Speakers. Back when we were at Oberon City a few years back. Ferarre was his name then, but now he goes by the name Zackary Schrum."

The Agent sat up abruptly and set her coffee cup on the table with a clatter. "Seriously?"

"It was definitely him. I asked the person who came to get me a few general questions about him. He arrived here shortly after I beat the snot out of him in his office on Oberon City. He's been working behind the scenes since then but only joined the Council of Speakers about nine months ago.

"From everything I can tell, it takes a lot of money and influence to get a seat at that table. Since he didn't have anything on that scale before, I'd be willing to place a rather large bet that the Cadre is behind his sudden rise in the world."

Falcone picked up her coffee mug and took a long sip, frowning as she thought. "That *is* very interesting. Did he recognize you?"

Brad shook his head. "I never took the face wrap off while I was in his office back then. The only thing he'd have to go on is my general height and build, and my voice. I watched his face pretty closely and I don't believe that he's suspicious.

"I could be wrong. The man might be the best actor to hit the stage in my lifetime. Odds are long but I suppose it's possible."

"Do you think he's the one who smuggled the nerve agent into the city?" Michelle asked.

Before he could answer, Falcone cut in. "Of course he is. This is no coincidence. In fact, once you start working in the intelligence field, you discover there is hardly ever any kind of coincidence. We're going to have to find a way to get our hands on him."

And this time, Brad promised himself that he wasn't going to let the rodent live. When dealing with pirates and slavers, it seemed no good deed went unpunished.

"Do we have any idea where he's living?" Falcone asked. "I can certainly have some of my contacts get the information for us, but the fewer people that know we're interested in him, the better."

"It shouldn't be too hard to find out, even if we're being careful," Brad said. "I'm wondering what his follow-up plan is."

The Agent cocked her head. "Follow-up plan?"

Brad set his forearms on the metal table and steepled his fingers. "If he had instructions to stop the Doctors' Guild from setting up shop, then he's going to be scrambling to find a new way to make that happen. The Cadre isn't just going to accept his explanation that we stopped plan A and they lost."

Falcone considered that for a moment before nodding. "Since the Doctors' Guild hasn't located alternative housing, they're still working out of the ships. The Pythons are responsible for their security now, so I suppose we should read them in."

"I can make that happen," Michelle said. "I'm meeting Colonel Ahmed later this evening to discuss a couple of logistical issues before we head out."

"That would be good," Brad said. "I'm certain Ferarre has people watching our ships." He turned his attention to Falcone. "If I might be so bold, what exactly were you working on today? I assume it was some variant of 'find the bad guys.'"

"Close enough," she agreed with a nod. "The agency doesn't have any paid informants on Oberon, and I was thinking to change that. If the Cadre is operating out of First Oberon, then I want to have my own eyes watching for signs of another attack before it happens.

"For something like that, you can't just pick someone off the street. First, you need someone that has enough access to know that something is going on. Second, you need someone that is steady enough that they won't inadvertently reveal themselves when something happens. Third, they need to be closed-mouthed so that no one knows they're spying for us.

"As you might imagine, that pretty severely cuts down on the number of potential candidates. Worse, many of the people that *are* qualified and suited to be a spy for you don't have the character. Or they have too much character, not that I expect to find that particular problem on Oberon."

That made sense to Brad. In very general terms, that was similar to how one hired people for a mercenary company. "Did you find anyone?"

"I found a few potential candidates," she said vaguely. "I wouldn't exactly call them hired at this point, but those type of folk would certainly be willing to do a little scouting for us. I'd wager that I can get Ferarre's new address within the hour."

Brad checked his wrist unit. It had been a long day. For his people, it had been an exceptionally long day.

"Put those feelers out. Michelle, that will also give you time to carry out your scheduled meeting with the Pythons. Then we can all have dinner and get some sleep before we can act on this. We definitely want to have as many locals as possible off the street when we start moving."

"I can do that," Falcone agreed. "What kind of operational plan are we looking at? A smash-and-grab? Your people blow a hole into his place and we snag him?"

"I'd rather not leave First Oberon with the hounds baying behind us," Brad said with a shake of his head. "We've already told everyone that we'll be staying for the next few days. Let's try something a little less obvious first.

"If we can slip inside his place, we might be able to get him before anyone is aware we have. That would give us days to ask some pointed questions."

A slow smile spread across Falcone's face. "I like the way you think. Shall we meet back here around 0200 local?"

"Sounds perfect. See you then."

———

As expected, Ferarre lived in one of the most exclusive and well-guarded areas of First Oberon. Unlike Olympus Mons City on Mars, the wealthiest people on Oberon didn't go deep. They built on the surface and used exclusive tunnels to get to the rest of First Oberon.

Frankly, Brad wasn't sure why they bothered. Uranus wasn't that much to look at. If this had been one of the moons of Jupiter or Saturn, that would have been a very different story. Well, he supposed people just had to make do with what they had.

Brad lay on top of a small pressure ridge in an armored vac-suit, examining these buildings through a military-grade optical enhancer. A hand-picked fire team was spread out of sight behind him.

He'd brought extra people when he'd left the pressurized domes who had taken pains to avoid being seen getting out onto the surface. They were off conducting the "exercise" he was using as cover in place of Brad and his primary strike team.

"They aren't much to look at, are they?" Falcone asked over the short-range radio link as she lay beside him, also examining the buildings. "I mean, seriously, why not just build down in the city? Those damned buildings had to have cost a fortune, and they're *ugly*."

Brad agreed. Built to withstand exterior conditions on Oberon, the buildings looked like toy blocks that some angry child had stacked roughly on top of one another and then knocked over in a fit of pique.

"I've seen two exterior patrols," he said after a few minutes. "They're using some kind of surface rover. Probably two or three people in each. They're taking a clockwise path around the entire group of buildings. Probably some kind of neighborhood watch."

"Ferarre will have some kind of internal security, as well," Falcone said. "Politics here is a contact sport. He's not just going to let anyone wander in and potentially murder him."

"That's where we have an edge," Brad said, putting away his optical enhancer. "Our equipment is a lot stealthier than the locals can get their hands on. It won't take us much effort to get past the roving guard.

"If you can get us inside without setting off any alarms, we can deal with what we find inside. My techs will make certain no one calls for help."

She set down her optical enhancer and rolled over far enough so that she could see him through her faceplate. She was grinning.

"You can take it as an article of faith that I'll get us into that building without tripping any alarms. However, we need to figure out which of the buildings he lives in, first. My contact told me roughly where he lived, but that's not enough detail to identify a specific building."

Brad smiled back at her. "I have a plan for that. With any luck, we won't have to do anything that might tip our hand. I'd hate to have to break into every building out here just to find the little bastard."

Falcone laughed. "Yeah, let's avoid that."

———

Sneaking past the guards proved to be relatively uncomplicated. The small rovers stayed on a predictable track, circling the exclusive neighborhood, and followed a regular schedule. All Brad had to do was wait for one to pass before crossing and moving out of sight between the buildings.

Once past the patrol, they moved slowly and only cautiously crossed any open areas. If there was a way to stick to the shadows, they did so. Uranus's blue-green light didn't make for very bright illumination, so he felt safe enough.

The communications specialist they'd brought along with them, Corporal Tisha Reece, located a handy com junction and began removing the access panel, while the rest of the fire team spread out to give her cover.

Brad had seen an expert hack into the Cadre's com and security systems when they'd attacked the Terror's base two years earlier. Deeply impressed, he'd invested some good money to make sure he had other talented people who could do almost as well. The corporal had proven well worth the training costs.

Reece plugged in several cables and began tapping on a tablet. "The communications are encrypted from end to end, it looks like. If I were trying to see the content of any calls, this would be a lot harder. But all I need to see are the routing tables. Those are in a simpler code. A standard code." She sounded almost offended at this lapse of professionalism.

"I found the one we're looking for. All I need to do at this point is determine which building matches the hardwired location."

"And how are you going to do that?" Brad asked, curious. "Just because a certain line is labeled as going to the target, how can you determine which of these physical residences matches up with the other end of the cable?"

The trooper turned and smiled at him through her helmet. "Someone helpfully put a map of this so-called neighborhood into the maintenance files and labeled which cables followed which route. I figured they'd do something like that. Otherwise, maintenance would be a nightmare.

"Here we go. It looks like the target is on the outskirts off to our left. Probably just inside the patrol area. Here's a map."

Brad and Falcone leaned in and examined the readout on the tablet.

"I can find that," Falcone said.

After the corporal had closed everything back up, the fire team made its way to Ferarre's home. Again, they saw no signs of activity on the surface. No surprise, considering the conditions they were working under.

The block walls of Ferarre's house looked like everyone else's: thick, uncolored stone. Each building they passed had had an emergency exit, basically a personnel airlock with a security system to prevent it from being opened from the outside without the right codes.

Corporal Reece popped an access plate and plugged her tablet into the system. Once she gained access, Falcone would work with her to disable the security system.

"Huh," Reece muttered. "That's funky."

"Is something wrong?" Brad asked.

"You could say that. It looks as if the security system is off-line."

Falcone edged over beside the trooper. "Let me take a look. It might be some kind of trick."

After a minute of tapping the screen, Falcone looked over at Brad. "It's not a trick. Someone deactivated the security system about two hours ago. Moreover, it looks as if they didn't do so from inside the building. I can see how they accessed it from this very port.

"This lock cycled twice after that. Once right after the security system was shut down and again about thirty minutes later."

That didn't sound good. In fact, it sounded really bad. For Ferarre.

"Open it up," he said with a sigh. "We go in according to plan even though I suspect our mission is already busted."

Falcone tapped something on the tablet's screen, and the exterior airlock door opened.

Tucked inside the small chamber was Ferarre's pajama-clad corpse. From the desperate and strangled expression on his face, his previous visitors had simply dragged the man out when they left and let the vacuum kill him. Then they'd stuffed his body back into the lock and departed.

"Well, this sucks," Falcone said.

"Less for us than for him," Brad said with a grimace. "I don't expect we're going to find anything, but let's make sure he didn't leave any evidence we can use to track the Cadre before we head back to the ship."

CHAPTER FOURTEEN

NEEDLESS TO SAY, there was a lot of excitement the next morning. Thankfully, they'd been careful in how they'd slipped out of the city, and no one really believed a platinum-rated mercenary company would slaughter people like that.

At that point, Brad decided that they were leaving for Io, Cadre fleet be damned. Unfortunately, he still had the crippled *Alan-a-dale* to factor in.

Thankfully, he'd come up with a plan to fool the Cadre. It took some sharp negotiation with Colonel Ahmed and the Pythons, but they struck a deal. *Alan-a-dale* couldn't move under her own power. Any ship towing her would be a huge disadvantage in acceleration. In other words: a big target.

So, when his ships left Oberon orbit, the Cadre warships that were almost certainly still somewhere near knew he wouldn't be going very fast. The spies they'd left in First Oberon would undoubtedly let them know the moment the Vikings departed, as well as giving them what they could about the mercenary company's course and speed.

Brad gave them exactly what they wanted.

His fleet of ships departed with a frigate in tow. Only the frigate was not *Alan-a-dale*. It was one of the Pythons' frigates.

As soon as the Vikings were on course away from Oberon and clear of direct view, they cut the Pythons' ship loose and accelerated. The other mercenary ship would circle back around and return to Oberon on a slower course.

The Cadre wouldn't be looking for someone coming back to Oberon. That sort of thing made no sense. They wouldn't figure out that the Vikings didn't have a ship in tow until it was far too late.

That meant that Brad's three ships slipped away from the area around Uranus without being tracked. It did leave one of their frigates in orbit around Oberon, but the Cadre wasn't interested in that one ship. They wanted Brad, and now he'd escaped.

Brad called ahead to Io and arranged a tow for his damaged frigate. It would take an extra week to get it safely to the Io shipyards, but that couldn't be helped.

The time wouldn't be wasted. By the time *Alan-a-dale* arrived, perhaps Falcone would have some information about the Cadre *Bound*-class destroyer.

No matter what happened, the frigate wasn't going to be helpful in tracking down the Cadre at this point. So long as they got it into a repair slip so that Hiroshi Kawa could start getting it back into fighting shape, that was good enough.

Saburo's father would also have to see about the repairs to *Bound by Law*, but since she was a former Fleet vessel, Brad was hopeful Falcone could get them to assist in providing spare parts. With luck, he'd have them both back into fighting shape by the time he needed them.

————

Brad's initial hope that they'd have actionable intelligence from the Agency about the Cadre *Bound*-class destroyer by the time they got to the Io Shipyards didn't pan out. They'd arrived without any word at all from the people sent to examine the Cadre destroyer's wreckage.

Perhaps they hadn't made it there yet. Brad didn't know. Falcone assured him that she'd have an update for him on the status of the investigation as soon as possible.

He arranged for a room just down the corridor from his quarters for Falcone and retired to his on-station quarters with his wife.

True to her word, Falcone had information by morning. She joined Brad and Michelle in their quarters for breakfast.

The little kitchen nook there wasn't very big, but Brad had paid good money to be absolutely certain his quarters were safe from any kind of electronic intrusion. No one would be listening in on this discussion.

Once they were all settled in over their meal and had blunted their hunger, Falcone started her impromptu briefing. The seriousness of her expression was somewhat belied by the way she was putting away her waffles.

"The Agency team made it to the coordinates you fought the Cadre," she said between bites. "The wreckage is spread out a bit, but they were able to locate several significant parts of the *Bound*-class destroyer that you destroyed. It proved relatively simple to find some significant components with serial numbers."

Michelle brightened. "So, you've identified the ship? That means we'll be able to track down who Fleet sold it to. We can put the screws to them and make them tell us what they know. No way the Cadre got that ship through legal means."

"That's even truer than you know," Falcone said grimly. "You see, that destroyer was lost in battle against the Cadre about a year ago. Lost with all hands. Literally destroyed when her powerplant exploded."

"Um," Brad said. "That ship was in pretty good condition for something blown to atoms."

"Exactly my thought," Falcone agreed. "Somebody faked the records of that battle so that the ship could disappear. Somebody in Fleet."

"Shouldn't somebody have noticed something like that?" Michelle asked. "What about the crew? If they were supposedly all killed, having them turn up somewhere later would be really bad."

Falcone nodded. "I suspect the ship was betrayed by somebody in the crew. Not a single one of them has turned up, so it wouldn't surprise me at all if the Cadre simply executed them when they took possession of the ship.

"We'll probably never know all the details. The only hard and cold fact is that if it happened once, it could've happened again. All of those ships that you fought could very well have gone through the same thing."

That was very bad news and Brad scowled. "Including a carrier that Fleet wants kept secret? Surely, they'd have noticed one of those going missing."

"So far as I've been able to determine, none of them is missing. I'm not certain what that means, but you can rest assured I've got talented and dedicated people asking very pointed questions on that subject to Fleet officers on Earth and Mars."

"It doesn't mean anything good," Brad said. "The Cadre has their claws deep inside the Commonwealth government and Fleet. If they can conceal the destruction of an entire vessel, even only a destroyer, that means they have so many people in place and in such positions of power that they're not concerned about information leaking out."

"That's terrifying," Michelle said. "How can we possibly fight somebody with that kind of power? Everdark, how did the Cadre even get that kind of power?"

Brad smiled grimly. "That's the big question, isn't it? We have several leads we can follow, but the end result seems clear. We need to find the Cadre's new base and destroy it. These ships have to be supplied somewhere. If we can locate that base and disrupt their logistics chain, that's really going to hurt their ability to use them."

"I think that the Cadre has been playing a long game," Falcone said. "At this point, it's obvious to me that they aren't the ultimate power pulling the strings. They're a tool that someone inside the Commonwealth government is using to execute their plans. Finding that person or persons has to be our ultimate goal."

"The first step in that has to be the Cadre," Brad said. "This carrier of theirs changes the game. It's a big ship, almost as big as the cruiser they have. *Lioness* is still out there too. Whoever is in control of the Cadre has to fuel her and the carrier. They're not like the smaller ships. They're going to take He-3 in fairly large quantities."

"That ties in with what the agency suspects," Falcone said. "There are very few locations where they can mine He-3. The Cadre attack on Saturn stole a bunch of equipment, or so we think.

"You remember the attack on Blackhawk Station, Brad? We never got a chance to directly question the woman that survived the attack on Ringbolt Associates after the attack. Svetlana Garrow. The Cadre assassin tried to blow you up, and your people got you out and off to Serenity Station. By the time the Agency moved in, Garrow was gone.

"The entire company area was thoroughly trashed during the raid, but we were finally able to determine what the Cadre had been after. Plans and equipment related to cutting-edge extraction of He-3. Based on what we're seeing now, it has to be something that relates to their being able to fuel and operate large vessels like the carrier and *Lioness*. Probably other ships, too."

"Cutting-edge in what way?" Michelle asked, taking a sip of her coffee. "Are we talking something to just make the process more efficient, or to expand the number of areas where it can be extracted from?"

Falcone pointed a fork holding a bit of waffle at Michelle. "That's a very perceptive question. Ringbolt Associates' plans were to cut into SaturCorp's business at Saturn. To do that, they needed something that made the operations profitable. That's where the increased efficiency came in.

"They hadn't expanded beyond test-bed operations, but they believed that they had the necessary technology to get more He-3 from a similar volume of gas than SaturCorp. They'd still need drop ships like the one you used to command, but they expected to be able to get almost twice the output from a similar volume of gas."

Michelle whistled. "That's huge. If they really could manage something like that, they'd put even big companies like JoveCorp and Satur-Corp at a massive disadvantage. They'd be scrambling to figure it out just to survive."

"And that's only the refining part," Falcone continued. "The extraction technology would allow them to expand operations to cometary bodies and still get enough He-3 to make the work worthwhile."

That news left Brad stunned. Something like that, even if the processing was inefficient, would allow the Cadre to put an extraction platform almost anywhere. Even out in the Kuiper belt. That would make finding them via the He-3 angle almost impossible. They needed to look at other angles.

"What's Fleet doing to confirm they're actually in control of all of their ships? That carrier didn't just pop out of nowhere. Someone is lying to them and they need to be sure that they aren't being misled on an epic scale."

Falcone nodded. "The Agency is helping with that. We're digging into the records and finding people inside Fleet that know others assigned to each ship. Not high-ranking people. Enlisted folk.

"They're sending messages to their friends and verifying they are all right. If any ships slipped into the Cadre hands, the crew won't be responding, so our contacts will know. It's going to take weeks to verify which ships are still under Commonwealth control, but we're starting with the drone carriers.

"Admittedly, Fleet is cautious about allowing people to communicate when they are stationed in critical facilities, but we'll make it happen and still stay under the radar."

That was one angle, Brad admitted, but there were other threads to pull on. "What about the VX-65 nerve agent? Does the Commonwealth really make crap like that? I was sure it was illegal."

"Just because it's illegal doesn't mean it's unavailable," Falcone said. "You can get anything you want in the Outer System, for a price. The Commonwealth outlawed these kinds of weapons in its founding documents. If someone is caught making it, that's a death sentence.

"And just such a group of people were caught a couple of years ago, tried, and executed. The exact same nerve agent. Seems a bit coincidental to me."

"There is no such thing as coincidence," they all intoned together.

"I'm so proud," Falcone said with fake cheer. "Now, this group of terrorists wasn't associated with the Cadre. Which in the end doesn't really mean that much. We all know that the Cadre will pick up what it wants from wherever they can get it.

"The original group's ideology was something of a crossover between nihilism and anarchy. Basically, they just wanted to kill lots and lots of people, preferably on Earth or Mars. They set up a research-and-manufacturing facility in the trailing trojans."

Brad rose and took his dishes into the small kitchen, washing them off as he thought. The King of Planets had a large number of rocky and cometary bodies gravitationally locked about sixty degrees ahead and behind it as it orbited the sun, each cluster hosting its own set of colonies like Serenade Station. The regions weren't at all close, and most people didn't associate the three distinct areas, even if they were all locked in the same way by the massive planet's gravity.

"Just a hunk of rock that nobody cared about," Falcone continued. "They masqueraded as a mining outfit and no one knew any different until an informant let the Agency know what they were really working on.

"We passed that information on to Fleet and they raided the place. Needless to say, those fools weren't interested in surrendering. They kept shooting until they couldn't shoot anymore.

"Fleet confiscated everything and dropped it all onto Jupiter. They rigged it in a capsule to go deep and fast so it would've burned up before it released any serious contaminants into Jupiter's atmosphere."

"Are we sure that Fleet really did that?" Michelle asked as she washed her own plates. "Right now, I'm not certain I'm willing to believe that."

"Neither am I," Brad said. "I think we'd best go check the place out for ourselves. If someone in Fleet claimed they cleaned it out but left all the equipment there, the Cadre could've been working on something all this time.

"And if they have been, they might still be there," he said with a wolfish smile. "If so, I think we can make them very unhappy to see us."

CHAPTER FIFTEEN

Brad pulled *Oath of Vengeance* and *Heart of Vengeance* in for this mission. *Bound by Law* was already in dock and getting her damage repaired. Which was perfectly fine because they shouldn't need a ship-killer this time.

The Cadre shouldn't have any way of knowing that Falcone had given them the data they needed to trace the nerve agent. That meant they wouldn't be on guard. Well, any more than people making contraband worthy of the death sentence would already be.

The trickiest part of this mission was arriving on station without tipping their hand that they were coming. The Cadre forces on the asteroid would be extremely leery of anyone trying to dock with them. So, Brad had to make absolutely certain they didn't see them coming.

Both of his ships were equipped with Fleet-grade stealth, so if they came in slowly enough, they shouldn't be detectable. The only way the targets—if there were any—would know that they were coming was to see one of his ships block a specific star, at least until they got very close.

He ordered both ships to come in on a direct path, taking the asteroid's orbit into account. As they got closer, the ships shouldn't seem to be moving side to side or up and down. They would just be growing larger.

The asteroid itself wasn't anything to write home about. The Jupiter trojans had some seriously large asteroids and cometary bodies, but this one was basically just a piece of debris that had probably been captured millions of years before. A rocky little husk that was barely two hundred meters across.

From the records that Falcone had obtained for them, the anarchists' base was well concealed. Since no one had any reason to bother with the asteroid, their work had gone unnoticed.

The interior was large enough for the research facility and perhaps two dozen people. After all, the fewer people who knew about what they were doing, the less chance they had of being discovered.

Not that that had helped them in the end. Someone had obviously betrayed them. Brad wondered if it was a Cadre-linked supplier of equipment and materials. If he was such a person, he'd make certain the anarchists got everything they needed, and then, once they'd achieved success, he'd turn them in.

If the Cadre worked it right, their contacts in Fleet would step in and arrest everyone. They'd leave people to dispose of all the hazardous materials and dangerous equipment. If those people truly worked for the Cadre, they'd file a report that said it was done and leave everything in place.

"We're about twenty minutes out," Michelle said. "Still no signs of activity. No power emanations, no lights."

Not that they had actually expected to see anything.

Brad opened a com channel to Saburo. "Are you ready to launch, Colonel?"

The Vikings' combat team leader and his team were already in armor aboard their assault shuttles. All they had to do was break free from the ships and start gently accelerating toward the asteroid.

"All set, sir. We're ready to launch on your command."

"Detach all combat craft in twenty seconds on my mark. Mark. Good luck and try to take some prisoners alive."

"You sure know how to take all the fun out of things, Commodore. We'll do you proud. Saburo out."

Heart of Vengeance carried a single assault shuttle, though it no longer carried troops unless they really needed them, while *Oath of Vengeance* had three. *Oath*'s small craft would be able to deliver quite the knockout punch for such a small facility, no matter how many people were inside.

Brad sat in his command chair watching the small craft inch forward on the main display. They were emitting no signals, so his tactical officer was manually putting in his best estimation for their positions.

Even though it was probably safe for Saburo to send signals back to the two warships, Brad had ordered radio silence. All it would take was one small mistake to let the enemy know they were coming.

Konrad Bogdanov updated the display every few minutes until the shuttles were almost on top of the asteroid. Then the man turned toward his commander.

"Sixty seconds out, Commodore. Still no sign that their approach has been detected."

"Should I start accelerating as soon as the attack begins?" Michelle asked. "We can be there in less than five minutes."

Brad considered that but shook his head. "If Saburo does his job right, they may not know he's boarded for a little bit. Let's give him a chance to secure as much of the facility as possible. Once he notifies us that he's in hostile contact with the enemy, we'll start accelerating.

"If it turns out that the asteroid is empty, then it won't make a difference. If it's full of hostile pirates, let's give Saburo the best chance possible to get full surprise."

He turned his attention to the tactical officer. "I want you to be ultra-attentive once the attack begins. It's possible the Cadre has external weapons platforms. If they fire, I want you to take them out as quickly as possible."

Both of his officers signaled their understanding.

Saburo and his men stopped the shuttles near the surface of the asteroid and made their assault in armored vac-suits. The original plans indicated that there were three separate airlocks: one for cargo, two for personnel. So, all the Colonel needed to do was send an assault shuttle to each.

"Incoming signal from Colonel Saburo," Xan Wong said from the communications console. "They're initiating the attack. The airlocks are still powered, so they're bypassing security and they'll head in at the same time."

That was the first clue that something was not as it should be. There was no reason for Fleet to have left that facility powered.

The next sixty seconds passed with syrupy slowness.

"All three teams are going in," Wong said.

This was it. If the facility was filled with Cadre pirates, all hell was about to break loose.

———

Brad waited tensely for the first update. He didn't have to wait long.

"We've got hostiles in here," Saburo said after just fifteen seconds. "We really stirred them up, too. We expected no more than a few dozen people, but I think we're dealing with at least twice that.

"No heavy weapons, but these people have some training. Marine-level at least. I think we're dealing with some of those Cadre commandos."

Perfect. Though Brad supposed this wasn't entirely unexpected. If this was as critical a facility as they'd thought, the bastards would protect it as well as they could.

"Take them out as quickly as you can," Brad ordered. "We don't want them to destroy any of the critical computer files if we can avoid it. These people are our lead to the Cadre base."

"Copy that, Commodore. Saburo out."

Brad turned his attention to his crew aboard *Oath*. "All ahead full. Scanners at maximum. They know we're here now, so let's see if they have any guardians for us to deal with."

"Scanners at maximum," Konrad confirmed. "Nothing in the immediate area around the asteroid. Not unless they're exceptionally stealthy."

"Don't discount that," Brad warned his tactical officer. "We've seen that the Cadre has access to some formerly Fleet vessels. That means that it's possible they have the same kind of stealth technology we're using. From this point forward, we need to treat operations against the Cadre as if we were attacking Fleet vessels."

From the look she gave him, Michelle wasn't convinced that that was the case, but she didn't argue.

Frankly, he wasn't convinced that they had that many Fleet vessels. But the fact that they had any at all was deeply disturbing. He didn't believe for a second that Fleet had misplaced one of their secret carriers. There was something far deeper going on than he'd ever imagined possible.

"We're three minutes away from the asteroid," Michelle said. "How close do you want us?"

"Within easy gatling range. If we have to withdraw and fire on the place, I'd rather leave something intact for us to salvage later."

"Contact!" Konrad said moments later. "Correction, two contacts. They're outside gatling range but inside extreme torpedo range. I'll need a minute to work up an estimate of their size, but based on their acceleration, they're probably corvettes."

Brad did some mental calculations in his head. If he went with the worst-case scenario, those were heavy corvettes or light destroyers and they might be as powerful as *Heart of Vengeance*. If it were just those two ships against his corvette and destroyer, this could get hairy but the outcome was probably going to be in his favor.

Unfortunately, his recent dealings with the Cadre had left Brad convinced that he couldn't assume anything. These two ships might be the only guardians this facility had, but then again, they might not.

If these ships entangled both his ships, others in the area could get *Oath* and *Heart* into their crosshairs. The best course of action for him would be to assume that was exactly what the Cadre wanted to happen.

As they say, hope for the best and plan for the worst.

"Keep the scanners going at maximum power, Konrad," he ordered his tactical officer. "It's always possible there are more ships waiting to get the drop on us. How quickly can we take these ships out?"

The tactical officer turned in his seat to face his commander. "If they want to stop us from capturing this asteroid, they can't just sit out there firing at us. They're going to have to come into our range. We could use the asteroid as cover and blast them with torpedoes as they close."

"We could," Michelle said, "but that would leave us pinned against this asteroid if other ships open fire from hiding. We'd have no room to maneuver and no speed. I think we'd be better off going out to meet them."

Konrad shook his head. "Then we wouldn't be in range to cover Colonel Saburo. No matter how we slice this, we're going to have to divide our attention. I'd rather stay close to our people and make sure that somebody doesn't pop out of nowhere and blow the entire asteroid to pieces."

"Throw the tactical representation onto the main screen," Brad ordered.

Once the man had done so, Brad considered the distances involved between the two enemy ships, the asteroid, and his ships. This would've been a really useful time to have all of his vessels there.

As things sat, he couldn't cover everyone well enough to be certain of the outcome. He was going to have to take some kind of chance one way or the other.

"Have *Heart* take position near the asteroid and provide cover for Colonel Saburo," he finally ordered. "They can add their fire to ours as we close with these other ships. That's going to make their fire less accurate, but it makes certain that these two ships aren't going to harm our people on the asteroid."

Two heavy corvettes—if that's what they were—against a destroyer like *Oath of Vengeance* would be a little bit too close to an even fight for Brad's taste. If they weren't as powerful as *Heart*, Brad would be able to press his advantage and really hurt them.

Well, he wasn't going to settle this by dithering. He gestured to both of his officers to execute his plan and sat back in his command chair to see what the results wound up being.

A minute later, Konrad smiled at him. "I think those are both light corvettes. They've got good acceleration for their size and their emissions aren't as well shielded as they could be. The second one is somewhat obscured behind the first, so it's possible that it's a heavy. We'll know as soon as they open fire."

With that, almost as if they were listening in, the two ships in front of *Oath* opened fire. The lead vessel fired two torpedoes, while the one behind it fired four.

So, one heavy and one light. They weren't going to be pleased that *Oath of Vengeance* could fire two more torpedoes than they could. This fight would be interesting, but it should be relatively secure in the outcome.

Konrad straightened abruptly. "New contact! There's a vessel coming out of stealth to our rear. It's not inside torpedo range yet, but it's damned close. They have us bracketed!"

That's what he got for thinking this would be easy.

CHAPTER SIXTEEN

BRAD OPENED a communications channel to *Heart of Vengeance*. Jason Finley's face appeared on the small repeater screen by Brad's knee.

"I see them," Jason said before Brad could speak. "I'm heading out to engage them now. We just have to hope that there isn't another one hiding out there in the darkness, just waiting for me to uncover the asteroid."

"Try to finish them as fast as you can," Brad said. "I don't want to leave Saburo hanging in the wind."

"Copy that. *Heart* out."

Brad focused his attention forward. "Fire all torpedoes, Konrad. Use the gatlings to take theirs out."

In some ways, a straight-up space battle didn't have a lot of mystery. Once the pieces were on the table, everything depended on the skills of the tactical officers and commanders. And, of course, what kind of weaponry those ships carried. Just based on the law of averages, *Oath of Vengeance* was going to win this fight.

That didn't mean that she'd come out unharmed. Without finesse, a space battle was like two men in a boxing ring, standing toe-to-toe and hitting one another in the face over and over. Somebody was going to win, but everyone was going to bleed.

A nimble fighter, though, could dance around his opponent while still punching his lights out, dodging every blow that came his way. That was how he saw the Vikings. Not only the finest crew possible, but engines and other equipment that had been enhanced to give them performance beyond what any average ship could manage.

In *Oath*'s case, that included her targeting systems. A lot of tactical officers would be forced to use their gatlings as water hoses, spraying everywhere and hoping that the other guy got wet.

Not Konrad Bogdanov and *Oath*. The destroyer had the very best scanners the Vikings could get outside of Fleet. Or possibly even inside Fleet.

Brad had tapped Kate Falcone for sources as they'd been upgrading their ships over the last two years. She'd come through in spades, in both quantity and quality. It wouldn't surprise him if she'd diverted Fleet equipment his way.

That wasn't even technically illegal anymore, as his people were reserve Fleet officers and the ships were counted as reserve units. The whole deal, after all, had been to provide a legal fig leaf for Brad's having used *nukes*. Anything less than that was fair game.

Konrad deftly guided *Oath*'s gatling fire to the enemy torpedoes. He stopped four of the enemy torpedoes before they even got close. He stopped one more just short of *Oath*, but the last one got through.

That's where Michelle showed her skill. A destroyer was a fairly large ship compared to a torpedo, but she made it dance around at the very last moment. His wife had come a long way since commanding a SaturCorp drop ship. Her deft touches on the controls made the destroyer swerve to the side at the last moment, almost as if it were skating on ice.

The enemy torpedo had been about to punch into the destroyer's aft quarter but found itself facing empty space. Not much empty space, but more than enough for the reactive armor to stop the fragments coming toward the ship when the torpedo exploded.

No doubt Mike Randall would complain about overstressing the engines, but Brad knew he'd rather do work tuning his beloved engines than patching holes in the hull.

With the enemy zero for six, Brad focused his attention on their own initial salvo. The enemy fired at them again right before *Oath*'s torpedoes entered terminal range. Konrad had already fired again, since *Oath*'s rate of fire with torpedoes seemed to be somewhat faster than the enemy's.

The Cadre's antimissile defense wasn't up to the same standards as the Vikings'. Of the eight incoming torpedoes, they only managed to stop four.

Konrad had targeted the heavier enemy vessel with five torpedoes, shunting the other three toward the lighter unit. In one of the flukes of space combat, the lighter unit stopped all three of the torpedoes coming its way.

That meant that the heavier ship took four torpedoes. Her reactive armor did the best it could, but nothing was that good. Explosions rippled along the heavy corvette's hull for a few seconds and then the ship exploded.

The two enemy vessels had positioned themselves close together to provide covering fire for one another. The survivor saw the folly of that particular strategy as she took the direct brunt of her comrade's explosion on their own hull.

"Enemy heavy corvette destroyed," Conrad said needlessly. "The lead ship seems to have lost some engine power, so I believe they've taken damage to Engineering. Eight torpedoes outbound to the enemy."

Brad wished he'd risked cramming *Law*'s combat teams aboard. They'd put every man and woman from *Oath*'s combat teams onto the asteroid, which left nothing to try and board the enemy ship. He'd just have to let this play out and see if they could recover anything from the wreckage when the fight was over.

A glance at the tactical repeater showed *Heart* was having a little bit rougher of a time. The ship behind them was a heavy corvette of the same weight class, and they were throwing identical numbers of torpedoes at one another.

"Bring us about," Brad ordered Michelle. "I want us back to cover *Heart* as quickly as possible.

"Konrad, keep using the gatlings on that second salvo and make sure that our torpedoes finish this guy off."

Brad knew that he was taking a chance that the enemy ship he'd targeted would get away or be able to fire at the asteroid, but it was a small one. The chances that the light corvette could stop eight torpedoes was vanishingly small.

Though, he had to admit that they'd showed far more skill thus far than he'd anticipated. Best not to be so confident. He'd keep a very close eye on the ship to see what happened when the second salvo hit it.

"Keep us close enough to help cover the asteroid," Brad ordered. "We'll have to split our attention until the guy behind us is gone."

This was pretty much the worst-case scenario that Brad could have anticipated. The enemy had spread the Vikings' attention all around the asteroid. There were several different ways the enemy might pull a surprise and kill a bunch of his people.

Heart of Vengeance and the other corvette were exchanging torpedoes in waves. The other vessel certainly seemed to be competently run. Whoever was using their gatlings for defense was good.

Honestly, they were too good. Better than Erasmo Poulos, *Heart's* tactical officer. So far, the enemy had managed to stop every single torpedo *Heart* had fired at him and he was continuing to close with the other ship even though *Oath of Vengeance* had turned toward their duel.

That was either suicidal stupidity or they knew something Brad didn't.

Brad felt his eyes narrowing. Had the Vikings really managed to slip up on the asteroid, or was this some kind of convoluted trap? A simpler explanation might be that they thought they could get the drop on Brad's ships, but that didn't explain why the enemy was pressing the attack when the battle was turning sharply against them.

"We hit the light corvette on our side," Konrad said. "Two hits. I can't believe the bastard managed to stop six of the other torpedoes. Their ship has stopped maneuvering, but they fired a third salvo before we got them."

The tactical officer grunted. "They targeted the asteroid. We still have two of their torpedoes coming at us, too."

Crap. Now Brad had to choose between rushing to the defense of his other ship or making absolutely certain none of the enemy torpedoes managed to get to the asteroid.

Under normal circumstances, he might be tempted to just let the torpedoes get through to the asteroid. There were only two, rock could absorb a lot of damage, and his people were in armored suits.

These circumstances were far from normal, however. If the Cadre thought it was worthwhile to fire at the asteroid, they had a reasonable expectation that their shots might be able to eliminate it. There was something down there that they definitely didn't want anyone else getting their hands on.

Konrad sat up a bit straighter. "The ship fighting *Heart* just fired a salvo at the asteroid too. Poulos missed them. We've got four inbound on the asteroid from almost diametrically opposed angles."

And Brad couldn't allow a single one of them through or Saburo and his men might all die. No pressure.

"Increase our acceleration," Brad snapped. "Michelle, get us as close to the asteroid as possible and put us in a position where we can bring our gatlings to bear on all four torpedoes. Focus on the ones closest to us right now, Konrad."

Oath of Vengeance leapt forward as Michelle applied full thrust. There was no way they were going to get back to the asteroid before the most distant torpedoes struck it, but they could improve the odds of Konrad taking them out first as much as possible.

With the last enemy ship charging toward the *Heart of Vengeance*, they couldn't count on them stopping the enemy torpedoes the had slipped by it. Jason was going to be focusing his full attention on the Cadre warship charging down his throat.

Brad opened a channel to Saburo. "I've got good news and bad news, Colonel. Which do you want first?"

"I'll take the bad news," his combat team leader said. "It'll go well with the bad news I have on my end."

Perfect.

"There were three Cadre ships waiting out here to ambush

anybody that came wandering along," Brad said, resisting the urge to ask what was going wrong for his combat teams. "One heavy corvette and two light corvettes. We took out the heavy completely and crippled one of the lights. *Heart* and the final ship are still duking it out, but I have every confidence who's going to come out on top.

"The bad news is that you've got four torpedoes inbound. We're going to do our very best to take them all out, but nothing in life is guaranteed. If the enemy thought the asteroid was worth shooting at, that probably means something really, really bad is going to happen if they hit what they were aiming for."

"I suspect I know what they're shooting at," Saburo said with a grunt. "The power plant is located close to the surface. If they crack the asteroid's shell, it's probably going to go off and gut everything in here. Including us."

"Can you shut it down?"

"Negative. We've got enemy holdouts in there, and we don't dare use anything too heavy or we might set it off. Some of my boys have a bunch of them pinned down in there. That might be stopping them from blowing the place themselves. As you might imagine, we're doing everything we can to keep them from getting near the controls."

It was Brad's turn to grunt. Either one of those situations could kill his entire ground force and one of his oldest friends.

"Try to take them out as quickly as possible," Brad said. "What about the rest of the facility?"

"We're making a lot better progress there. The plans that Agent Falcone got for us are incomplete or perhaps the Cadre has been expanding. It's a lot bigger in here, with more labs and manufacturing areas, than we expected.

"Thus far, we've killed two or three dozen trained fighters and captured maybe a dozen noncombatants. Not sure what in Everdark they're doing in here, but it probably has to do with manufacturing that VX-65."

That was a safe bet. They wouldn't be using commandos to manufacture the deadly nerve agent. There would be chemists or whatever the appropriate science was.

"Speaking of the nerve agent," Brad said, "make certain that somebody doesn't let any loose or you'll lose every single prisoner."

He wasn't worried about his own people if that happened. Their armor would protect them. The captured noncombatants, on the other hand, were vulnerable. It would be just like the Cadre to let loose a nerve agent to kill their own people so they couldn't talk.

"Do the best you can and let us know if your situation changes. If you have to, get our people out of there. Jump into space and we'll find you."

Each of his troops had a transponder built into their armor that would aid in recovery operations if that happened. It was far better to chase them all over this corner of space than to have anyone killed.

Brad refocused his attention on the incoming torpedoes. Konrad had already stopped the two targeting *Oath* and was focused on the closest two headed for the asteroid. In just twenty seconds, his tactical officer wiped one of those out of space and refocused his attention on the remaining one on their side of the asteroid.

The tactical officer also had gatlings firing at the more distant pair, but hitting those was much more chancy. It would also take longer to see the results of his fire.

With his man doing as much as he could, Brad turned to the scanner readings coming from the disabled Cadre corvette. It hadn't fired any more torpedoes, but that didn't mean that they were sitting idly by.

Michelle wasn't going in a straight line as she headed for the asteroid. They wouldn't want to be caught in someone else's gatling fire because they thought they were safe.

That made Brad think and he felt his eyes narrow. If that power station was so close to the asteroid's surface, it might be vulnerable to gatling fire, and asteroids couldn't evade.

Taking temporary control of *Oath*'s torpedoes, Brad fired four at the disabled Cadre warship. If it was already dead in space, this wasn't going to materially change things. Well, except for any survivors there, and he wasn't too worried about people who had ambushed him. If they were working on doing something sly, this might just save his people's lives.

His caution proved warranted when the torpedoes were almost halfway to the corvette. His scanners started picking up debris flying off the surface of the asteroid. He'd been right!

Brad had no idea if it was anywhere near the power station, but they had to take out that damned warship. It was a race against time now.

CHAPTER SEVENTEEN

THE ANGLE the mass-driver rounds were impacting the asteroid at could be worse, Brad supposed. There was a lot of rock they'd have to chew through before they could get to the power room. The torpedoes, on the other hand, would directly strike the target unless he stopped them.

"Konrad, you really need to knock out those torpedoes," he said softly but with a lot of emphasis.

The tactical officer waved one hand over his shoulder and kept his attention focused on his console. "I'm working on that, boss. Thirty-five seconds until impact."

Brad's mental timer slowly counted down as the torpedoes raced toward the asteroid. At about twenty seconds out, Konrad took out one of the torpedoes. At this range, the mass-driver slug that either would or wouldn't stop the remaining torpedo had already been fired. All they could do was pray.

As time ran out, Brad realized they weren't going to get lucky. And then, at the last moment, one of the mass-driver rounds clipped the torpedo. It wasn't enough to destroy it, but it altered its trajectory and sent it slamming into the asteroid in a slightly different area.

They all stared at the screen, waiting to see if the asteroid blew up and took their friends with it. It didn't, but that certainly didn't mean everything was okay. The torpedo must've breached the base in a different area, because the asteroid began spewing atmosphere and debris.

Brad opened a channel to Saburo. "Talk to me."

As he waited for a response with growing worry, he noted that the torpedoes he'd fired at the Cadre corvette that had been firing the mass-driver rounds were almost on top of it. The enemy had taken two of them out, but that wasn't going to help him.

Both torpedoes slammed into the light corvette and it exploded. Two down and one to go.

"We're a bit shook up, Commodore," Saburo finally said. "The facility took a hit and we've lost atmosphere, but I stuffed the noncombatants into one of the compartments and sealed the hatch. Unless something is seriously wrong, we'll probably still have someone to talk to.

"We took advantage of the distraction and rushed the power room. The fighting is over. We lost a few people and have some injured. How's it going out there?"

Brad sat back, relieved. He never liked losing even a single person, but that was better than losing everyone. At least the boarding action was a success. With a little bit of luck, it would change the course of this investigation and lead them to the new Cadre base.

"I think we've about got it in hand," Brad said. "Double-check everything and be certain you've secured any nerve agent. I'm going to be coming over to take a look for myself as soon as we take care of the last enemy ship."

Saburo nodded in a small video display. "We'll have everything secured by the time you get here, sir. Go finish kicking their asses."

"We'll do our best, Colonel. *Oath* out."

Brad turned his attention to Konrad. "Fire a full spread of torpedoes at that last ship. Finish them."

"Yes, sir. Firing now."

Eight torpedoes flashed away from the destroyer and headed for the remaining enemy corvette. With *Heart* keeping it pinned down, his salvo should be more than enough to finish this fight once and for all.

Being cornered only made the remaining Cadre corvette fight harder. Any chance it had of fleeing was gone. At this point, they had to know they were going to die.

One of *Heart*'s torpedoes smashed into the enemy and crippled an engine. In exchange, the Vikings' corvette took a glancing hit amidships. It looked as if her reactive armor might have mitigated the damage somewhat.

Being crippled at exactly that moment proved to be a very costly and fatal event for the final Cadre ship. They didn't stop a single one of Konrad's torpedoes. The ship's destruction was abrupt and total.

Brad opened a channel to *Heart of Vengeance*. As soon as Jason's face appeared, Brad knew the damage had been light. His former tactical officer had a relieved expression.

"We got clipped, but it isn't too bad," Jason said, confirming Brad's guess. "We're losing some air, but it's not going to hamper our operations. We're still fully combat-effective. No reported injuries."

"That's good," Brad said as he rubbed his face. "It sounds as if Saburo lost some people and they have some injuries. They have the asteroid secured, so I'm going to recall a couple of the assault shuttles and head over to find out what's going on. Get ready for some of the wounded to be coming your way.

"While I'm examining the facility, I want both ships searching the debris field and keeping watch for other ships. If there any survivors, pick them up. If we can identify who we're dealing with, that will be worthwhile. These bastards were a little bit more competent than I'd have expected from the Cadre."

The other man nodded. "Michelle and I can handle that. I look forward to hearing what you find over there, sir. I hope it really helps us screw the Cadre up."

"Me, too. *Oath* out."

Brad rose from his chair and stretched his back. Sitting there throughout the fight had his back in knots. He stepped over beside Michelle's console.

"Have Saburo split the wounded and send some to *Heart* and some to us. The dead come back to *Oath of Vengeance*. Start a search pattern around where we took out those two ships. If we can pick up survivors, great. If not, too bad for them."

He looked over at Konrad. "I want you to keep an eagle eye out for threats. If any section of one of these wrecks is large enough to have weapons, make certain that they don't come to bear on our ships. Also, be wary of new ships. Full scans all the time."

It took twenty minutes for the assault shuttles to detach from the asteroid and begin their journey back to their motherships. Brad left Michelle in charge of *Oath* and went down to oversee their arrival.

The medics took seven people with injuries ranging from minor to serious to the infirmary. Other troopers carried out bags containing the bodies of four of their comrades. Those also went to the infirmary to be stored until they could get back to Io.

Once that sad task was accomplished, Brad accompanied the troopers back to the asteroid facility. It was time to see what they were dealing with and ask some hard questions of the noncombatants.

The assault shuttle carrying Brad docked at a personnel lock. There was no need to sneak aboard now, since they had complete control.

Brad still wore a combat vac-suit because they hadn't finished patching the damage caused by the torpedo yet. The section he was exiting into was still pressurized, but a single failure elsewhere in the facility could leave everyone in a vacuum with no warning. Best to be exceptionally careful.

The corridors around the airlock showed signs of heavy fighting: gouges on the floors, burns on the bulkheads, and divots blown out of ceilings. The fallen enemy fighters must've been gathered somewhere else, but the blood from where they'd died still covered enough places to make this place look like a torture chamber.

Saburo met him a moment later. The Colonel's armor was blackened in a couple of places and certainly looked as if it had taken a few glancing shots. The man had his helmet off and resting in the crook of his arm.

"I just finished a quick tour of the compartments we can access.

Some are sealed off because of vacuum, and a couple of others are locked down because the people formerly running this place considered them dangerous, I think. There are biohazard warnings on those areas, so I'm betting that's where the nerve agent is being concocted and stored."

Brad nodded and took off his helmet so that he could speak more clearly with his friend. "You said you had about a dozen noncombatant prisoners. Scientists?"

"Looks like. They basically shat themselves when we showed up. The guards tried to kill them all. We found half a dozen of the science types with lots of bullet holes, so there must've been orders to take them down fast. We surprised them and the guards couldn't finish the job."

"Make certain to record good video of everything you see. Falcone is going to want to go over everything. She's going to regret her bet that this place was empty.

"I know she needed to stay on Io so that she could try and track where those damned enemy ships might be hiding, but that's not going to keep her from bitching now that we found something and she's not here for it."

Saburo laughed. "That woman could be a mercenary, with the amount of bitching she does when things don't go her way. I'd thought spies were a bit more accepting about setbacks."

"Agent Falcone is a woman of many depths," Brad said piously. "Let's go see these noncombatants. I have some unpleasant questions that I'd like to get answers to. When I make threats, keep a stern face."

The Asian man escorted Brad through several corridors and to a compartment where two of the Vikings troopers stood outside, their weapons at the ready. The officer opened the hatch and gestured for Brad to precede him.

The noncombatants were all seated in rolling chairs on the far side of a conference room, under the watchful eyes of four additional troopers. The prisoners looked terrified.

With good reason.

Brad set his helmet down on the table and rested his hands on his hips as he stared coldly at each of the prisoners.

"My name is Commodore Brad Madrid of the Vikings Mercenary Company. As you are no doubt aware, you are my prisoners.

"I suspect this facility of manufacturing an outlawed nerve agent called VX-65. I'm going to ask each of you some very pointed questions, and if I'm not happy with the answers you give, I'm going to put you into an airlock and slowly release the atmosphere until I hear what I want."

One of the men, and older fellow with shocks of white hair, scowled. "This is outrageous."

Brad gave him an arctic smile. "I couldn't agree more. Using your skills to create a banned weapon of mass destruction *is* outrageous. Do us all a favor and save your outrage. It will do you no good here."

Ignoring the man's bluster, Brad turned to Saburo. "Have two of our troopers escort that one to a different compartment for me. Make certain none of the others speak to one another. If they refuse to shut up, gag them."

As tempting as it might be, Brad wasn't going to be stuffing anyone into an airlock. He wasn't going to give the rage inside of him that much hold over him ever again. But that wouldn't stop him from threatening the hell out of them. These were no innocent civilians—and the Commonwealth *could* execute them for manufacturing chemical weapons. They probably wouldn't, but they had to know that a firing squad was definitely a potential future for them all.

Brad watched the two troopers manhandle the selected prisoner out of the room and followed them down the corridor to what looked like someone's office. After they'd dragged the man inside, Brad seated himself behind the desk and steepled his fingers on its surface.

"I'm not even going to pretend that I'd offer you a seat. My associates will hold you there while I ask questions, and should I be dissatisfied with the answers I receive, they will escort you to your final resting place.

"Now, who are you? Keep your answer short and sweet. Save your excuses for someone that cares."

The man drew himself up as much as he could while the troopers held on to his arms and shot Brad a haughty look.

"My name is Dr. Nicolas Bradburn and I am in *charge* of this facility.

You claim that you are a mercenary commander? Then I shall see you expelled from the Guild and executed for treason!"

"Really?" Brad asked, drawing out the word slowly. "That's showing a lot of chutzpah in the face of reality, Doctor. What makes you think the Commonwealth is going to do anything to me when I captured you working in a Cadre facility?"

"Preposterous! This is the Raeburn Research Laboratory. The Commonwealth founded and funds this facility. You've killed a number of scientists working for the Commonwealth and executed Commonwealth Marines. It is *you*, sir, who are a pirate!"

Could the man really believe that? Had the Cadre fooled the people working here so completely that they believed that they were working for the Commonwealth?

"If this is a legitimate Commonwealth facility, how do you explain the fact that you are working on banned weapons of mass destruction?" Brad asked, leaning back in his seat to consider the scientist. "No one in the Commonwealth is supposed to be developing nerve agents."

Bradburn sneered. "We have a Commonwealth charter for this work, and you are a murderer."

The supposed scientist jerked himself forward, only to be stopped by the troopers holding his arms as he snarled at Brad.

"And I shall enjoy seeing you put out of an airlock for this atrocity," the man said with smug satisfaction.

CHAPTER EIGHTEEN

FALCONE SLAPPED a printout down on Brad's desk. "As difficult as this is to believe, these idiots might have some reason to really believe they are working for the Commonwealth government."

Without picking up the printout, Brad crossed his arms over his chest and stared at her. "You've got to be kidding me."

She dropped into the chair in front of his commandeered desk at the Raeburn Research Laboratory. "I've been over their computer systems with a fine-toothed comb. They've been sending reports to what they believe to be the Commonwealth about their progress, been receiving orders and instructions on what to do, and seemed to have every reason to believe that they were operating under lawful authority.

"Which isn't to say that they really are. My superiors have spoken with official representatives from the Department of Commonwealth Defense and other divisions of the government. They have no records of this facility and strongly deny ordering *anyone* to do research into banned weapons of mass destruction of any kind."

Brad felt his expression sour. "What about the scientists? Did they really believe that they were working for the government, or should they have known they were working for the Cadre?"

"Oh, they should've known that they were working for the Cadre," Falcone said with a snort. "Unfortunately, it seems as if people with scientific degrees can be a little short of what the rest of us call common sense.

"When someone shows up at a university or corporation claiming to be from the Commonwealth and offers one a job to work on something that is completely illegal, I would certainly hope that one would at least call the government and ask about the people offering the employment. Only, that doesn't seem to have happened in this case."

Falcone looked disgusted. "Not a single one of these idiots contacted the Commonwealth to verify that the job offer was legitimate. A smooth-talking recruiter—probably the same woman from the descriptions—spoke to each of them over a year ago and had them on their way here within a week.

"They even signed nondisclosure agreements, and half of them are refusing to speak with us at all because they're afraid we're going to put them in jail for talking."

Brad shook his head. "I think I could probably point out which ones we're talking about. They cooperated with the wrong people and refused to cooperate with the right ones. What about the guards? The scientists thought they were Commonwealth Marines. Have we been able to trace any of them?"

The woman nodded. "About half of them actually were Commonwealth Marines at one point. Mostly people that were thrown out for one reason or another. Not the kind of folks you'd like to meet in a back alley."

"Considering that they gunned down half a dozen scientists when we breached the airlock, I'd imagine not."

Brad rubbed his face tiredly. It had taken almost a week to get Falcone out there, for her to send detailed information and requests to the Inner System, and get answers back. His hope that they'd find a lead to take them directly to where the Cadre warships were hiding had been dashed.

The three ships that had been guarding this facility were Fleet surplus. There hadn't been any survivors, unfortunately. None of the computer systems on those vessels had been salvageable.

They'd had experts go over the computer systems on the asteroid, but they might as well not have bothered. The idiot scientists had maintained everything and they didn't know anything about the Cadre.

Worryingly, there had been no indication that any of the nerve agent had left the facility. He had people now going through the stockpiles and determining how much might be missing. First Oberon might not have worked out for the Cadre, but Brad was worried there would be more successful attacks elsewhere.

"Where do we go from here?" he asked slowly. "We've got nothing."

"That's not entirely true," Falcone disagreed. "I've been following up on the He-3 trail. Those capital ships need fuel, just like you said. It has to be coming from somewhere.

"Neither JoveCorp or SaturCorp would knowingly support the Cadre, but I've had people watching all the tankers that are getting filled with refined fuel. There are some anomalies. I'm sure this won't come as a shock to you, but they're all based out of Blackhawk Station."

He felt himself frowning. "Actually, that is surprising. After the Cadre tried to take the entire place out, I'd have expected them to be careful about who they dealt with."

"It's been two years since the attack," Falcone disagreed. "People can't maintain peak awareness over that kind of time. They've slacked off. Oh, I'm sure they still got a very firm set of controls over their defensive platforms, but other companies have moved in to take Ringbolt Associates' place.

"One of them—and I can't tell you which one at this point—is probably working with the Cadre, because they've been shipping tankers out to Fleet installations that Fleet never asked for and that never arrived to deliver their cargo. That means the Cadre is the most likely recipient."

A knock on the hatch interrupted them. Dr. Merlyn Grass stood outside in the corridor, frowning through her glasses at them.

Brad gestured for the woman to come in. "What can I do for you, Doctor?"

"I have bad news," the scientist said, wringing her hands. "I've just completed an inventory of all biohazard storage facilities. A significant quantity of the VX-65 nerve agent is unaccounted for. I'm still not certain what the material in the containers actually is, but it's definitely inert and not harmful in the same way as the nerve agent would be."

Falcone leaned forward in her chair. "Just how much nerve agent are we talking about? I've provided you an estimate of what I believe was used at First Oberon. Is the missing amount comparable?"

The mousy woman shook her head. "Worse, I'm afraid. By my estimation, if you include what was released at First Oberon, there is enough nerve agent unaccounted for to conduct an additional three attacks of the same severity."

Brad sighed. One more complication that could end up killing tens of thousands of people. What in Everdark did the Cadre gain from doing this? If one was looking at money, their piracy and terrorism made no sense. There had to be something more going on behind the scenes.

"How much nerve agent is still locked up here, Doctor?" he asked tiredly.

"Roughly ten times that amount. I've been operating under the assumption that we're not going to leave that here when we depart. I've gathered it all together in reinforced containers for disposal."

Brad glanced at Falcone. "What does the Agency have to say about that? Are we good to destroy it? Let me be clear: that's my preference."

The Commonwealth Agent nodded emphatically. "I've been given instructions to make sure that that happens. When we depart for Io, I believe we should drop it into Jupiter's atmosphere. Not only that, I want to see this entire facility destroyed so completely that there is no chance anyone will be able to make it operational again or relocate the equipment."

"Then that's what we'll do," Brad said decisively. "Dr. Grass, if you'd have your people take anything that you'll find useful elsewhere but that is not specific to developing and manufacturing nerve agent, I'm more than happy to let you take it with you when we depart for Io. We'll be planting charges to obliterate this facility before we depart. How long will it take you to get everything ready?"

The woman flushed a little. "Actually, I'd assumed that would be what we were doing and have already seen to it. The equipment is still in open containers so that you can examine it and verify that it is not specific to nerve agent manufacture. I'd estimate that with a thorough inspection, we can be ready to depart in only a few hours."

"Good work, Doctor. I'll let Agent Falcone verify everything and we'll plan on pulling out for Io in three hours. That will allow everyone more than enough time to double-check without feeling rushed.

"We'll take a slight detour and drop the nerve agent into the Jovian atmosphere before completing our journey to Io. If you would, please pass my thanks to everyone for their hard work. We deeply appreciate it."

Dr. Grass nodded. "Thank you for the opportunity, Commodore. And, of course, the money you paid us for coming out here in doing this. It's going to assist our research quite a bit. We're also happy to serve the Commonwealth."

Falcone rose to her feet. "Commodore, I'll leave you to what you're doing and go make sure that everything is as we expect. If you could make certain that we're going to be ready to head for Blackhawk Station once we drop the scientists off, I'd like to get there as soon as possible without tipping our hand."

Kawa Repair and Construction had finished the repair work on both of the damaged Vikings vessels in the last twenty-four hours. They'd be ready to depart as soon as the scientists were on a shuttle back down to Io.

Brad smiled. "I can't wait to see what they've done with the place."

———

Somewhat to Brad's shock, they managed to drop the nerve agent into the Jovian atmosphere without any problem. It burned up cleanly along with all the equipment critical to its manufacture. He'd halfway expected the Cadre to turn up and try to take it back from them.

They arrived at Io on schedule and sent the scientists down on a civilian shuttle. *Bound by Law* and *Alan-a-dale* were waiting.

Once they'd snuck away from Oberon, he'd arranged for a tow for *Alan-a-dale*. Hiroshi Kawa had worked his people overtime to make certain the corvette was operational in time. Saburo's father had definitely earned his bonus this time.

To mask their destination, and to guard against the Cadre ambushing them again, his ships acted as if they were headed toward the asteroid belt before engaging stealth and changing course.

Even then, they didn't head directly for Saturn. It was far better to arc above the plane of the ecliptic for a while. Every kilometer that they put between themselves and where the Cadre expected to find them meant a significant reduction in the chances they'd be detected.

Going out of the way did increase the amount of time it took to get to Blackhawk Station, but that beat another ambush. It also made it far less likely that the Cadre would change their fuel delivery schedule because they got worried.

If the Vikings could tag a tanker heading out to meet the Cadre's heavy warships, then they could turn the tables and ambush them.

That still left them the delicate task of identifying which tanker to trail. Falcone had narrowed their search to a single company—Draco Limited—but Brad wasn't convinced she'd found all of the information they needed to make this operation a success.

Thankfully, he knew someone he could rely on to answer any questions he might have. Lisa Simon, the tactical officer of *Bound by Law*, had once been a senior security officer on Blackhawk Station.

She undoubtedly still knew people in their security department and could probably be confident of their character.

He took a shuttle over to *Law* to both keep their discussion private and to have a chance to look over the repairs. She met him in her commanding officer's office.

"I'd forgotten how big this was," Brad said as he took a chair. The three of them were seated in the open area in front of Brenda Andre's desk.

"That's not a plus," Andre said. "Fleet made a bad call on this. I'd rather have more bridge space."

While he could certainly see her point, Brad disagreed in principle.

The extra office space was useful to a mercenary commander. Presentation was actually important, as much as it annoyed him.

He turned down her offer of coffee and turned to Lisa Simon. "I'd rather not have our ships show up at Blackhawk Station. Any sighting will get back to the Cadre, and I don't want them to know that we're on their tail. If they feel spooked, they'll cut and run.

"That's why I've come to you for help. I feel confident you still know a lot of people there. Do you think you could get someone there to give us an idea of when certain tankers are going to be leaving?"

Simon nodded. "Absolutely. The management of Blackhawk Station may have scapegoated me, but I had an excellent relationship with everyone in security. I can think of half a dozen people off the top of my head that would be willing to pass information to me without saying a word to anyone.

"As a plus, I've actually been in communication with a few of them over the last couple of years. Me sending a message now isn't going to stand out at all."

"Excellent," Brad said with a smile. "Here's what I'd like you to do. Send your message to our office on the Io Shipyards and we'll have them forward it. I trust our encryption. They can forward your message on to Blackhawk and it will seem as if we're still near Io. Their return message will have to be forwarded back to us, but we have to consider communications security at Blackhawk to be compromised."

Simon leaned back in her seat slightly, her eyes unfocused as she considered what he'd said. After a few seconds, she nodded. "I have someone in mind. Management promoted him to lieutenant after they fired me. Excuse me; I should've said 'when we mutually agreed that it was best for me to move on in search of other opportunities.'"

Simon said the last with accompanying air quotes. The sight made him smile wryly.

"Make sure that he is exceptionally discreet," Brad added seriously. "It's almost certain that at least one company there is either a shell working directly for the Cadre or has senior people in their pay. It wouldn't surprise me if the Cadre has infiltrated management at Blackhawk Station."

His warning made Simon's smile widen. "If they are, I'll bet someone suspects. If so, I'd love to snag them up with the Cadre scum we're going to track down."

"Me too," he said with a matching grin. "Remember, someone might be watching for our communications, so keep things low-key. If you have a personal cypher your friend already has, please use it but still be as discreet as possible."

"Count on me, Commodore. I still have a lot to pay the Cadre back for, and I'm not new to the security game. No one will know about this from my end."

"Excellent," he said, turning his attention to Andre. "Now, Captain, I'd like to take a tour of the ship and see the repairs. After that, I'll take you up on that coffee."

CHAPTER NINETEEN

BRAD WAS PLEASED to see that Lisa Simon's activities bore fruit before they got to Blackhawk Station. She was quickly able to establish communication with one of her former coworkers and used a shared encryption key that the man already had to send him a file that she implied had some…ahem…"intimate images."

Not, she'd assured him, that she'd *actually* sent him naked pictures of herself. Whether she did or not was none of Brad's business. All that he cared about was that the ruse got their request for specific information on tankers going in and out for Draco Limited.

Over the course of the next three days, her friend in Blackhawk Security got her a complete list not only of which ships the company routinely used and what their schedule had been in the past, but also their intended schedule for the next few months.

Even though Simon trusted the man, they didn't tell him that they were most interested in the tankers that were supposedly servicing Fleet bases and units. Operational security for this mission needed to be tight.

Once they had the schedule, Brad closeted himself with Falcone and Simon. The former had experience with picking out patterns and unusual twists of data. The latter, even after all this time, still had an incredible grasp on how things worked at Blackhawk Station. Odd patterns there would stand out to her.

"For such a little company, they seem exceptionally busy," Simon said after studying the data. "SaturCorp is a huge organization that has existed for decades, and they only have about twice as many tanker flights as Draco Limited. That is really strange."

"That's not the most interesting part," Falcone said, tapping the screen of her tablet. "When you look at SaturCorp's flights, they usually involve multiple tankers going to large facilities. That's how the company makes a profit: they deliver in bulk.

"Draco Limited, on the other hand, seems to be delivering their He-3 via single tankers. Not only that, it seems as if they're going all over the system. Even to some locations that don't really make sense based on Saturn's orbit."

"What do you mean?" Brad asked, trying to see the pattern that had caught her eye in the data. Nothing stood out to him.

"Just look at these deliveries to the belt. Jupiter is much closer to the asteroid belt, and JoveCorp is in a far better position to fill many of these orders. Oh, not all. Orbital mechanics see to that, but some of Draco's flights almost directly bypass Jupiter to get to the belt. That makes no sense at all. It has to be costing someone a lot of money to use them rather than JoveCorp."

"Why would a small company based out of Saturn be making such long trips deep into the system if they didn't have to?" Brad asked.

"Camouflage?" Simon asked. "To make deliveries to places someone can't trust JoveCorp or SaturCorp to see?"

Falcone pointed at the other woman. "Exactly! Some of these deliveries are almost certainly to Cadre facilities. Probably not many, but still. They need a lot of unrelated traffic to hide their critical deliveries.

"It's always better if no one sees you doing something you want hidden, but if you can't hide, make certain there are plenty of other things going on to attract any unfortunate attention. The Agency teaches that to all their agents and it works.

"That's why pattern recognition is such a crucial skill for an agent. We have to dig the important things out of the muck and recognize that they matter. This matters."

Brad studied the detailed list of tanker flights. These were the filed flight plans, so there was no guarantee that the tankers actually went anywhere close to the listed destinations.

In any case, there were a lot of them. Anyone not knowing that the shipments to Fleet installations were bogus would probably never notice them in the noise of the other transactions.

"Let's look exclusively at what's going on with Fleet," he said. "Thanks to Kate, we know none of those deliveries ever happened. That means any deliveries listed for Fleet have to be going somewhere else. Let's clear the chaff out and focus on the wheat."

The data that Simon had acquired covered a six-month period starting four months earlier and projecting two months into the future. Falcone tapped on her tablets screen for a few minutes and the data on Brad's and Simon's tablet changed.

Virtually all of the entries disappeared. There were far fewer deliveries to supposed Fleet facilities than Brad had anticipated. Five spread out over the last four months and three upcoming.

Unfortunately, the next scheduled departure was three weeks in the future. The most recent departure was two days before.

Falcone rubbed her face and stretched her back. "Dammit. Two freaking days. That damn tanker could be anywhere. So much for the plan to get ahead of it and shadow the damned thing."

"Let's not give up just yet," Brad said, his voice calm and soothing. "The tanker filed to go to the far side of the belt. That leaves a lot of the system to cover, but it also means they might really follow the course for a bit before they deviate."

He opened a com channel to the bridge. "Michelle, have all the ships alter course to the coordinates I'm sending you. It looks as if our target has been in motion for a few days already. Full stealth, but have everyone looking for the bugger."

"Copy that," she said.

Brad ended the call and looked back at his two planners. "Rather than assuming we won't catch them, let's plan on what we need to do *when* we catch up with them.

"As someone working for the Cadre, they're probably not too worried about pirates. That might mean they'll keep a less stringent watch, but we can't count on it. Any competent bridge officer will see us in time to start screaming for help. If they let the Cadre know that we're coming, that's going to make our work a lot more difficult."

Falcone nodded. "It would if they were able to get a signal out. I think we can prevent that."

He shot her a look, his eyes narrowed. "I'm not exactly certain how the Agency can derail the laws of physics. What do you have in mind?"

"Something we've been working on for quite a while. A powerful multi-spectrum jammer. If we can get it into the general vicinity of that tanker, they can scream their fool heads off and it won't make one bit of difference."

Brad wasn't convinced. Radios on spaceships had to be very strong to get a signal across the Solar System. Jamming one might be possible, but it wouldn't be subtle.

"Something like that needs to be more powerful than the ship's radio. Everybody in the system is going to know that we're jamming them. They may not know specifically what's going on, but the Cadre has to have an idea of where their ship is. If they're paying any attention at all, this is going to be like shooting off a flare in the middle of the night."

Falcone grinned. "That's not what the science geeks tell me. It doesn't drown out the enemy's signal. It subverts it. That's why it has to be very close. They call it destructive interference.

"Basically, it acts like noise-canceling headphones. It senses an incoming radio wave and projects a counter-wave to wash it out. That means that if it works as advertised, there's no signal to get out. Well, not beyond a fairly short distance, I suspect."

Brad tapped his fingers on his desk as he considered what she'd just suggested. If a jammer pushed a canceling signal, it might severely blunt the range at which the original transmission could be detected as more than background noise.

The problem he saw was coverage. The jammer would be on one side or the other of the tanker. They had no idea where any Cadre vessels would be located. The coverage had to be complete or they risked ruining everything.

"Just how powerful is this jammer? he asked. "If it needs to be at close range, exactly how are we going to get into range to place it? This sounds like a catch-22 situation."

"It's a lot more powerful than one might think," she said. "Still, you're right in that it has to be almost on top of the ship. One might be sufficient for this, but two or more would be better.

"The units are small enough to fit inside a standard torpedo. If we can get two of them into the vicinity of the tanker, one on either side, I'd feel pretty confident that no signal is going to get out. I brought four units just in case."

He rubbed his chin. "Just in case, huh? When exactly did you bring these on board?"

"When you called me out to the asteroid. By that point, I already knew that we'd be heading to Blackhawk Station at some point. So, I made sure to come prepared. It shouldn't take Mike Randall long to get them installed."

"Do you have anything *else* to declare?" he asked sternly. "I might be working for the Agency on this matter, but these are still *my* ships."

She smiled, unrepentant. "Not at this time, though I reserve the right to change that answer if I need to."

He threw up his hands in surrender. "Some things never change. Let's just hope that we have a chance to try out your new tech."

———

Eighteen hours later, *Alan-a-dale* spotted the tanker. It had altered course, but the deviation was relatively small. It still seemed to be heading for somewhere in the belt, but much closer than the original course would have called for.

It took two more hours to get all of his ships onto parallel courses outside of the range that the tanker could pick them up with the crap scanners they probably had.

All four of his ships were basically sitting at cardinal points around the tanker and shadowing her. If they had to accelerate toward the slower vessel, they could get into weapons range in less than fifteen minutes.

He was sitting in his chair on the bridge of *Oath of Vengeance* in his combat armor when it came time to execute phase one of the plan. When they'd spotted the tanker, they'd distributed the jammers out to all of his ships. Now each of them would fire a torpedo at the tanker.

Mike Randall had stepped down the acceleration of the torpedoes so that they would close at a much slower rate. That should make them significantly more difficult to detect, though useless as weapons now.

"All right, Konrad," Brad said. "Signal the other ships via tight beam. Execute phase one in sixty seconds from my mark. Mark."

"Copy that," his tactical officer said. "With the reduced torpedo acceleration, it will take about half an hour for them to drift into position. They'll remain in coverage range while our shuttles close after that for about another half-hour, so our window is short."

The launch was so gentle that Brad couldn't tell they'd fired. The ships were on passive scanners, so the tactical repeater on his chair only had an estimated position for the four torpedoes as they crept in toward the unsuspecting tanker.

Every time Brad glanced at the time, only five minutes had gone by. The thirty minutes felt more like three hours.

To his relief, the torpedoes arrived on station without incident. They wouldn't begin transmitting any signal-canceling radio waves unless the tanker transmitted something. That basically meant he wouldn't know if this was going to work until it was too late.

"Signal *Law* that we'll launch shuttles in five minutes, Michelle."

"On it," his wife responded. "Be careful."

Brad rose and made his way back to the assault shuttle Saburo had assigned him to. Technically, he was along solely as a passenger, but they all knew just how intense the fighting could get if things went sour.

Besides his combat armor, Brad was armed with his mono-blade, pistol, and a rifle. All of the bullets were low-powered so that they wouldn't risk blowing holes in the side of the tanker. Explosions on tankers tended to be somewhat large affairs and to be avoided at all costs.

Saburo was on one of the other three assault shuttles *Oath* carried, but would be close enough to communicate via low-powered lasers for the entire flight.

Each shuttle had enough room for a dozen combat troops, give or take, so that drove the size of the ground combat forces on the destroyers. At Saburo's recommendation, each shuttle carried a squad of nine —basically two fire teams of four each and a noncommissioned squad leader—and an officer. Add in Saburo and Phan, and you had thirty-two people with room for four more.

Once Brad was strapped in, he linked his com to Saburo's. "What's our status?"

"We detach in thirty seconds," his combat team commander said. "I'm letting Lieutenant Phan command our prong of the attack and will only take over if something goes wrong. Pretend I'm not here."

Brad snorted. He doubted Phan would forget her commander was looking over her shoulder.

He felt the shuttle detach from *Oath* and begin thrusting. It was light for that sort of thing, but they weren't using much acceleration. The goal of this exercise was to use the assault shuttles' stealth to get as close as possible to the tanker before they had to board.

In a perfect world, they'd make it all the way to the tanker's hull, but that wasn't realistic. He'd settle for getting within five minutes' hard burn.

It had been a while since Brad had gone along on a mission like this, but he had to confess that he was looking forward to the action. Commanding a quartet of warships was satisfying work, but taking a personal hand with pirates always gave him a rush.

The timer inside his helmet was counting down, but not with their actual arrival time. Instead, it listed how long it would take to get to the tanker if they went to maximum thrust at that very moment. That made the timer countdown oddly slow.

Even though they were starting out about twenty-five minutes' slow thrust away, the timer read less than ten minutes at the beginning. As time dragged on, the number dragged toward zero.

When they crossed the five-minute marker without any sign that the tanker was aware of their presence, he rejoiced inwardly. When the timer showed less than three minutes, he was exuberant. Every second they took away from the pirates' reaction, gave them less opportunity to destroy critical information.

"All troopers prepare to board," Lieutenant Phan said in a low tone over the coms. "Fire teams one and two will lead the way. If we remain undetected all the way in, we will proceed to the airlocks and conduct a soft intrusion, just the same as Major Doary and her people.

"If the enemy shows any indication that they've detected our approach, we'll go in hard and fast. We'll use charges to blow the airlocks and secure the critical areas of the ship as quickly as possible. Once inside, everyone has their assigned targets."

Brad couldn't see the woman, but her calm tone belied the fact that they were about to get into a shooting match with pirates. He'd always appreciated her unflappable composure.

"This is Commodore Madrid," he added. "Remember that we want prisoners. If you see any indication of someone with a weapon or feel threatened, you are cleared for lethal force, but I would prefer that we take as many people prisoner as possible.

"It's entirely possible that some of the crew is not aware of whom they're working for. If someone surrenders, put restraints on them and continue with the mission. Your safety comes first. Remember that. Good luck."

"Fire teams one and two will capture the bridge, three and four will secure the computer center, and five and six will assist two fire teams from *Bound by Law* in securing Engineering," Phan said. "Major Doary's remaining four teams will be scouring the surface of the tanker to disable any method of communicating with other ships or people in the system. Both ships' heavy-weapons fire teams will go wherever we need as a reserve force. As one might expect, we don't need heavy weapons on a tanker, so they have a regular load-out of weapons.

"Fire team four," Lieutenant Phan continued. "Your primary mission is to keep the Commodore safe as you back up team three. *Safe* being a relative term in the middle of a firefight, but you get the idea. Cover his back and make sure that he doesn't get in over his head."

"Thanks," Brad said dryly.

"It's all part of the service, sir. Good luck to you, too."

He couldn't believe his eyes when they hit the one-minute mark. If anyone was on the bridge, they should've seen the approaching assault shuttles. Everlit, the automated collision alarms should be signaling something even though the closing rate was very low.

A whole new kind of anxiety ran through Brad when they hit thirty seconds. Action was imminent, so Brad did a second check on his weapons and the release on his restraints.

The assault shuttles made it in to just under ten seconds before the tanker showed any indication that it had detected them. At that point, it attempted to change course and accelerate.

Lieutenant Phan gave the order and the assault shuttle rocketed down onto the tanker's hull. They'd already picked out appropriate locations to put down.

Brad wasn't certain if the tanker was unarmed, but their surprise meant that no one had a chance to shoot at them, for which he was grateful. Losing a shuttle full of people would suck.

Once the shuttle slammed into the tanker's hull, everyone was moving. Brad rose to his feet and followed the lead teams out. This was it.

CHAPTER TWENTY

THE LEAD FIRE teams wasted no time in blowing the outer airlock door. They quickly slapped explosives around its perimeter and set them off. The chamber must've had pressure, because the hatch promptly went spinning off into space.

Everyone huddled close to the breached airlock as they spread a portable airlock over their heads and sealed it to the hull. They'd practiced this operation hundreds of times, and it took only thirty seconds.

Once it was sealed, someone planted a shaped charge on the inner door and slipped out of the airlock just before it went off.

This charge was much smaller than the one they'd used to pry off the outer door. As a rule, a ship used security features only on the outer doors. No one worried about someone in a spaceship getting into the airlock from the inside.

That meant they only had to have enough explosive to breach the hinges and latch. The portable airlock huffed outward as the atmosphere in the ship rushed out to fill it. In moments, the pressure had equalized and they had access to the tanker.

"Fire teams one and two on point. Go! Go! Go!" Lieutenant Phan said over the dedicated platoon channel.

The assigned troopers moved into the ship quickly and efficiently.

Brad, being the supercargo, followed along at the rear. The troops from his shuttle had several targets. The bridge was the main one, but the computer center was just as important. In the long term, probably even more important than the bridge.

On a tanker, the computer wasn't going to be that impressive, but that didn't mean there wasn't some critical piece of information on it. If they could keep the enemy from wiping it, that might give them just the lead they needed.

Fire team one headed for the bridge, while fire team two set off for the computer center. Lieutenant Phan followed the team heading toward the bridge to provide exterior security for the operation. Saburo was doing the same with one of the Engineering teams. Fire team four—Brad's team—followed the team assigned to the computer center.

On a regular ship, the distance would be fairly small between the airlock and the bridge or computer center. The tanker, however, was of a significant size. That meant they had to go through several corridors to get to the target.

Brad expected to see crewmen, but the corridors were ominously empty.

The first indication of resistance came over the com when fire team one ran into several people defending the bridge and began exchanging fire. As per Brad's orders, they'd instructed the people to surrender, and received a hail of bullets as their answer.

The firefight was short and decisive, from everything Brad heard. His people were armored; the crew were not. Worse for the defenders, there was nowhere in the corridor that they could use for cover. They had to stand there in the open, shooting at the Vikings. Always a bad idea.

Brad wasn't entirely surprised to find the same situation held true at the computer center. Fire team two returned fire as soon as the enemy started shooting. He hoped they were being careful not to shoot the computer. The confrontation wasn't in Brad's line of sight, and it was over by the time he could see what was happening.

Two crewmen in regular vac-suits lay sprawled in front of the hatch leading into the computer center. They'd been shot numerous times and were obviously dead.

"The hatch is locked," one of the troopers in fire team two said.

"Use a breaching charge," Brad said. "Keep it light. We don't want to wreck the computer."

The man fitted a charge over the lock, and everyone stepped back while he triggered it.

Brad felt the *whump* of the explosives going off through his armor, even with his back turned. By the time he looked back at the hatch, his people were already pouring into the computer center.

Based on the shouts for someone to surrender, there was someone inside. Since his people didn't open fire, Brad made a second assumption that the person had surrendered or wasn't armed.

"Make sure that no one comes up behind us," Brad instructed the corporal in charge of fire team four. Then he went inside.

The interior of the computer center—which was really too grand a phrase—consisted of several battered computer cases on racks and a cramped desk bolted to the bulkhead. It was only marginally larger than the guest bathroom in Brad's apartment back on the Io Shipyards.

Needless to say, a fire team of mercenaries pretty much filled the room.

Brad stepped over to the computer interface, looked at the screen, and his heart sank. The graphic being displayed was one for wiping the system and it indicated the dump was complete.

Well, it seemed as if the computer center was no longer a primary target and this opportunity had slipped between their fingers.

"Fire team four will remain on station with me," he ordered. "Fire team two, find out where Lieutenant Phan wants you and get moving. We've got this under control."

"Copy that, sir," the corporal in charge of the other fire team said. He gestured for his people to move out, and in moments, they were gone, leaving Brad alone with the prisoner while his people guarded the corridor outside.

Brad stood watching over the prisoner. The mercenaries had bound the man's hands behind his back. This one wasn't in a vacuum suit. Instead, he wore regular shipboard coveralls. He looked terrified.

He had every right to be.

"Finally," Brad said as he squatted down. "Alone at last. Why did you wipe the computers?"

In spite of his fear, the man jutted out his chin in defiance. "To keep someone like you from using it against us."

Not exactly the kind of words Brad would have expected of an innocent spacer.

"My name is Brad Madrid and I command the Vikings Mercenary Company. This vessel is supporting Cadre operations. You, sir, are a pirate. If you'd like to avoid a very brief trial resulting in your execution, I'd suggest that you start giving me reasons why I should let you live."

If anything, Brad's words terrorized the man even more but he continued holding his defiant expression. "You'll get nothing from me. Do your worst."

Brad smiled coldly. "Well, since you insist."

———

In spite of his ominous tone, Brad didn't stick the man into a handy airlock. They found an area to hold the prisoners as they rounded the crew up. To keep them from speaking to one another, all were bound and gagged. Let them sweat things for a little while as Brad and his crew continued to clear the tanker.

There was significantly more fighting than one would anticipate from a tanker, so that was additional confirmation that these were Cadre pirates fighting for their lives because they knew the fate that awaited them if they were tried.

Both the bridge and Engineering were sealed when his people arrived, but the hatches weren't sufficient to keep out determined troopers. A couple of shaped charges blew the hatches and got his men and women into the secured areas.

That didn't mean they captured them without bloodshed. Surrender was the exception rather than the rule. The butcher's bill was going to be high once they started counting up how many people had decided to fight back.

Brad's initial impulse was to go to the bridge, but the corporal in command of his fire team seemed disinclined to allow him out before they'd secured the ship. It seemed that Saburo had given the man orders.

While he was waiting, Brad examined the computer room in more detail. The units themselves might not contain any helpful information but that didn't mean there wasn't something to be found.

And, in fact, he *did* find something interesting.

On a shelf below the built-in desk was a small set of backup disks. They were labeled for previous flights, so it was unlikely they'd have any detailed information about the current mission, but they still presented an opportunity to perhaps get something from a previous run.

He'd gotten a bit rusty over the last couple of years, but his computer knowledge was still good enough to isolate the station in the room and load the tapes for a manual review.

A quick call to Falcone back on *Oath of Vengeance* got him the dates of a few previous supposed Fleet deliveries made by Draco Limited. Several of them were included in the backup tape set.

As Brad loaded one, he wondered what the man who had wiped the computers had planned to do with the tapes. Had he intended to destroy them in some fashion? Probably. The fact that Brad's assault shuttles had given them no warning hadn't given him time to deal with them.

There was a fair bit of operational data on the backup tape. Basically, readings from all the instrumentation and equipment inside the ship. Including, to Brad's pleasure, some astrogation data.

According to the tape, the tanker made a trip to the asteroid belt on the trip where they'd supposedly been making a Fleet run. The destination was an unnamed asteroid that only had a numerical designation. The data from the scanners gave him a decent look at its size and shape, but the tanker had turned the scanners off shortly after arrival.

Based on the timestamps, they hadn't turned them back on for another ten hours. At that point, they'd departed back toward Black-hawk Station.

Rather than bug anyone back on *Oath,* he waited for Colonel

Saburo to declare the tanker under control. That took another fifteen minutes.

"I'm sending everybody looking for stragglers," Saburo said when Brad called him. "On a ship this big, there's an ass-ton of places someone might conceal themselves. You can move around now, but stay vigilant."

"I've done this before, Mother," Brad said reprovingly. "I'll be happy at this point if I can just move up to the bridge and double-check a few things."

"I'm serious, Commodore. It's only takes one person popping out of nowhere at the wrong time to ruin someone's day."

"I'll be careful. Madrid out."

Brad gestured to the corporal, and they started out for the bridge. Because Saburo had been so adamant, Brad went slowly and allowed a bit more paranoia to color his actions than he normally would.

That proved a wise decision when a supply locker burst open as he was passing by and an older man with a ragged beard lunged out at him, a bright blue monofilament blade snapping to life as he moved.

The man was far too close for Brad to duck back, so he grabbed the man's wrist in both his hands instead. The bright line flashed between their faces as each struggled to control where it went.

Almost without thought, Brad brought his knee up into the man's groin three times in quick succession. That pretty much took the fight out of him. Moments later, Brad had possession of the mono-blade and the pirate was doubled over on the deck.

Everything had happened so quickly that none of the mercenaries had had an opportunity to shoot the attacker. Once he was down, they had the self-control to restrain themselves. The embarrassed corporal in command of the fire team secured their newest prisoner and handed him off to one of his people.

"Sorry, sir," the man said over the command channel.

"Don't worry about it," Brad said as he deactivated the blade and stuffed it into one of the outer pockets on his vacuum armor. "Let's just get to the bridge before any more surprises pop out."

Everyone was on a hair trigger the rest of the way to the bridge.

The corporal was visibly relieved when Brad stepped onto the bridge and was under the protection of two fire teams.

The tanker's bridge was smaller than *Heart of Vengeance*'s and in significantly poorer repair than the corvette had been when Brad had taken possession of it. In addition, a number of consoles had fresh holes in them and were smoking. The main screen was shattered. In addition, two Cadre bodies lay on the floor.

Brad focused his attention on fire team one's commander. "Report."

"There were three people in here when we arrived, sir. One of them was working on a console while the other two tried to keep us out. All three were hit during the exchange of fire. The survivor probably isn't going to make it, but we shipped him off to what passes for a medical cubby on this tub."

Brad nodded his understanding and searched for a console that was still operational. The one serving as an engineering backup panel seemed to be undamaged, so Brad sat down and brought up the ship's systems.

With the computer wiped, there wasn't much to see, but he could still determine their present course. The ship had dodged a little bit trying to lose them at the last moment, but that didn't stop him from seeing their rough heading.

He didn't have a complete listing of asteroids in his back pocket, so he sent a request for the location of the asteroid from the tape back to *Oath of Vengeance*. It only took Michelle a minute to give him the information he was looking for.

The tanker was headed toward the same section of the belt as the asteroid they'd visited on the previous trip. That was careless of them and provided him with an opportunity to surprise whomever they were coming to refuel.

He grinned at Michelle over the com channel he'd opened. "We've got a break. Send over enough people to run the tanker and we'll take it to the rendezvous they've already set up. If we play our cards right, we're going to be able to ambush one of their capital ships.

"Maybe the carrier. Maybe *Lioness*. Maybe only another ship that is going to move the cargo to a different location. In any case, we have a chance to catch them off guard. Did any signal get out?"

His wife shook her head. "Falcone says the jammers worked as designed. No one heard them when they started yelling. She's on her way over, by the way."

"That's fine. She and I need to go over this ship with a fine-toothed comb, and I know she'll want to intimidate our prisoners. I'll give you a call when we have more information. For now, keep us on course for the rendezvous and get the ships back into stealth."

He leaned back in the battered couch after he'd disconnected and smiled. This was just the break they'd needed. Now he could make the Cadre pay for his uncle and so many of his friends.

CHAPTER TWENTY-ONE

IT TOOK Lieutenant Phan and Major Doary about an hour to completely secure the ship and search every nook and cranny for people and self-destruct devices. They found a few of each.

The most important things they found were the explosives in critical areas meant to destroy the ship. On anything other than a tanker, they'd probably be in the engine room. And, to be fair, there were some in there.

There were also a number of significantly-sized charges on the exterior of the tanker. Since helium, no matter its form, wasn't explosive, that caused Brad to look a little deeper into what the tanker was carrying.

Not all of the tanks were filled with He-3. A few had hydrogen. Others had oxygen. With an explosive device located on the hull between tanks containing each, that made for a rather large explosion if someone decided to destroy the ship.

They had cleverly installed vents on the interior of the ship and no doubt planned to vent the tanks before blowing the charges. The mixture would act much like a fuel-air explosive, even in a vacuum, so long as they timed things correctly.

Clever and deadly. Definitely not innocent bystanders.

There weren't that many tanks given over the potentially explosive mixture, and that made sense. This tanker still had to deliver a virtually full load of He-3, or the Cadre might as well not bother. Still, it was clever.

To be certain they hadn't missed any, Brad ordered that every tank be checked and anything that was not He-3 be vented slowly into space. A hit in battle would have almost as significant an effect as the charges.

The haul of prisoners was smaller than he'd anticipated. The tanker had had a crew of thirty-two individuals. Twenty-one of those had died in the fighting. Seven more were in critical condition, with four not expected to survive.

That only left four uninjured people. One of them was the man Brad had captured in the computer center. He'd probably be the best one to start questioning with, since they'd already developed a relationship.

Once Falcone arrived aboard the tanker, Brad met her in the computer center to discuss strategy while she examined the backup drives for any other interesting tidbits he might have missed. Since there was only one chair, he stood off to the side, next to the wiped computer system, while she worked.

"It doesn't seem as if anyone really wanted to surrender," Brad said as an opening. "I think we have one senior officer in custody. He was trying to do something on the bridge and got shot up by my people before he could finish.

"Based on what we found on the hull, my guess is that he was going to blow up the ship. It makes me really glad that we got as close as we did before they spotted us. If they'd known we were coming for much longer, they'd have blown the hull before we touched down."

"Or just as you touched down," she added, glancing over at him. "It's what I'd do. Take as many of your boarders with me as I could."

"Damned bloody-minded spies," he muttered. "Still, you're probably right. I just wish that we'd captured more senior people. The odds of anyone knowing where the important Cadre installations are go down significantly once we exclude the officers."

She nodded as she tapped on the virtual keyboard. "Maybe we'll get lucky with the guy from the bridge."

Brad somehow doubted that.

Based on the medical report he'd received, his medics were doing everything they could, but the guy was probably going to die no matter what they did. At this point, he'd ordered them to focus on trying to get him awake enough to question before he died.

"We've got the guy we captured in this compartment," Brad said. "He's the one that wiped the computer systems. I suspect he's got the best chance of knowing something interesting out of the people capable of talking, if we can convince him to tell us what he knows."

"Don't you worry about that," she said with a cold smile. "I can be very persuasive."

He knew from experience that she could be damned scary when she wanted to be. "I've already set the groundwork for you. I told him that if he didn't cooperate, we'd stick him in an airlock."

Falcone laughed. "I'm not certain you'd have done that even back before you got a handle on that temper of yours. There's too much of a good guy deep down inside you.

"You're not going to execute someone because they're uncooperative, no matter what they've done in the past. If you're not fighting, you're not going to kill them."

That was probably true. He'd have difficulty killing anyone in cold blood, even Cadre scum.

Two years earlier, after the deaths of virtually everyone he'd known and loved, he'd come close to losing his soul. Even now, the therapy he went through when they were back in the Io Shipyards occasionally uncovered dark bits that he had to work through.

Sometimes, his sessions were solo. Sometimes, he and Michelle were there together. Having her in his life made him feel a lot more stable. She was a rock.

His Agency partner, on the other hand, would do whatever she felt needed to be done. If she decided the prisoners needed to be spaced, Brad had no doubt she'd carry out that sentence without a single sign of regret.

That wasn't to say that she was a soulless monster. He didn't think that at all. She *would* regret it. She was just a lot tougher than he was when it came to doing bloody tasks that needed doing after the shooting stopped, and wouldn't hesitate to do it, regret afterward or no.

Falcone leaned closer to the screen and made a soft sound with her tongue. "Okay, I've loaded all the backup data into a general holding program that I brought over from *Oath of Vengeance*. Looking at the dates listed on these entries, this tanker is the one that made all the fake runs to Fleet bases.

"I'm not certain that exonerates any of the other tankers' crews, but it certainly means that everyone on board *this* ship is as dirty as Everdarkened shit. Referring back to your earlier comment, if I need to make some salutary examples to get people chatting, I won't have any problem sticking one of these bastards through an airlock to get some cooperation from his fellows."

Brad leaned forward and examined the data on the screen. "It doesn't look as if they always went to the same location, but they do their meetings in pairs. Every two trips, they switch locations. This is the second jaunt to that one asteroid. That's sloppy. They should pick a different location every single time to keep people like us from tracking them down."

Falcone shot him a wry smile. "You pick some interesting times to fuss about other people's professionalism. Why can't you just be happy that they screwed up and we have an opportunity?"

"Oh, I'm happy. I just wanted to point out where they could improve, because at some point in the future, they just might. We need to be ready and we can't count on them being sloppy. Is there anything else in there that looks interesting?"

She shook her head. "No logs written by human beings, so everything is simply mechanical output. How the reactors were doing, life-support processing, various other internal stuff that might be useful for maintenance.

"When they got on station, they shut off the external scanners. No data at all. It looks as if they wanted to make absolutely certain no one got a glance at who they were meeting."

He nodded. "That probably wasn't to prevent the data from being captured by the logs. Whoever was in command of this tanker likely wanted to be certain none of his crew spotted some detail they weren't supposed to know. There are various levels of involvement even for Cadre pirates, and loose lips sink ships."

His com signaled.

"Madrid."

"Corporal Jimenez, sir. The prisoner from the bridge seems to be waking up. I think this is a last rally before he goes down for the count, so if you want to ask him any questions, you might want to hurry."

Brad looked at Falcone as she stood. "We're on our way."

————

The compartment that passed for medical center on the tanker seemed as if it were only suitable for very minor injuries. What high-level gear it had was for poisonings, vacuum exposure, and burns, the major threats aboard a tanker. It wasn't really up to the task of keeping someone alive that required surgery.

His people had set up areas in the corridor where the prisoners could be cared for. There just wasn't enough room for all of them in the compartment.

It only took a glance to confirm what they had told Brad earlier. Of the critical cases, two seemed to have died, based on the sheets over their bodies.

The last two with severe injuries—including the man they'd come to see—were in very bad condition. If they survived the next few hours, Brad would be very impressed with the medics' skill.

The pirate that they'd captured on the bridge of the tanker lay on the only table inside the compartment itself. Based on its design, he didn't think the table was meant for surgical procedures. It was too short for anyone to actually lie on, because their lower legs drooped toward the floor.

Corporal Jimenez stood beside the table, her hand sitting next to the pirate's head. The tall woman had taken her helmet and gloves off and set them nearby, allowing her long black hair to hang down her back.

Brad couldn't imagine how much a pain in the ass it was to stuff that back into a helmet, but that wasn't his problem. If Saburo didn't mind, he didn't.

"Talk to me," he said as he examined the pirate.

The sheet covering the man was stained in blood. Based on the fact that some of it was fresh, he assumed the bastard was still leaking.

"We stopped as much of the bleeding as we could, sir, but he's still losing something internally. His organs are beginning to shut down. He was semiconscious a minute ago, and I expect that he's probably going to wake up again before he passes. I could probably make certain of that by giving him a stimulant, but it would hasten his death."

Her distaste at the idea was obvious to anyone with eyes.

With all the doctors Brad had met over the last few years, he understood why. Healers wanted to save lives, not make people die faster. Corporal Jimenez might not be a doctor in the strictest sense but was obviously cut from the same mold.

"I happen to have some experience with administering stimulants," Falcone said. "Where are they?"

The corporal pointed toward an open medical pack sitting on a counter. "They're in the bag, ma'am."

"Why don't you go see to your other patients?" Brad asked. "We can handle this from here."

He figured he might as well take the load of what they were about to do completely off the woman's shoulders. She was a good trooper and he didn't want to cause her needless pain.

Falcone rummaged through the pack after Jimenez departed and pulled out a vial and injector. She eyeballed the patient and drew some of the clear liquid before putting the vial away.

She pulled the bloodstained sheet down enough to expose the man's neck. "Based on experience, we're not going to have long. Don't beat around the bush. Three minutes is about all we can hope for."

Brad was somewhat skeptical that they'd get any useful information from the man. "He has to know he's dying. He's not going to talk, except perhaps to gloat."

"That, my young friend, is defeatism," she said reprovingly. "We may be able to convince him that he's going to survive. I suggest you lead with that. Ready?"

"Me? You've got a lot more experience at this sort of thing than I do."

"I'll chip in," she said as she injected the stimulant into the man's neck. "It's been my experience that these Cadre types respond better to men than women. He might just try to dominate me, whereas he'll argue with you. As I said, time is short."

Brad let that sink in while he waited for the stimulant to take hold. The Cadre did have women in their ranks, but they weren't exactly known for gender equality. He supposed that Falcone could be right.

They'd find out shortly.

The powerful stimulant brought the dying man back to awareness in less than thirty seconds. The man's breath wheezed wetly in his throat as he struggled for air. His gaze initially settled on Falcone, and despite his condition, he still managed to sneer.

"You'll get...nothing from...me."

"We'll see about that," Brad said as he leaned forward in a manner meant to intimidate the man. "I am Commodore Brad Madrid of the Vikings Mercenary Company. Sadly for you, I must inform you that even though your injuries are severe, we expect you to make a complete recovery. Well, completely enough so that you can answer every question I have"

"Is that...so?" the man asked, his eyes narrowed. "I've heard...of you. Fuck off."

The man ground his teeth and glared at Brad.

"We've already captured..." Brad started, but stopped abruptly when the man started foaming from the mouth. "Holy crap!"

Falcone swore something significantly more pungent and tried to pry the man's mouth open. He resisted and began shaking uncontrollably.

"Poison!" Falcone said, stepping back. "Dammit."

They watched the Cadre officer die. Once he'd stopped moving, she tossed the empty injector onto the counter next to the pack.

"I can't believe I just saw that," she muttered. "Something right out of a clichéd old vid. He had a hollow tooth filled with poison. Probably cyanide. Who does that kind of thing?"

Brad crossed his arms and stared at the dead pirate. "I suppose we can assume that he knew something they didn't want anyone to learn and he was dedicated enough to commit suicide. That's new. I wonder if this is a new tactic or just something we've never had the opportunity to observe before."

She shrugged. "I guess we'll find out when we jump whoever is meeting this tanker. We need to examine every other person on this ship. If they have hollow teeth, I don't want them to have an opportunity to use them."

"We can try," Brad said with a nod. "Other than the other man in critical condition, everyone else could've already used one. We'll hope for the best, but I think the bastards got us again."

CHAPTER TWENTY-TWO

A SEARCH of the prisoners and bodies revealed two others with false teeth containing what Brad assumed was poison. One of the men had been located in Engineering and the other deep in the bowels of the tanker. Both had been killed in the fighting.

Whatever deep knowledge the Cadre had wanted kept to themselves was gone. They'd question the other prisoners, but the odds of getting the critical information he'd hoped for had probably died with the man on the table.

With only seven survivors, three of whom were in critical condition, the interrogations they now planned probably weren't going to reveal any deep, dark secrets, but you didn't know until you started asking questions.

Falcone took a tour of the tanker and selected the galley as the best place to question the prisoners. Unfortunately, a number of crewmen had chosen the galley to make their final stand. It smelled of death and blood.

While the scents weren't exactly unknown to Brad, he'd delayed the start of the interrogations and ordered several of his troopers to perform basic cleanup tasks before they started.

Once the corpses had been removed and their blood washed away, he picked a table near the bulkhead, and the two of them placed their tablets on the chipped plastic surface. Two troopers in armor stood inside the hatch leading to the corridor, and two more stood behind Brad and Falcone.

When one added in the two guards who would escort every prisoner, he believed that would be enough intimidation to keep them in line. Of course, these were hard-core Cadre pirates. They knew what their ultimate fate would almost certainly be.

"Before we get started," Brad said, "I want to get one thing straight in my mind. Are you going to make an example out of any of these people to try and get the others to cooperate? If so, I don't want my people executing prisoners, no matter how much I believe they need to eventually be executed. That would be disastrous to their morale."

Falcone shook her head. "If I thought one of these people had critical information that I needed in a hurry, you bet your ass I'd do that. Frankly, I doubt any of the survivors know anything about who they were meeting.

"Judging by the false teeth, only the captain, executive officer, and chief engineer were deeply enough into the Cadre to know anything truly important. I'm hoping to get things the prisoners picked up that they didn't realize was important, or important things that their superiors inadvertently allowed them to see."

"And exactly how do you intend to get them to cooperate? Promise them their lives in exchange for life in prison without mentioning the mines on Mercury?"

Two years before, she'd made that kind of deal with another Cadre prisoner. Brad wondered if the woman was still alive.

"It worked last time," Falcone said with a grin. "Details are important in contract negotiations. If you want something, you have to fight for it and have something worth bargaining with to get some favorable clauses."

Brad knew that very well. Of course, the details he negotiated on behalf of the Vikings rarely had such potentially lethal loopholes as the mines of Mercury. The mercenaries risked death every time they went into the field, but a good negotiator made certain they had a good idea of what they were getting into.

"Do we start with the guy from the computer room or save him for last?" Brad asked.

"Let's start with him," Falcone said after a few seconds of thought. "We're not going to tell any of the other prisoners what was discussed with those that came before or after, so it doesn't really matter. I'm curious to see what he has to say for himself."

Brad glanced over his shoulder and nodded to one of the troopers standing behind him.

Adrian Orlosky, a huge bear of a man, nodded his understanding and raised his wrist-comp to his lips, murmuring softly.

A few minutes later, the hatch leading into the compartment opened and two troopers frog-marched the prisoner in to stand in front of the table. The man had the beginnings of a black eye.

Brad shifted his gaze to the most senior of the troopers escorting the prisoner. "Did he give you any trouble?"

"Nothing we couldn't handle, sir," the woman said. "The prisoner seemed to think that he had a chance to make a break for it. We corrected his misunderstanding."

That was probably exactly what had happened, but Brad made a mental note to tag Saburo about it. He knew his combat team commander would make certain that was all it had been.

Brad shifted his gaze back to the prisoner. "It seems we meet again. Are you still confident that I'm not going to get what I'm looking for?"

To his credit, the man didn't wilt under Brad's stare. "I said it then and I'll say it now. You won't get anything from me."

"At least you have the courage of your convictions," Brad granted the man. "Allow me to introduce my associate. This is Agent Kate Falcone of the Commonwealth Investigative Agency. She believes— and our previous history together confirms her confidence in the matter—that she can get what we want from you.

"The process is never pretty and often fatal to those who disappoint her. As a mercenary commander, I dislike the sausage-making process, but my hands are legally tied. When it comes to dealing with Cadre prisoners, she has the authority to decide your fate. I suggest you keep that firmly in mind during the next few minutes, as it might just save your life."

Falcone leaned forward and smiled like a shark. "For the record, I never kill anyone that doesn't thoroughly deserve it. It's already clear to me that you work for the Cadre. That, my friend, means a death sentence. The only thing we're negotiating at this point is whether I carry it out here or send you somewhere else to go through the formalities first.

"If you can't give me something worth my time, we can go directly to the nearest airlock and carry out the sentence. Five minutes and you're floating in vacuum, strangling to death on your own blood."

Her smile widened. "I'm told that that's a *very* ugly way to die. That in and of itself makes it incredibly appropriate for Cadre scum like you. So, go ahead. Tell me that you don't have anything worth my time and we'll get you out of here pronto. I have other prisoners to question and I haven't had lunch yet."

The man was obviously having some kind of inner struggle. Unlike the fatally injured prisoner in the infirmary—the captain, they'd guessed—Brad wasn't certain this guy had the conviction to go to the grave with his mouth closed.

Falcone allowed the silence to drag on for about twenty seconds before she nodded and stood. "Very well. Troopers, you know where to take this man."

"Wait!" the man said, resisting the mercenaries as they started to turn him around. "I have some information that I'm willing to give you in exchange for my life."

"Why didn't you just start with that?" Falcone asked as she sat back down. "I'm always willing to make a good-faith effort with someone that's willing to cooperate.

"Let me warn you, though, that you're going to have to have some decent information, or all you'll be buying yourself is more time in a cell waiting for someone else to kill you."

Brad sat forward when the man nodded. "Let's start with something simple, shall we? What's your name and what do you do on board this ship?"

"My name is Rory Zacharias and I'm the navigator aboard *Sidhe*." The man slumped in the mercenaries' grasp as he spoke, his defiance visibly leaking away.

"Why were you wiping the computer when we captured you, Mr. Zacharias?" Brad continued in a reasonable tone. "What information were you hoping to deny us?"

"The captain ordered me to dump the computer. We already had programs built into it, so that wasn't much of a problem, though I still can't believe how little warning we had. I only finished just before the shooting started. I never had a chance to get my hands on the backup data."

He raised an eyebrow. "That's the first part of what I have to offer. In the computer room, on a shelf under the desk, are our backup disks for previous trips. I wasn't supposed to keep them, but there should've been plenty of time to get rid of them."

Brad smiled coolly. "Sometimes luck is bad, both in us sneaking up on you and because we've already found them, so they don't count."

"We've identified the asteroid you were going toward and determined that it's the same one you went to on your previous trip. Interesting how you go to a single destination twice before changing. Why not change every time?"

"You'll have to ask the captain," the man said with a shrug. "That's above my pay grade."

"Sadly for you, he is no longer with us," Falcone said as she leaned back in her seat. "I hope you have more than that to offer. You'll be disappointed at how this deal goes if you don't."

"Who were you meeting?" Brad asked. "And who have you met in the past on these missions?"

The prisoner looked uncomfortable. "The captain always shut off the scanners when we arrived on station. No one was allowed to see exactly who we docked with. It was a security measure because they're not sure they can trust everyone on the crew."

"I see. So, you don't actually have anything else of value to us? Agent Falcone?"

"Just wait a second, dammit," the man said peevishly. "I've already told you that I'm going to tell you what I know. It'll go faster if you'd stop threatening me and give me time to actually tell you."

Bemused, Brad nodded. "By all means, then. Please continue."

"I can't tell you exactly who we were meeting, but I've overheard the captain talking with them during the refueling operations. Just snippets, as he usually stays on the bridge alone during refueling operations. These people don't talk like regular pirates."

With a look of vague interest, Falcone gestured for the man to continue. "If you had to guess, what kind of person or persons have you been dealing with?"

"It's like out of one of those vids about Fleet. They're all professional-like. 'Come to heading seven three niner and hold station' kind of stuff. Everything they say is short and sweet, and they keep using words in a way that makes me think of those vids."

Brad glanced at Falcone. They knew they were dealing with ships that Fleet had lost. Was it much of a stretch to expect that those vessels had ex-Fleet personnel on board? Someone with knowledge of how those carriers worked had to be guiding the drones. That just wasn't the kind of skills a pirate had.

"How many of these runs have you made?" Falcone asked. "When was the first one that you participated in?"

"It's all in the discs," the man said with a shrug. "Eight? Maybe nine? Long enough that they were starting to trust me. The captain said he wanted to talk to me after this mission about moving up to a higher level of trust. Guess that ain't gonna happen."

"I'm afraid not," Brad said. "If you can't tell us anything about the ships or people you're meeting, what about Draco Limited? Someone there has to know what you're doing. Does it go all the way to the top, or is there someone specific that you work for?"

The man shook his head and smiled wryly. "As much as those people at Blackhawk Station go on and on about the pirate attack two years ago, they're deaf, dumb, and blind. Every single one of the management types at Draco are members of the Cadre. Every single ship they have—even the ones doing the milk runs—are commanded by Cadre members. All the senior officers on board: captain, exec, and chief engineer.

"They moved into the offices of the place the Cadre cleaned out two years ago, and no one had a clue. It just blows my mind."

That news didn't surprise Brad all that much. He'd suspected that Draco was a wholly-owned Cadre subsidiary.

"That *is* useful information," Brad said, "but I think you have more to add. If you were being considered for more trust, then you've seen things. You know things. This is your chance to trot it out. Sell us now or off you go."

The man seemed to consider something for a moment and then sighed. "I didn't really see anybody's faces, but I had to deliver something to the captain and heard the new Cadre leader talking for a little bit before the captain muted whatever he was listening to and turned the monitor. You know, the Phoenix."

Falcone leaned forward. "You're sure that it was the Phoenix? It could've been anybody."

The man shrugged slightly. "It sure sounded like the dude was claiming that he ran the Cadre. So far as I know, only the Phoenix has the balls to make that claim."

Considering that Falcone had said the Agency didn't even know if the Phoenix was a man or a woman, that sounded like useful information to Brad.

"What'd he sound like?" Brad asked. "Anything like the Terror?"

The prisoner laughed. "I only heard a couple of sentences, and there's only so much that I can guess about some guy I barely saw. One thing I can say for sure: he wasn't raving like the Terror usually did. Then again, I have no idea how the Terror behaved in private."

"But you saw his face?" Falcone asked.

"Well, not really. The captain swung the monitor around real fast, so I only caught a glimpse. That doesn't really count. Just enough to say he was a dark-haired skinny bugger in a vac-suit."

"I decide what counts. You just bought yourself a reprieve. I'm going to have these troopers put you into a different cabin while we decide exactly what we're going to do next."

The two troopers took that as their cue to escort the prisoner out.

Brad waited until they were gone to speak. "Do you really think that's going to lead us to identifying the Phoenix?"

She shrugged. "All it takes to unravel a case like this is one teeny thread. Who knows? Maybe one of the other prisoners can give us more information. If not, we might get something when the ship or ships this tanker was supposed to meet show up. I'm not counting anything out at this point."

Sadly, none of the other prisoners had anything useful to add. That was disappointing for Brad, but it did clear the decks for the next stage of the operation. Now he only had to figure out how to lure a Cadre warship into range for his ships to jump it. And, of course, to actually capture it and some of its crew.

CHAPTER TWENTY-THREE

JUST IN CASE the asteroid was under observation, Brad ordered a slow approach with his corvettes leading the way. They coasted in with their passive scanners cranked up to maximum sensitivity, and only after they'd determined there was no one waiting did he authorize the tanker to go in, with the destroyers bringing up the rear.

Unlike what people saw in the vids, the asteroid's makeup was not homogenous. It wasn't a hunk of rock or metal, but a conglomerate of dust, pebbles, and larger chunks held together by its own weak gravity. It spun lazily in the dim sunlight, completely unremarkable.

Now the waiting game started. The only way he figured they could capture whatever ship came to meet the tanker was an ambush. And that meant getting a lot closer than they could get with his ships, even with their advanced stealth technology.

Contrary to popular belief, the bodies in the asteroid belt were scattered far and wide, with ones large enough to shield a ship from observation typically not being in handy striking range. That made this task even more difficult but was probably why the Cadre had chosen the location for its illicit refueling. They'd see treachery a long way off.

The only certainty was that the warship—whether it turned out to be their carrier or their cruiser—would have to dock with the tanker.

That was the only way to transfer the He-3. That was the Vikings' opportunity.

To prevent a possible collision between the tanker and whatever ship it was fueling, the hoses were relatively long, but when it came to space, those kinds of distances were still very short. No more than a couple of hundred meters.

With that in mind, Brad had stationed every trooper they had on the tanker. By pulling people from various sections of his four ships, he was able to give the tanker a minimum crew. Enough to get this job done, if not enough people to fly the ship for very long.

Once the shooting started, it was all too likely the tanker would be destroyed. That meant the crew manning the ship would be joining the attack. Their job wouldn't be shooting at the enemy, though some of them had proven very adept from the additional training Saburo had given them over the last few years. No, their job would be attempting to disable the vessel and any self-destruct charges while the troopers took the fight to the enemy.

Unfortunately, he still needed to stash his ships somewhere nearby. Far enough away that they wouldn't be detected, but close enough to respond if the larger warship had smaller escorts. Which it likely would.

He didn't expect that the Cadre would open fire on one of their major warships until it became clear they were in danger of losing it. That meant that even after the attack started, there would be a window where his ships could distract the smaller vessels and give him a chance to capture the larger one.

Based on their track record thus far, Brad was a bit skeptical that they'd succeed in actually capturing one of the Cadre's larger vessels. The pirates were a bit bloody-minded for that. They'd do whatever they could to destroy their vessels first.

All one had to do to recognize that was look at what they'd done to the tanker to prevent its capture. *Lioness* or the carrier would be even more protected.

That kind of behavior was worrying. What exactly was so important? This new behavior hinted at something far more sinister going on than he'd originally anticipated. Something he and Falcone needed to get to the bottom of as quickly as possible.

If, of course, the ambush didn't go completely sour. While the local area of space wasn't completely empty, they were having to rely on his ships' stealth capability far more than he preferred. Sitting still in space at a distance usually worked, but not always.

A rap at the hatch of his appropriated office distracted him from his dour thoughts. It was Falcone.

"We just got a tight-beam com from *Oath of Vengeance*. They're here."

"What kind of information could they give us on the Cadre ships?" he asked as he stood.

"Not much. Passive scanners are crap at this range, and they all seem to be using heat-dampening stealth. It looks like three ships, but there could be a fourth one. Your tactical officer wasn't willing to commit. He did say that one of them looked pretty big during his initial calculations."

So, not a transfer from this tanker to another one. He'd worried about the Cadre being that paranoid.

They stepped out into the corridor and headed for the bridge, such as it was. He'd brought Mike Randall over to get the damaged consoles back online, and the troopers had cleaned up the blood spilled in the takeover.

He didn't expect to see anything directly through the tanker's scanners. They were pathetic. The incoming vessels would be on top of them before he'd see them on passive scanners.

Aurora Farkus, *Oath*'s backup pilot, glanced up from her console as Brad and Falcone walked into the bridge. "Still nothing on passive scanners, sir. Not only are they coming in under stealth, they're using the asteroid to block visual of their approach. It looks as if they're sending a scout to check us out, based on the information Konrad sent me."

Brad took his seat and brought up the feed coming from *Oath of Vengeance*. It was just as sketchy as one might imagine.

If forced to make a wager, he'd bet one of the escorts was a destroyer and the other a corvette. The shadow that might be a third one behind the large ship could be either. He should probably bet on it being real and being a second destroyer, just to be safe.

He opened a channel to Saburo. "Rise and shine. Our guests have arrived."

"Copy that. We'll be ready in ten minutes."

"No rush. It'll take at least double that for their scout to get decent images of us," Brad said. "Then we have to actually link up with them before we board. I figure at least an hour."

"That's fine, but I don't want my people feeling like they can amble along to the fight. Trust me, *hurry up and wait* isn't just a motto. It's a way of life."

Brad laughed as he killed the line and settled in to observe the approaching ship. Odds were very good that either this ship or the big one was going to open communications with the tanker before things got rolling. That was where the biggest risk was going to come in.

While he'd been talking, Falcone had settled in at the remaining console. She'd been working on splicing together audio of the captain they'd recovered from the backup disks so that it seemed as if he was saying different things. She'd coordinated with Brenda Andre over Fleet protocol during refueling operations. That gave her a potential set of responses that made sense.

The only problem was going to be dealing with the visual aspect. They didn't have any recordings of the communication between the tanker and any of the vessels it refueled. Even if they had, they wouldn't have risked using them. Minute changes in hairstyle or clothing or even the people on the bridge of the tanker would have quickly given them away.

Since that wasn't going to work, they were going to bluff their way through with a com failure. If the other team didn't buy what they were selling, this could get ugly fast.

The tanker's passive scanners finally picked up the scout as it was coming around the asteroid to get a good look at them. The vessel broke out of stealth and went to active scanners, bathing the tanker in signal.

It must've been relatively satisfied with what it saw, because the scans dialed back their intensity and the ship settled into an overwatch position. As Brad had suspected, it was a light corvette.

"Incoming signal," Farkus said. "They are requesting visual."

Brad raised an eyebrow at Falcone. "Are you ready?"

"I sure as Everlit hope so," the Agent said. "Here goes our canned response."

The response she'd put together had the captain explaining that they'd had an equipment failure with the camera on the bridge. It was a straightforward as they could make it. The only question was if the other ship would accept the answer and be lulled by hearing a familiar voice.

After a few seconds, Falcone sagged a little bit. "They acknowledged the failure and said to get busy getting it fixed. They didn't sound suspicious."

Score one for the good guys. Now they just had to hope that their ruse held long enough for the tanker to begin fueling operations.

The situation became more defined over the next half hour. Two other vessels, in addition to the corvette, were running escort duty for the larger ship. They were still on the other side of the asteroid, so the tanker couldn't get a direct view.

With the Cadre corvette sitting virtually on top of them, it was far too risky to receive any sort of communication from any of the Vikings' ships. At this point, his people probably knew exactly what was coming to meet the tanker and couldn't tell him.

Well, he'd find out soon enough.

"I think I've pegged one of the escorts," Falcone said. "I'm not a naval type, but the scanner signature is pretty close to *Heart of Vengeance*. I'm guessing it's a heavy corvette. The other one, it's still a little bit light on the data, but I think it's bigger."

Brad nodded and rose to look over her shoulder. "Back before I became a mercenary, I used to have a thing for Fleet ships. I was always studying their stats and information about them. Of course, I was doing the same for merchant ships, so I suppose I was just a space nut."

The readings on her console did look like a destroyer of some kind and a heavy corvette. If so, the escort forces were almost as powerful as what the Vikings had brought along with them. And the way that the escort vessels were keeping an eye on the general area around the asteroid was far too professional for Brad's liking.

It was a good thing that his people and he had come up with some options to deal with the escorts. The key, though, was that all of their planning revolved around keeping the enemy unaware that they were in a trap until Brad sprang it. If one of the escorts spotted something anomalous, the game was up.

It took another twenty minutes, but Brad finally got a good look at the ship coming to pick up a load of He-3. It was that damned carrier.

"Well, well, well," he muttered. "Hello, mister carrier. Isn't this interesting. And just a little bit more dangerous than I'd hoped."

Falcone turned in her chair to face him. "How do you mean? We knew they had the ship. Shouldn't our planning have revolved around meeting it?"

"Oh, we planned for it. I'd just hoped we'd get the cruiser instead. One decapitating blow and we've had the Phoenix. Now? We can probably take this ship off the table one way or another.

"That's going to hurt the Cadre, but they've already proven how good they are at recovering from blows like that. The carrier is definitely second place in my mind. Though to be fair, I really want to know where they got it. If we can put a name to it, we'll roll up some of the people working with them at Fleet."

"We have a new signal," Farkus said. "It's coming from the carrier."

"Let's put this one on audio," Brad said. "I'd certainly like to hear what the enemy commander sounds like."

"*Sidhe*, this is *Longbow*," a man said in a calm, professional voice. "I understand you're having com problems. Is that correct?"

Falcone's fingers danced on her console.

"Yes," the dead captain said. "We're working to rectify the problem and I hope to have it operational within the hour."

"Copy that. Since I can't visually confirm who I'm talking to, even though I recognize your voice, I'm going to have to ask you to authenticate with the code phrase."

"Shit," Falcone said. "I never saw anything about a code phrase in any of the communications that were recorded. What do I say?"

Brad's mind raced. If they gave the answer wrong, this mission was completely blown and so were they. Not only that, they couldn't delay answering without raising suspicion.

"Since we don't know, we might as well try bluffing our way out," Brad said. "Tell him there isn't one."

His gut tightened as her fingers danced across the console. If they got this wrong, the carrier would launch drones long before his ships could intervene.

"What in Everdark are you talking about?" the dead captain asked. "I don't have one of those."

The silence dragged on for a few seconds before the man responded. "And you knowing that is just as good as having one, don't you think? We'll be in position to take on He-3 in twenty-five minutes. Start fueling operations as soon as we're ready. I'd rather not wait out here any longer than I need to. *Longbow* out."

Brad let out the breath he'd been holding. "I think we just got all the good luck we can count on for this mission. Based on the enemy locations, which of our ships is in the best position for us to signal?"

"*Bound by Law*," Farkus said. "They won't be able to respond, but they should be able to signal the other ships."

"Give them our new schedule. Once we start the fueling operations, Saburo will lead the troopers over. Call it fifteen minutes after we start. We'll be right behind him.

"I want *Law* to open fire on the destroyer so that the first shots impact fifty minutes from right now. With any luck, the destroyer won't see what's coming and it will die fast. That'll leave our two destroyers and two corvettes to stack up against the two Cadre corvettes."

Falcone stood. "What about the carrier? We can't count it out until we disable it. If we can disable it."

"Oh, I'm sure they're going to be involved in this fight," Brad said.

"But their main armament is drones. If we can disable the ship quickly enough, we'll take them off the board."

"I thought you said we couldn't count on any more good luck going forward."

He allowed himself a small smile. "There's good luck and then there's things you just simply have to get done. Trust my people. We'll get this done."

Brave words. Now they just had to make the magic happen.

CHAPTER TWENTY-FOUR

O_VER THE NEXT TWENTY-FIVE MINUTES_, the carrier grew large in their
passive sensors. Much larger than ships in space normally appeared.

When hostile vessels exchanged torpedoes and mass-driver slugs,
the ranges were measured in the tens of thousands of kilometers. Now,
with the massive vessel virtually on top of the tanker, the distance was
less than two hundred meters.

At that laughably short distance, a torpedo would barely have
enough speed to penetrate the tanker's hull. Mass-driver rounds, on
the other hand, would blow huge gaping holes all the way through the
tanker. Which was the primary reason Brad was taking every single
person on the initial attack.

Falcone had given him a little bit more information on the class of
ship he was looking at while they were waiting. The *Spearthrower*-class
drone carrier was one of the heavier units in use by Fleet. It only had
four torpedo launchers and twenty eight-barrel fifteen-millimeter
gatlings as its onboard armament, but those weren't the primary firepower ships like that carried into battle.

The thirty Javelin interceptor drones inside its hull each hosted a
four-barrel fifteen-millimeter gatling and a single torpedo. Individu-

ally, they weren't all that powerful. In a swarm, they could wreck even big ships in seconds.

The drones were remotely controlled by "pilots" on the carrier. Six people controlled five drones each. Those people and their controls were the weak point that Brad intended to exploit during the attack.

The feel for the ships that Falcone had gotten was by necessity incomplete. Fleet wasn't sharing any information that they didn't have to. Certainly not deck plans.

Records from the last time the Vikings had engaged this ship gave them a good idea of how the engineering and launch facilities were laid out, in a big-picture kind of way. That in turn pointed to several areas of the ship that would be protected enough to shield both the bridge and the control facilities.

Frankly, Brad wouldn't be surprised if the two were combined. It made a kind of sense for the ship's commander or any admiral on board to have direct access to the pilots during battle.

Based on the information Falcone had received, they believed Fleet had only eight of these carriers. It would still be a while before Falcone's contacts managed to verify which one was out of contact, but they'd have more data to trace this ship soon.

Because of Fleet's reluctance, they weren't even sure if *Longbow* was a Fleet name. It might be that the Cadre had renamed the ship after they'd taken possession, much as they had done for the cruiser *Lioness*.

"Five minutes, Commodore," Saburo said over the comlink. "If you and Agent Falcone could make your way down here, we're ready to kick this party off."

"We're on our way," Brad said as he rose to his feet and locked the console out of habit. He waited at the hatch for Falcone to join him.

She exited the bridge and strode purposefully toward the airlock they'd be using. Both of them were already clad in armored vac-suits so they'd be ready to exit the ship as soon as they arrived.

"I rerouted the ship's communications to my suit," Falcone said. "If they call, I'll answer them through my suit com. Not that I expect them to do so at this point in the refueling operations. The He-3 is already flowing. There's no need for them to say anything unless a problem develops or their tanks are full."

"How long will it take to fill their tanks?" Brad asked as they headed down a ladder toward the appropriate deck.

"That really depends. Most ships refuel long before they actually need to do so. They certainly don't want to get below one-third capacity. My guess is that that ship is probably sitting at about fifty percent.

"If that's the case, it would probably take anywhere between half an hour to an hour to fill them. I can't be certain, because I'm not sure what their capacity is."

Brad nodded. "That's good. We should already be on board their ship before they feel the need to chat."

Saburo and the rest of the crew was waiting for them outside the cargo lock. With all of the ground combat mercenaries and mandatory crew for the tanker present, they had almost eighty people standing by, all armed and ready to take that carrier away from its Cadre crew.

Brad clapped his hands to get everyone's attention. "Listen up. Once we leave this tanker, we're committed. No one is coming to rescue us. We either take that carrier or they take us.

"Pay close attention to what's going on around you. If you see something the rest of us need to know, pass it up the chain of command fast. If you get an order from us to do something unexpected, do the very best you can, because we'll be counting on you. We're playing this by ear and we're going to need to know what each group is seeing."

He paused for a moment to allow that to sink in. "We don't have deck plans, but we know where Engineering is. The teams headed there need to strike hard and fast. Protect our engineers because they're going to do their flat level best to disable the drone controls and communications.

"That's going to save our friends from getting their Everlit guts shot out of them. Nothing we can do will stop that carrier from launching drones. Our best bet is to make sure they don't get close enough to our ships to fire them. Does anyone have any questions? Anything at all?"

Orlosky raised a big, meaty hand. "What about prisoners, Commodore? Do we assume everyone we meet is Cadre? This used to be a Fleet ship. Do you think they might still have Fleet prisoners aboard?"

Brad raised his palms in a gesture of uncertainty. "Who knows? Keep your eyes peeled, and if you see someone that looks like a prisoner, let us know. Anyone armed, take them down hard. If someone surrenders, tie them up and keep pushing forward. We'll clean up once we're done.

"Also, let's think about computer files. Several of the fire teams are heading to areas where the computer center might be located. If you find it, cut it off from the rest of the ship. We'd like to keep them from remotely wiping the data. Shut the servers down and make sure they stay down.

"I'm proud as Everlit stars of you all. I have no doubt we're going to triumph today. Good luck."

Saburo turned to face his people and raised his arms over his head. "I expect the very best from each and every one of you today. You're Vikings. Go show those bastards why they should be afraid of us. Now, everyone into the cargo lock.

"We'll exit the ship in three groups. Remember to keep radio silence. At this range, they're going to be able to hear you sneeze. Once everyone is out onto the hull, we'll go down the hoses like little ants. Then when we get to the carrier, everyone move to your designated entry points and wait for my signal. Vikings!"

With that, the Vikings cheered, locked their helmets into place, and started loading themselves into the cargo airlock.

Brad, Falcone, and the rest of the non-ground combat forces would be in the last group. He really hoped no one on the carrier was keeping a visual eye on the hoses. If so, the Vikings would be in for a *very* warm welcome.

———

Gathering on the hull of the tanker took a surprisingly short period of time. Brad had overseen a couple of drills on the way to the asteroid and watched Saburo work his people hard. Everyone knew precisely where they needed to be and what they needed to do.

Even so, he thought they just cut a minute off their best time.

The hoses carrying the He-3 from the tanker to the carrier had a couple of contradictory characteristics. They had to be flexible in order to be stowed, but to serve in transshipping fuel, they needed to be rigid.

The pressure of the He-3 was part of how that was achieved, but each section of tubing also had stiff metal rods that locked magnetically into place at the flip of a switch. Thankfully, the tanker's autopilot was sufficient for station-keeping purposes. The alignment between the ships had to be precise.

Under normal circumstances, the hoses could be jettisoned by the ship being refueled in case of emergency. His engineers had made certain that was no longer possible. If the carrier tried to jettison the refueling tubes, they'd jam in place.

Of course, the things weren't strong enough to actually keep the big ship in place, but they would buy the boarders another fifteen or twenty seconds before the carrier's engines pulled the massive ship loose from the tanker.

That might not sound like much, but when one was scurrying for cover, fifteen seconds was an eternity.

Thankfully, once they got onto the carrier's hull, there wouldn't be any defensive measures waiting for them. No one expected enemy combat troops to just appear out of nowhere in deep space.

In any kind of reasonable situation, a ship's commander knew that they'd see oncoming enemy forces long before any kind of boarding action started. That's why Brad's plan even had a chance of success. No one expected it.

If the enemy ship had cameras watching the fuel lines, they'd almost certainly be placed close to the ship itself. After all, what they were really looking for were leaks or some other kind of mechanical failure.

With that in mind, Saburo and his people got about three-quarters of the way across and then let go of the hoses. The small reservoir each suit had to generate thrust was more than sufficient to get them safely to the carrier with plenty of reserve to spare.

Brad dragged himself along the hose he'd chosen with ease. He'd long before mastered working in zero gravity. In fact, none of his people seemed to be out of practice. He made a mental note to mention that in their files. All their extra training had paid off.

His anxiety calmed the closer he got to the location where they were jumping for the carrier. He'd just about decided this was actually going to work when the hose flexed under his hands.

For a moment, he thought someone ahead of him had used their legs to jump off and sent a ripple down the hose, but it wasn't going to be that easy. The rear of the carrier lit up as its engines came online. It was trying to tear free.

"Heads up!" he snapped over the general com. "They're onto us. All entry teams move. Don't wait for us. Go! Go! Go!"

Someone on the carrier must've seen something that they shouldn't have. That spoke to a higher level of professionalism than Brad would've expected. Once more, the Cadre had surprised them.

Brad gathered himself to get free of the hose, but the ripple going through its length suddenly doubled. With a jerk he could feel through his gloved hands, it rebounded from somewhere behind him. This particular hose had probably just snapped free of the tanker.

Without waiting to find out if his guess was correct, Brad engaged his thrusters and sought to get clear of the hose.

Unfortunately, it had the jump on him. The hose curled in on itself and snapped forward, sending Brad hurtling toward the carrier's hull. He instantly reversed his suit's thrust but doubted it would be enough to offset all the momentum the hose had just imparted to him.

He didn't have time to look and see how many other people were in dire straits. He'd find out soon enough. They could pick up those who missed the carrier after the fight was over.

From her cursing, Brad suspected that Falcone was one of those people.

"Falcone, what's your status?" he asked.

"I'm screwed," she snarled. "That damned hose just sent me toward the asteroid. The carrier is going to be moving too fast for me to catch up. Get them, Madrid. Don't waste this chance."

"Trust me when I say that I'll capture this ship or die trying. Hang on until we can come back for you."

With alarming rapidity, the carrier grew larger in front of him. He flipped over and aligned his legs with a clear spot. This was going to be a significant impact.

It came faster than he'd expected, too. Brad rebounded off before his magnetic boots could clamp on. While he hadn't broken a leg, he was going to be walking funny for a while.

In his rush, he completely lost track of where he was supposed to go. He had some of his troopers in sight, already on this carrier, so he'd follow them.

It turned out the group he was following was the one directly under Saburo's command. He recognized the Colonel's vacuum armor from some of the artwork he'd added to spice it up.

Neither Brad or Saburo minded a little bit of individualization. So long as it didn't damage discipline. Besides, Brad thought the art was beautiful.

The etchings along the stretches of armor were in the Japanese style and showed samurai warriors in battle. Brad wasn't certain who Saburo had hired to create the art, but it looked original.

Saburo's teams had zeroed in on a personnel lock toward the forward half of the carrier. His men were already placing breaching charges around it to gain rapid entry.

Brad sighed in relief when his boots clamped on to the carrier's hull. He'd been worried that it might slip away before he got back to it. That was probably an unreasonable worry, but it was still relief.

He hadn't had a chance to take a single step when he felt vibration through the hull. A glance overhead showed the tanker coming apart as mass-driver rounds tore into it.

Saburo had seen it as well. "Well, there goes our ride. I suppose we'll have to make sure we don't walk home."

"Charges are ready," Orlosky said.

"Blow it," Brad ordered.

The troopers all faced away from the lock, and a *thump* rattled the hull.

Brad turned back and saw the exterior hatch sailing away on a jet of leaking air. They'd ruptured the inner door. That might make access more difficult, but they didn't have a choice. It was do-or-die time.

CHAPTER TWENTY-FIVE

THE BREACHING team slapped a temporary airlock over the gaping, air-spewing hole in the side of the carrier. There wasn't room enough inside it for everyone to fit, so the initial forces would have to secure a beachhead inside the carrier.

Brad kept a wary eye on the tanker as it came apart over their heads. The He-3 it contained wasn't explosive in and of itself, but it *was* stored at high pressure. That, coupled with the mass-driver rounds drilling through the hull, made for quite a show.

Fragments large and small were spinning away from the doomed ship in every direction. Even though the carrier was opening the distance between it and the tanker with every moment, plenty of those bits and pieces were colliding with the warship.

Including a few somewhat *sizable* fragments.

Something that resembled a hull plate took out an auxiliary communications array less than twenty meters from the airlock with a crash that Brad felt through his boots. That shot debris in every direction.

Something caromed off the top of Brad's helmet before he could duck. He listened closely in case it had fractured his protective armor, but heard no indication of leaking air. Dammit, that was far too close.

While he came out of the impact fine, the portable airlock did not. It now sported half a dozen holes small and large across its surface and was doing nothing to slow the loss of the carrier's atmosphere.

"Cut it loose," he ordered. "We'll just have to deal with any airtight doors once we get inside."

The mercenaries quickly unsealed the airlock and cast it away. The amount of air coming out of the damaged lock was significantly higher now. Apparently, the first group of troops had been forced to cut the airlock's interior door the rest of the way open.

Rather than fight the air rushing out, they waited for the flow to stop on its own and then headed in as quickly as they could.

The corridor just inside the carrier reminded Brad of his visits aboard various Fleet vessels. That shouldn't be shocking, he supposed. It wasn't as if the Cadre was going to redo the paint after they hijacked the ship. Decorating wasn't their strong suit.

Saburo was already moving his troops toward where they suspected the bridge and pilot control for the drones was located. It was critical that they stop the enemy from using those weapons against his ships.

By now, the mass-driver slugs that *Bound by Law* had fired earlier should have impacted the Cadre destroyer. If they'd caught it flat-footed, that ship was now a floating mass of wreckage in much the same condition as the tanker. The rest of his ships would be firing torpedoes.

If they weren't lucky, his ships had just revealed themselves and were going to be in for an exceptionally tough fight.

Being trapped inside the carrier, Brad would have no insight into what was going on around them until they secured the ship. So, he supposed he'd best get busy doing exactly that.

There were no signs of Cadre pirates around them, but that was only to be expected. Once the airlock started leaking air, the vacuum alarms would've begun screaming and every person in the area would've headed for the nearest airtight door or suit.

Anyone trapped in a cabin by the loss of pressure wouldn't be a threat. They couldn't go anywhere.

That didn't mean that mobile defenders weren't headed their way. Brad expected to run headfirst into a buzz saw. The Cadre had to stop them from seizing the bridge and Engineering. If they didn't, this fight was going to end a lot more quickly than the pirates wanted.

"I have a deck map," somebody said over the command com. "One of those 'you are here' kind of maps. I'm sending it to everyone."

The overlay in Brad's HUD showed a map off to the side. He enlarged it long enough to get a feel for how the ship was laid out. The dot that indicated the viewer's location was toward the aft of the ship, so he knew the finder hadn't been one of his people.

That didn't keep him from locating where they were probably standing. He might be off by a deck or two, but the bridge was somewhere aft of their location and in toward the centerline of the carrier.

"This is Madrid," he said over Saburo's command link. "Somebody get me a deck number."

"I passed one inside the lock, sir," Orlosky said. "We're on deck seven."

A few moments of examining the map told Brad that they needed to be on deck nine. "Find a way to get down two decks. The bridge is somewhere toward the center of the ship and aft of our current location. If I'm right, the drone control area won't be too far away."

"This is fire team six," a voice said over the general channel. "We found the drone launchers. They're empty. It looks like the enemy has launched."

Now the clock was really ticking.

Saburo urged his people on and they quickly found a stairwell leading down. It was unguarded on this level because of the breach.

"It looks like the airtight doors closed inside the stairwell," the Colonel said after a quick check inside. "We can get down one level, but not two. Everyone into the stairwell and we'll try closing this hatch to see if we can get past it."

It only took a minute to get everyone inside the stairwell. Brad brought up the rear and sealed the hatch behind himself. "We're in."

"Working on the door," Saburo said. "It's locked, but I have a master key. Everyone face away."

The mercenary officer must've used a fairly small breaching charge to rupture part of the door, because the air pressure began to rapidly rise around Brad but they didn't have to deal with any debris. Moments later, Saburo had the airtight door open.

The mercenaries streamed through it and forced the hatch on the correct deck. They walked right into an ambush, it seemed. The sound of booming shotguns and activated mono-blades filled the air but didn't stop any of the mercenaries from rushing forward.

Brad was on their heels, his pistol in one hand and his deactivated mono-blade in the other.

The pirates had the Vikings in a crossfire from behind two improvised barricades set up to the right and left in the perpendicular corridor. Some of his people were already down, but the rest were charging toward both positions, firing as they went.

It looked as if the barriers weren't very protective, because every shot that hit one went right through. Half the people behind them weren't even in vac-suits, much less armored ones.

A few of them were wearing regular body armor and carrying rifles. Those became his people's primary targets. The shotguns were an annoyance, but they weren't going to penetrate the mercenaries' armored vac-suits without heavier ammunition then they'd have been carrying without specific reasons.

That's when pirates on either side hurled grenades into the middle of his people. The first one went off and dropped half a dozen mercenaries. The second one landed almost at Brad's feet.

He reached for it, but trooper Orlosky was faster. He snatched it off the deck and put his own body between his comrades and the grenade just as it went off. Blood and bits of armor splashed across Brad's faceplate.

Not only had he lost another of his troopers, he couldn't see a thing.

———

Unable to act, Brad knelt and dug into the pouch at his belt. He knew that there was a rag in there somewhere. It wouldn't be enough to clean his faceplate, but anything was better than being blind.

While he was struggling with that, someone slammed into him from the side and sent him sprawling. The rag he'd just plucked out of his pouch came loose and he dropped his pistol.

"No laying down the job, sir," Saburo said over the command channel. "Up you go."

Someone—Brad assumed it was Saburo—yanked him to his feet. Brad scrubbed his hands furiously across his faceplate. That smeared the blood everywhere but did create a few streaks that he could mostly see through.

His combat team commander was already gone, chasing his men to where they were overrunning one of the barricades.

Brad finally spotted his pistol lying on the deck and took two steps to retrieve it. As he was standing up, he saw that the assault on the second barricade had been less successful. More pirates had reinforced that particular group, and they were now charging toward the Vikings, screaming at the top of their lungs.

Circumstances were far less than optimal, but Brad started shooting pirates and activated his mono-blade. He stepped clear of any of his troops and swung at the first pirate even as he emptied his pistol into the crowd behind the man.

The first pirate proved to be less of a challenge than Brad had feared. While he couldn't see everything through his faceplate, Brad saw enough to block the man's strike in such a way that his own blade snapped into his face when he drew back.

The bearded man screamed as the blue filament sliced deeply into his face. He slapped a hand across his injury and staggered back, only to be beheaded by one of the pirates behind him.

It looked to Brad as if the blue-on-blue incident had been accidental, but one never knew with pirates. A fight to the death might be the perfect place to settle a score.

This next man was far superior in skill to the bearded fellow, so Brad changed his opinion over the next several blows. The pirate was too good to have accidentally sliced off his cohort's head.

The Vikings around Brad held firm and stopped the charging pirates. The fighting was intense for about thirty seconds and then the enemy broke, fleeing the field of battle.

Brad supposed Saburo's returning forces probably had something to do with that. The Colonel and his men had killed all the people behind the first barricade and been able to turn their full force back to their other enemies.

"After them!" Brad said. "The bridge is in that direction. Keep chasing them and try to catch them with the hatch open."

If they had to blow the hatch leading onto the bridge—which would certainly be armored—then they were going to wreck the controls and kill everybody in a position to know what in Everdark was really going on.

As his men rushed to keep the pirates too busy to turn and fight, Brad found a dead pirate's shirt to wipe his faceplate relatively clean. He needed to be able to see what the enemy was doing rather than hopping around half-blinded. He took the time to reload his pistol, holster it, and grab a fallen rifle.

That delay put him near the back of the group heading for the bridge. With the map clear in his mind, he wasn't surprised when he came around a corner in the corridor and found the entryway to the bridge defended.

Unlike the impromptu defenses, these people were in full armor and carried rifles issued by Fleet to their marines. Whoever had designed the approach to the bridge had made certain that the corridors came in at an angle and gave the defenders a place to hide.

The Vikings had a place to hide too: behind the fleeing pirates that they were chasing.

That defense proved less stout when the pirates at the bridge hatch opened fire directly through their comrades. They'd waited until a thin man not wearing armor reached them.

In seconds, the remaining ambushers were down.

But that still gave the Vikings a chance to bring their own weapons into play. On board a ship, one had to be careful how much force one brought to bear, but that didn't mean you had no teeth.

Saburo, who was a maestro of unorthodox weaponry, hurled a

grenade into the area where the defenders were hiding. Not only did it explode, it scattered intensely luminous particles that stuck to *everything*.

And as Brad could attest, getting something on one's faceplate really ruined one's ability to aim.

The grenade also had an audio component, but with the men ahead of them in sealed armor, that wasn't nearly as debilitating as it would've been under other circumstances.

With the aid of that distraction, Saburo's troops pushed forward and exchanged heavy fire with the defenders. Singly and in pairs, his mercenaries started dropping. Four, five, seven were down.

The losses were not one-sided. The enemy was dropping at an even faster rate. That made the unarmored man, who was now glowing brightly, tap a code into the hatch leading onto the bridge. It opened.

Knowing that time was exceptionally short, Brad hurled himself forward. One of the dying pirates fired his rifle at Brad. The slug struck him a glancing blow to the leg. Based on the stab of pain, something had gotten through, but he wasn't sure how bad it was.

Someone behind Brad shot the defender just as Brad knocked the man over with his shoulder and rolled onto the bridge of the carrier.

It was larger than the bridge on the cruiser *Freedom*, though it was laid out in a similar pattern. There were more stations and that meant more people. Brad saw he was dealing with almost a dozen people. All of them were rising from their seats and grabbing for pistols.

"Everyone freeze," Brad shouted through his exterior speaker. "Anyone that surrenders now gets to live."

Though he doubted that would work, Brad hoped to gain enough time for his men to follow him in. His hand slapped on the control to the hatch, aborting the command to close it.

As quick as a snake, the man who had been seated at the command chair raised the pistol in his hand and shot the pirate who had retreated onto the bridge in the side of the head.

That gory betrayal froze everyone for a few seconds. Just long enough for Saburo and some of his men to get through the bridge hatch behind Brad.

The pale, red-headed man who had just murdered his associate dropped his pistol and raised his hands. "I surrender. We all surrender."

Brad wasn't certain that everyone else agreed with that statement, and for another few seconds, it looked as if there was going to be a firefight. Then, one by one, the pirates dropped their weapons and raised their hands above their heads.

CHAPTER TWENTY-SIX

"Step away from the consoles," Saburo barked. "Anyone twitches wrong, we open fire."

Longbow's bridge crew slowly obeyed, but the man in command slowly rotated to face the boarders, holding his empty hands out.

"Commodore Madrid, I presume?" he asked in a calm Martian accent. "Look at the display."

He pointed. Brad followed his gesture and saw, for the first time since he'd abandoned the tanker, the tactical plot. The Cadre destroyer was gone, like he'd hoped, but the enemy corvettes had proven more dangerous than he'd expected. No one had predicted they'd be the brand-new *Invictus*-class ships, and they'd focused their fire on their opposite numbers in the Vikings. *Alan-a-dale* was leaking atmosphere, and *Heart of Vengeance* had clearly taken hard hits.

And a swarm of green icons were charging toward his people, a minute at most from contact.

"The drones are in terminal acquisition," the Cadre officer told him. "With the signal from *Longbow* cut off, they will go into full autonomous mode. Your ships? They can't win that fight."

"Saburo, shut them down," Brad snapped.

"That won't save you," the redheaded man noted. "The corvettes' commander is Lionel Madrigal. He's a fanatic and he has nukes. If the drones shut down completely, he'll know what happened and he'll burn his ships up to nuke your destroyers.

"How many friends are you prepared to lose today, Commodore? I can save them all…if you'll let me."

He gestured to a cluster of control consoles to one side of the bridge. Their screens looked almost like the officers had been playing one of Michelle's strategy games, not commanding a warship—which meant they were the control systems for the Javelin drones.

"You expect me to trust you?" Brad snapped.

"You can read the display as well as I can," the stranger replied. "Thirty seconds, tops. Your call, Madrid."

It was possible the man was lying. It was possible that the drones weren't in autonomous mode *yet*, and if Brad let the officer access the drone control systems, he'd turn them on Brad's people.

But he was right. The two corvettes had survived everything Brad's fleet could throw at them for far too long, and if they *did* have nukes, they'd be able to at least take out his destroyers.

The destroyers that happened to have Brad's *wife* aboard.

"Do it," he snapped, before he could change his mind. "But if you betray me…"

The man shrugged and crossed to the consoles, seemingly unaware of the guns pointed at him. He tapped a series of commands, and a warning sign popped up on the screen.

"Activate Prodigal Protocols," he said aloud to the screen. "Authentication Michaels-Lambda-Niner-Fuck-This-Garbage."

For a moment, nothing happened—and then the colors on the screen swapped. The two Cadre destroyers were suddenly bright crimson, and the Vikings' ships were the solid blue of allied units.

The drones' profile didn't change, and for several eternal seconds, Brad was convinced the Cadre officer had just put on a light show to fool them.

And then fifteen drones launched on each Cadre corvette at point-blank range. The torpedoes didn't have much velocity after only a few seconds of acceleration, but the Cadre appeared to have access to the high-density chemical warheads Fleet used for overkill.

The hundred-kilo warheads were equivalent to five hundred tons of old-style TNT. Each.

Each corvette took the equivalent of a small nuclear bomb, vanishing before they even realized they'd been betrayed.

The Cadre officer tapped a few more commands and stepped away from the console.

"It might be valuable, Commodore, if you order your people to leave the drones be," he said calmly. "They're on their way back to *Longbow* in autonomous mode, weapons locked down."

"Who *are* you?" Brad demanded.

"Commander Connor Michaels, Independence Militia."

"Bullshit," the Commodore snapped. "This is a Cadre ship and you're Cadre."

Michaels sighed.

"As you mean the term, yes," he agreed. "Right now, Commodore, the Phoenix has no reason to think anyone in this convoy survived. That gives us a margin of opportunity."

"'Us,' Commander?" Brad asked, only half-willingly.

"I'm assuming you have an Agency operative with you? I need someone with authority, Commodore Madrid. I'm willing to cut a deal...but the moment the Phoenix realizes I'm alive, you won't be able to meet my price."

The redheaded man smiled sadly.

"Shall we talk in private?"

———

It would take several hours to rendezvous the various ships, and something in Michaels' demeanor led Brad to think they didn't have that much time. Fortunately, the SAR shuttle that had picked up Falcone and the other Dutchmen was headed to the carrier already, and it only took another ten minutes to be sure the whole ship was secure and get her aboard.

Longbow wasn't in great shape after being boarded...but she was more intact than he'd hoped. There was a lot of the normal combat damage, but they'd taken life support, Engineering, and the bridge intact. She looked like crap inside, but she could fly and she could fight.

Of course, all of her systems were locked behind encryption several light-years beyond Brad's own ability. That, of course, was why he had Corporal Reece.

Falcone entered the bridge less than five minutes after they'd secured the ship, her helmet off but ready in her hands in case someone did anything stupid.

"What have we got?" she asked.

"Senior officer wants to cut a deal," he summarized. "We disconnected the systems to the Captain's office and shoved him in there. The rest of the prisoners are locked up elsewhere, just in case."

"We took more of those on the bridge than anywhere else," Saburo told them both grimly. "And most of what we've got are juniors. I don't think we have a single officer alive who wasn't on the bridge, and not many of the noncoms."

"This ship had a crew of three hundred in Fleet service," Brad noted. "How bad is it?"

"We have fifty-two prisoners," his ground commander told him. "Half are wounded. We've got eighteen dead and fifteen wounded of our own, but this boat at least has a Fleet-standard medbay. All of the wounded should live—ours and theirs."

"We're not even into communications yet," Brad told Falcone. "Reece is on her way up and that's going to be her first port of call, but I figure we want to talk to the officer together."

"Agreed. Usual terms, I think," she said harshly.

Which meant a promise of life…with the unspoken small print of it being life in the Mercury mines. It wasn't a nice deal.

"It's your game," he told her. "Your rules."

He wasn't going to shed a lot of tears for pirates, even if he wasn't *quite* up to tossing them out the airlock himself.

"I want to check one thing first," she said, stepping over to the command chair. She rotated the seat to a specific angle and clicked something. "Original builder's plates," she said as she slid the chair forward.

"Fuck me."

"Kate?"

"Take a look," she told him.

Brad stepped over to study the plate she'd uncovered. It gave a date—about six months earlier. There *should* have been a yard name, but that was missing.

What wasn't missing were the hull number and commissioned name.

DC-010 Longbow.

"I thought Fleet only built eight of these," Brad said slowly.

"So far as I know, that's exactly right," Falcone replied. "Let's talk to this Michaels. I have all *kinds* of questions for him now."

———

Michaels, it seemed, was quite familiar with the Captain's office he'd been put in. In the ten minutes it took Brad and Falcone to join him in the office, he'd turned the desk around, set two chairs "behind" it for them, grabbed a seat for himself, and made coffee.

"Can we trust the coffee?" Falcone asked as she eyed the cups.

"There's nothing in it," Michaels replied. "It's Fleet-grade, so black as tar and bitter as betrayal, but Joyce had cream, sugar, and booze around if you want them."

"*Bitter as betrayal* seems appropriate," the Agent told him. "You want a deal?"

"Yeah. And we're not doing it on your terms, before you tell me you'll spare our lives and send us to the Mercury mines."

Brad swallowed a choking laugh. Apparently, Falcone had a *reputation* now.

She leaned across the desk.

"And why do you think that's what I'd offer? Or that you're worth better?" she asked, the sweetness in her tone dangerously deceptive.

"We've met, Agent, though I doubt you remember me," Michaels told her. "I was one of the five pilots on *Spearthrower* when you took us after those wreckers on Venus. I remember the deal you gave their leader, and I owe my people better than that."

"I haven't met many pirates who think that much of their crews," Brad replied.

"I can explain the difference, Commodore, but that falls under the things I have of value to trade," the Cadre officer replied. "And we're running short on time if you're going to meet my price."

"And why would that be?" Brad asked.

"Because once the Cadre kills my family, I have nothing to even try to live for," he said flatly. "So, let's talk terms, shall we?"

That was a verbal punch in the gut Brad hadn't expected. He thought he'd concealed his reaction, but from Michaels's eyes, Brad had failed.

"Talk," Falcone ordered.

"I can tell you where this ship came from. Where her crew was recruited. I can unlock her systems and give you control of her," Michaels laid out. "I'll tell you *everything* I know."

"And in exchange?" the Agent asked.

"Three things." He held up a finger.

"One, I want full amnesty for the crew. I doubt any of the serious cases survived, but I'll review the list and let you know if there's anyone left aboard you can't risk setting free. The rest I want you to deliver safely to Earth with new identities and clean records."

He held up a second finger.

"Two, I want to live. I'm pretty inarguably guilty of treason, regardless of the ameliorating circumstances, but I want a promise of life for myself and any other surviving officers and noncoms. I'll accept we need to go to prison, but we *don't* go to a death facility like the Mercury mines."

He held up a third finger.

"Third, and if you fail at this, it's a deal-breaker, I have a wife and two little girls on Mars. All of the middle and junior officers aboard *Longbow* have families. Didn't think of that when we were being fed the line of bullshit, and when the brick finally dropped, the Phoenix happily told us they were being watched."

Fuck.

"They haven't, so far as a crap-ton of the money I made for this Everdark-cursed gig can tell, actually seized anyone's families yet, but they know where they are. Thanks to said crap-ton of money, I *also* know where the families of every member of *Longbow*'s crew are."

Michaels smiled thinly.

"So, this is my real price, Agent Falcon: your Agency saves my family and makes at least a real damn effort to save the families of the rest of our crew.

"Meet my demands, and this ship is yours, and I'll tell you everything I know."

Brad shared a glance with Falcone, then sighed as a thought struck him.

"That's between Agent Falcon and her boss," he said. "But I do have one question for you: do you know if that poison tooth has a remote control?"

The Cadre man's smile thinned to white.

"Oh, it almost certainly does," he told them. "Every officer and noncom you've captured will have one. That's why I'm pretty sure none of the hardcore cases are still alive—but you may want to get some pliers in here if you want to get those answers from me."

———

Falcone looked furious as she stalked out onto the bridge. Her entire body language changed as the door closed and she shook her head.

"Who the fuck does that *pirate* think he is?" she demanded aloud.

Brad sighed.

"Unless I missed the pieces he gave us, he *is* an ex-Fleet officer who bought a line of bullshit when he should have known better, and then got trapped with his family's lives on the line," he told her. "He's Cadre, he's a pirate, he's even—at least at some point—a Dark-cursed volunteer…but he wants out."

"The only way out of the Cadre is in a fucking body bag," Falcone snapped.

"That's what the Phoenix wants," Brad said quietly. "Kate, if they have capital ships—drone carriers, another cruiser, heavy destroyers… a lot of their crew have to be like Michaels. Blackmailed or with hostages. They have to know we'll cover for them if they turn.

"Plus, he's right on the time limit—and regardless of what Connor Michaels has done, his family doesn't deserve to meet a Cadre assassin."

"It's not your damn call, Commodore Madrid," the spy snarled.

"It's yours. And we need his data. So, make the call," Brad told her calmly. "Think with your head and not your hate."

He held her gaze for several long seconds, and she made a shaky, chopping nod.

"I seem to recall saying something similar to you once," she noted. "And…you're right. I'll ping Mars. We'll probably need a recording from his family before he'll talk."

"Likely," Brad agreed, and stepped over to look at the builder's plate that told him the ship was utterly impossible. "And I think we need him to talk.

"Saburo." He gestured the Colonel over to him. "Let's get medics to check over the prisoners—I don't want anyone who doesn't want to be questioned biting on a tooth, and I *really* don't want anyone who *wants* to talk be killed by a damn remote control."

CHAPTER TWENTY-SEVEN

With orbits the way they currently lined up, the round-trip time for a radio message to Mars was almost an hour. The Commonwealth Investigative Agency's people were good, but they couldn't move out and take a list of just under a hundred names into protective custody, potentially while under fire, and get back to Brad immediately.

The Vikings took the time to move their four ships in and around *Longbow* and make sure their own communications were tight. Brad's little fleet had taken more of a pounding than he'd hoped, but most of it was thankfully superficial.

All of his ships could fight. *Heart of Vengeance* was short a lot of her reactive armor, but her systems were intact.

The only casualties had been in the boarding op, bodies that were slowly transported back to *Oath of Vengeance* while Brad paced the deck of the captured carrier.

"I don't suppose Fleet will let us keep her?" Michelle asked over the radio. "Just think what we could jack our rates to if we were the only mercenary company in the system with a *carrier*."

"Given that Fleet doesn't even like to admit they have carriers?" Brad replied. "I'll be happy if they buy her off us and don't just confiscate her."

"I can probably guarantee that," Falcone told him as the Agent appeared, leaning against the command chair Brad had co-opted. "There's no way I can get them to let you keep her, sorry. Not with those semi-sentient killing machines downstairs."

Brad had carefully chosen *not* to go inspect the returned Javelin drones. Falcone had taken a closer look.

She hadn't come away looking overly happy with their existence.

"And that's before I mention that Saburo's Geiger counters tell me there's nukes in the torpedo magazines?" Brad said sweetly.

"Nobody wants you anywhere *near* nuclear weapons again, Brad," Michelle told him from *Oath*'s bridge. "Not Fleet—and definitely not the Cadre!"

Falcone checked something as her wrist-comp beeped, and lost some of the color on her face.

"Well," she said, then swallowed hard. "We know that the Cadre now knows the convoy went dark. I doubt they know if anyone survived, but every tooth implant your medics removed just went off as one.

"And we didn't even pick up the signal."

"That's...not good," Brad noted.

"Low frequency, multi-emitter," Reece guessed, the tech currently half-buried inside the communication control consoles. "Probably bounced it from four or five sources timed to hit here at the same time. Interference would make identifying a source impossible, and the low energy would make it hard to detect at all."

The Vikings' commanding officer looked at the image of his wife and the Commonwealth Agent standing next to him. "Did that make sense to you?" he asked. "Because it *almost* made sense to me."

And if any of the three women listening to him believed that, well, they wouldn't be working for him.

"There we go," Reece announced. "Someone who put this together was a *paranoid* bastard."

Michaels had given them codes he insisted should activate the carrier's communications suite. They'd very clearly worked...and the console had shut itself down moments later.

"We guessed that," Brad told her. "What did you find?"

She held up a plain black box the length of her hand.

"Dead man's switch. The moment the captain died, the communications system sent an alert pulse and shut down. We'll want to check the other systems, too. We need Michaels's codes, but if they dead-man-switched key systems in case of a mutiny…"

"Paranoid bastards," Brad agreed. "Who *was* the captain?"

"The skinny fucker Michaels shot," Falcone told him. "I'm hoping for an ID back from the Agency, but I'm guessing he's ex-Fleet like his third officer."

The communications system came back online as she spoke.

"Any old messages in the buffer?" the Agent asked hopefully.

"Switch wiped the local memory when the captain died, sorry," Reece replied. "Physically burnt out the boards. There'll be backups in the main core, but…who knows what code ran when that switch got yanked."

"So, we may have a lobotomized ship?" Brad asked. "Even if Michaels gives us his codes?"

"Unlikely," Falcone said. "They wouldn't want the ship to be completely useless if something happened to the captain. The Cadre wouldn't accept a single point of failure. I'm guessing we just weren't supposed to be able to communicate until a Cadre pickup force arrived, but we'd still be able to complete whatever mission they were on."

"If there's any more traps aboard this ship, find them," Brad ordered. He wasn't planning on *keeping* the ship, but having a Cadre capital ship had all sorts of possibilities buzzing around his brain.

"We'll have her clean by tomorrow," Reece promised. "Now I know what to look for, I can check over systems pretty quickly." She shook her head.

"If we don't get an officer's codes to get into the systems, though, it'll be *weeks* before we can take control of her."

"Let's hope your friends on Mars did their jobs," Brad said to Falcone. "Still waiting on that update?"

"I have faith," she told him. "They'll get it done."

It was another hour before the message from the Agency finally arrived. The man in the video was noticeably older than when Brad had last met him barely eighteen months before. Randy Cartwright had had faintly reddish hair and freckles when the Agent had helped Brad infiltrate a Martian suburb to chase the Cadre.

The freckles remained, but the hair had gone white and there were new stress lines around his eyes. Cartwright hadn't had a good year.

"Madrid was always a good source for a headache, wasn't he, Kate?" he asked quietly. "We went for the names on the list. We've successfully extracted sixty-three of them. The rest?"

He shook his head.

"They're gone, Kate. Some of them have been gone for days, others for weeks…months. I don't know if they're alive or dead, but from the context you sent me the damn list in, I'm guessing alive. In a fucking Cadre box somewhere."

Brad inhaled sharply. That would be his own personal worst nightmare, one that had come very close to true when the Terror had used Michelle as bait to lure him in. That hadn't ended well for the Terror, but it seemed the Phoenix didn't fall far from the tree.

"We got Michaels's family," the Martian continued. "Half a step ahead of a squad of Cadre commandos—aiming for live extraction, I *think*. And I mean the hard-asses, too. We dropped our Marine overhead on the bastards. No prisoners, and they got at least half of their team out.

"I hope these people are worth it, Kate. I've got five of mine and six of Admiral Weber's in hospital—and three Marines in body bags."

"*Fuck,*" Falcone murmured. "They really went after those families hard."

"I checked a bunch of your other data. Some of it officially, some of it not. Bailey says she never said a damned word about any carriers, but so long as *that's* clear, she knows where all eight are and validated their locations as of twenty-four hours ago.

"Fleet isn't missing a carrier. There was a prototype that she is over ninety percent sure was melted down—and the only reason she isn't a hundred percent sure is that she trusts Madrid."

Commodore Bailey, CO of the battleship *Eternal,* was the senior starship commander of the Martian Squadron. She and Brad went back a while with an acrimonious relationship that had included everything from threats and cursing to Bailey almost having to execute him for illegal use of nukes.

"Oh, and Bailey most definitely did not provide a database of all Fleet personnel who retired, were made redundant, or officially died in the last four years. And it's definitely not attached to this message."

Cartwright sighed.

"There's also a message to Michaels from his wife and kids. Hope it helps. I have found entirely new reasons to hate the Cadre today."

The message ended and Brad looked over at Falcone. "The attachments?"

"The thoroughly illegal database we definitely don't have and a video for Michaels. Which do you want to tackle first?" she asked.

"ID the captain, then we'll talk to Michaels," Brad decided. He wasn't sure they needed that ammunition, but it could come in handy.

Falcone was already setting to work and inhaled sharply as she got a result almost instantly.

"Lieutenant Arthur Vong, how far off the beaten track you fell," she said softly. "Right on the edge of Bailey's search parameter. He was cashiered for selling drugs aboard *Freedom* four years ago."

She snorted. "Michaels outranked him in Fleet grade and time, but he'd been with Cadre longer. They clearly trusted him, a lot given the damn dead man's switches."

"Michaels is in there too?" Brad asked.

"Yep. Last Fleet role was as CAG for *Spearthrower*, but he took a voluntary early retirement package that was being offered as part of the first round of cuts. He's right. We worked together at Venus, about three years back."

"And folks got sent to the Mercury mines?" the Vikings leader asked.

Falcone winced.

"They were luring high-altitude craft in the Venus atmosphere too low, hacking their systems so they ended up in pressure zones they couldn't handle—and then grabbing the wreckage in ships designed for the Venusian surface," she noted. "At least two hundred dead we knew about, and we needed to find their base—but every one of them was a sick bastard who'd earned a bullet."

"I wasn't arguing," Brad told her. "I just want to know how deep a hole you dug with this guy."

"That depends on whether he still thinks he's an officer…or if he realizes he's fallen into the category as those wreckers."

———

The video from Michaels's wife was about what you'd expect. *This is today's date. We're alive and fine. Why in Everdark are Marines kicking down my door and asking me to record this video?*

It was enough. More than enough, as the Cadre officer literally had his head in his hands after the first few seconds. Brad carefully did not notice the tears streaking his face when he looked back up at them.

"Thank you," he said quietly. "And the rest?"

"I am prepared to consider a guarantee of life in a medium-security prison for yourself and your people," Falcone said stonily. "I cannot—I *will* not—promise full amnesty for pirates and criminals."

Michaels sighed.

"Do you really think the electronics technician running machine shop three on this ship can be considered directly involved?" he asked. "Yes, there are people aboard this ship guilty of real and serious crimes, but a lot of the crew are accessories at most. The Independence Militia ships don't carry boarding troops. We don't see the aftermath.

"They have true Cadre ships accompanying us for that, and Cadre commandos," Michaels noted. "They use us for fire support, and there's a psychological element to it, too."

He sighed. "They know damned well that we can lie to ourselves so long as we don't actually participate in the thefts and massacres, hide behind the rags of our honor and our duty to protect our families."

"This ship alone is responsible for at least half a dozen raids I know of," Falcone told him. "Enough of that blood is on your people's hands that I won't offer more. Your family is safe. Most of your crew's families are safe, and the Agency is looking for the rest.

"You'll go to a medium-security facility on Deimos, one the Agency has thoroughly vetted the staff of. You'll serve time for your crimes, all of you, but you will live."

It was harsher than Brad might have offered, given what they now knew about the crew of *Longbow*...but it was more merciful than he'd give most Cadre, too.

Michaels considered for a long time, then nodded.

"All right. Do you want me to talk or unlock the ship first?"

"Talk," Falcone ordered. "I'll have questions, but let's start at the beginning, shall we?"

He exhaled, putting his hands on the desk. He studied them for a long moment, then pulled a bottle of whisky out of the desk and poured a generous dollop into his coffee.

"The beginning, huh?" Michaels said softly. "There's a lot of beginnings, and most won't make sense to anyone who isn't a Fleet officer." He gestured to Brad. "Madrid will get some of it, but we all know his reserve commission is a fig leaf.

"But...there's a lot that goes on in the Outer System that Fleet knows about but can't deal with. We say we don't have the hulls, we say we don't have the hands...but truthfully, what we lack is the *will*. The Commonwealth has the industrial capacity to mass-produce corvettes, at the very least. The Fleet, before the cuts, was two hundred and forty-three ships strong.

"One set of estimates I was privy to said that with a less than one percent increase in the overall Commonwealth budget, they could build, crew, and arm a hundred corvettes and twenty destroyers in two years. A fifty percent increase in the numbers, if not the tonnage, of the Fleet, enough to secure the Outer System and actually provide order across Sol.

"Of course, part of the reason we don't do it is that the Outer System would fight us," Michaels admitted. "So would the Jovians, if we handled it badly. It wouldn't be a police campaign. It would be a fucking war."

That...understated things, Brad suspected. If it was done carefully, with appropriate respect for local authorities like the First Oberon Council of Speakers, it could easily birth a new golden age for humanity.

Even *he* didn't think the Commonwealth could do it that way. It would be war. The Mercenary Guild would split down the middle, with half of the companies taking contracts from whatever entity organized the rebellion and half fighting for the Commonwealth.

It was a nightmare scenario.

"That's…why there's no will," Michaels noted. "I understand that now. I didn't two years ago. I was Martian-born, Martian-bred. My Fleet service had been almost entirely inside Mars's orbit; all I saw was the news.

"And then the cuts came, and the offer of voluntary retirement with partial pension." He shrugged. "There were a lot of recruiters around at the time. The Mercenary Guild and the Jovian governors understood the assets available…and what they were losing in the strength of the Fleet.

"I don't think anyone would have flagged the Independence Militia recruiters as anything different, but it was all cloak-and-dagger even then," Michaels admitted. "It was supposed to be a privately funded counter-piracy force in the Outer System, but the recruiters hinted at a different purpose. If you pushed hard enough—I didn't, but others did—it was strongly implied they were building a revolutionary fleet to declare independence from the Commonwealth."

He took a sip of the coffee he'd filled with alcohol.

"You signed on for a revolution?" Falcone asked, her voice disbelieving.

"No, I was one of the stupid ones," he admitted flatly. "I signed on to an anti-piracy fleet. They sold me a hard bill of goods, Agent. They needed someone with carrier experience, and Fleet wasn't downsizing the carriers or the cruisers."

"So, you trained the enemies of the Commonwealth," she said.

"Yes," he agreed. "By that point, I knew what I was doing, too," he said levelly. "But by the time I was out here aboard *Longbow*, they told me what would happen if I tried to quit. Or sell them out. Only way out of the Cadre is a body bag, Agent Falcon, and my family would be in bags too.

"They tried to keep the Independence ships' hands clean, but the officers all had to know what we were in for. Blackmail. Hostages.

Money's enough for some, and others they'd recruited as Independence turned out to be perfectly suited for the real Cadre."

Michaels finished the coffee.

"They needed real officers and real crew," he told Brad and Kate. "Drone carriers, destroyers…these aren't ships you want regular pirates manning, and they aren't ships regular pirates *can* crew. And they only have so many 'true' Cadre to go around."

"Where in Everdark are they even *getting* the ships?" Brad asked. "I know where every *Bound*-class ship went, yet I've taken down two in Cadre colors."

"The cuts help cover what they're doing," Michaels said quietly, "but they're not getting surplus ships. *Longbow* and *Trebuchet* were never Fleet carriers. The destroyer squadrons? They were never Fleet ships."

Two carriers. That was what that set of names meant. The Cadre had *two* Everdarkened carriers.

Well, one now, Brad realized with a cold smile.

"What were they?" he demanded.

"Clean build," Michaels told him. "I was one of the first people to ever set foot aboard this ship, Commodore. She deserved better than what the Cadre made her." He sighed. "The officers and men who became the Independence Militia deserved better, too, but enough of them have just plain given up that they're a lost cause."

"Am I understanding you correctly, Commander Michaels?" Falcone demanded, her voice very cold and very still. "Are you saying that one of Fleet's suppliers is knowingly building warships for the Cadre?"

"I imagine a lot of it's covered by orders from the Independence Militia, and I bet at least some of it looks like legitimate Fleet construction orders…but the guys at the corporate head offices have got to know," he confirmed. "Two carriers that I know of. Twenty-three destroyers. Forty corvettes.

"That's the Independence Militia's strength. Some of those ships are truly Cadre. The rest…" He sighed. "We're Cadre too; we're just not fanatics. I don't even know what those fuckers have to be fanatics *about*."

"That's treason. That's…worse than treason," Falcone said.

"Which yard?" Brad asked.

"I don't know," the Cadre officer replied. "What do I know? I know that they had enough damned cutouts that they've used the same delivery location every time. I took delivery of *Trebuchet* for the Cadre —we always covered the swap-over with a carrier or *Lioness*."

"You can tell us where?" Brad demanded.

"I can tell you where," he confirmed. "I can tell you *when*—there's another delivery coming up, and from the rumors I've heard, we're expecting another carrier.

"And if you'll trust me, I can give you a face and a voice they know. I've made the pickups before. The Cadre may know I'm dead or turned…but there's too many cutouts in place for the yard folks to know that."

CHAPTER TWENTY-EIGHT

Whatever her actual provenance and intended crews, *Longbow* had been built to a Commonwealth Fleet template. The *Spearthrower*-class carriers had been designed as task group flagships, so they had some of the best virtual conferencing gear Brad had ever seen.

It put the extraordinarily expensive suite he'd installed in *Oath of Vengeance* to shame, but it let him pull all of his senior officers into a conference as they considered their next move.

"I need full status reports, people," he told them. "We have a unique opportunity laid before us, but if trying to take advantage of it is suicide, we'll hand it over to Fleet."

None of his officers looked happy at that idea. Brad hadn't hired anyone who didn't want to stick it to the Cadre.

Jason Finley shook his head. Brad's old tactical officer looked exhausted but determined.

"We've patched up everything on *Heart* that can be patched," he said firmly. "We ran out of replacement reactive armor strips, but we've got at least a basic layer over the entire ship. Couple of weak spots, but I do generally try *not* to get hit."

"Can we reallocate spares from the other ships or *Longbow*?" Brad asked. He was pretty sure he knew the answer, but he figured he'd ask.

"Cross-compatibility from the larger ships' armor is…mixed at best," Michelle told him. "If we went through everyone's stockpiles, we could probably find some pieces small enough to fit, but that could tie up our engineering department for days—and we've *always* got better things for the engineers to do."

"We're fine," Finley added. "A little thin in places, but like I said: our first defense is not getting hit. It's usually easier."

The two corvettes that had survived to engage Brad's people had been nasty pieces of work with big engines and heavy torpedo armaments. They'd lasted a lot longer against two destroyers and two corvettes than he'd expected, and hammered his ships hard before Michaels's betrayal had taken them out.

"*Alan-a-dale* is in about the same state as *Heart*," Jace Olhouser noted. "We're down a torpedo tube—there's no way we're getting the starboard tube put back together outside a shipyard—but our armor is in better shape than *Heart*."

Brad nodded and glanced at his wife and Captain Andre. "Our destroyers?"

"*Bound by Law* never even entered their range," Andre told him. "In hindsight, we should have moved in closer before the penny dropped, and we might have kept the corvettes from getting hammered."

"Probably not," Michelle replied. "They ignored *Oath*, and we were dumping torpedoes and slugs into them right alongside the corvettes. Whoever was in command saw our weak spot and went for it, hard."

"Not hard enough, thankfully," Brad said. "From what Michaels said—and the radiation in the debris agrees with him—the bastards had nukes. I guess he figured the drones were going to make up the difference."

"If they hadn't turned on him, they would have," Michelle said grimly. "When are you coming back aboard, Brad? I'm not entirely comfortable having our CO—or my *husband*—on a Cadre ship we're not entirely sure is trap-free."

"Soon," he promised. "But it all depends on what we decide to do, people. Kate? Brief 'em."

The Commonwealth Agent nodded and stepped up to take over

control of the briefing console. A map of the Solar System came up with a green icon flashing on it.

"Okay everyone. We're here. The way back end of the Everdark and beyond. Turns out that part of why *Longbow* was here to refuel, specifically, is that the next place they were going was here."

A red icon flashed up on the screen, even more in the back end of nowhere. If there was anything at the set of coordinates Michaels and *Longbow*'s computers had given them, it wasn't in the Commonwealth databases.

"We're just under three days from there. The nearest Fleet concentrations I know of are a minimum of four days away—and that would be them blasting through the area without slowing down. Great for scouting and okay for blowing things up, not so great if we want to capture ships."

She smiled grimly.

"And believe me, we want to capture ships. In just over two and a half days, a convoy will reach that spot with the plan of rendezvousing with *Longbow* and her escorts. That convoy is from the Cadre's supplier and will contain an unknown number of warships, but Michaels believes it will include a new heavy unit, almost certainly a carrier."

Which was terrifying. The fact that the Cadre had one carrier had been a shock to Brad and everyone else. Two was a nightmare. Three… Brad didn't have words for what the Cadre's ability to acquire three carriers was.

At least he'd taken one away.

"While the Cadre knows that *Longbow*'s task group has been destroyed, we don't know how close their nearest forces are. We, however, are in position to arrive, with the ship the convoy is expecting, less than twelve hours late."

"You want us to fake being a Cadre pickup group?" Michelle asked. "That seems…doable. *Oath* might give the game away, though. She's unique and the Cadre knows her."

"The good news is that it doesn't sound like the people dropping the ships off are Cadre," Brad pointed out. "They work for the yards. We don't know which yards, but capturing those ships should answer that question.

"According to Michaels, the suppliers bring three ships of their own: two escorts and a passenger liner to carry their transit crews. Usually, the Cadre pickup team will tow the ships to a second location the suppliers don't know about, where they will meet Cadre crews."

He shook his head.

"Most of those crews are 'Independence Militia' with Cadre commanders," he told his people. "They got themselves a shit deal, but there's nothing we can do for them. Everlit, the information security these guys are running is hard enough that Michaels was the *third officer* on this carrier and can't give us the coordinates of a 'Militia' base."

"Because that shouldn't be a huge warning sign for the idiots who signed on," Olhouser grumped.

"Make no mistake," Brad warned Olhouser, "I've got some sympathy for how deep the bastards have dug themselves, but I doubt there's an 'Independence Militia' ship out there without innocent blood on their hands. The Cadre will have made *damn* sure of that."

"Their existence means we're prepared to consider surrenders and the Agency may cut deals with them," Falcone told the mercenaries, "but they are at *best* enemy combatants. Clear?"

"Clear," *Alan-a-dale*'s commander said with a pleased expression.

"I think *Oath* will be less of a problem than we think," Brad continued. "Or, at least, no more of a problem than having one more destroyer than *Longbow*'s original group causes, anyway. We'll follow along behind everyone else stealthily while *Longbow* and the rest of our ships close.

"While there are only passage crews aboard the ships, we're almost certainly outmassed and outgunned by the convoy. We want them to hand the ships over and get back onto their transport home.

"Then you punch out the escorts and *Oath* makes an assault approach on the transport, getting close enough to guarantee clean landings for Saburo's people."

"What about my teams?" Doary asked.

"I need you to stay on *Longbow*," Brad admitted. "Crewing her is going to be the biggest problem out of this."

"Not really," Falcone noted. "If the Militia crew want amnesty?

They can bloody well earn it by flying the ship into battle for us—with Major Doary's troopers holding guns to their backs, just in case."

———

The surviving crew from *Longbow* had been locked into their own quarters after Brad's people had swept them for surprises and over-ridden the locking mechanisms. The codes might not be the same ones Fleet used, but the mechanisms were the same—and Fleet allowed for the possibility of house arrest for *anyone*, apparently.

Brad did the Cadre officer the courtesy of knocking before he and Falcone entered, though they didn't wait for a response.

Michaels was sitting in a chair, reading an old-style paperback with several exploding spaceships on the cover. He laid the book aside as they came in and looked at them levelly.

"I'd say *mi casa es su casa*, Commodore, but Everdark…what *was* my ship is now your salvage. How can I help you?"

"I'm just here to pitch the plan," Brad told him with a chuckle, gesturing toward Falcone. "Agent Falcone is the one who can help *you*."

The third officer's quarters on a Fleet capital ship were quite luxurious to Brad's merchant-raised and mercenary-trained mind. There was a lounge area with a couch and several chairs, one of which Falcone took over as she sat down and studied Michaels in silence.

"Agent, Commodore…" Michaels held up his hands, palms up. "I'll argue for my people and I'll argue for my family, but I know damn well what I walked into and I know damn well what I've done.

"My reasons seemed good enough at the time, but I'm at best a privateer and a traitor—and at worst, a pirate, a murderer, and arguably a spy in time of war." He grimaced. "Do I just about summarize the charges, Agent Falcone?"

The spy chuckled. There wasn't much humor in the sound.

"Honestly, I think you might be overselling it," she noted. "Both *spy* and *time of war* would be hard to convince a judge to buy into. I probably wouldn't even try for *murderer*. *Pirate* and *traitor* is enough to shoot you, and I promised I wouldn't do that."

"A mercy I seem to recall promising to earn," he replied. "You have full access to this ship. If you have questions about the Cadre, I'll answer as best as I can. I warn you, though, even the 'trusted' Independence officers were…second-class so far as the Cadre was concerned."

"Oh, you and I are going to be having some long, *long* conversations over the next couple of days," Falcone promised. "For now, though, Commodore Madrid has a plan. One for which he could use more hands on deck."

"Hands, I would guess, familiar with *Longbow*?" Michaels guessed.

"You may be too smart for your own good," the spy told him.

The redheaded man sighed.

"You were kind enough to give me a list of the survivors," he reminded them. "Fifty-one people other than me. There are four I suggested, strongly, that Colonel Saburo keep under very close watch. All four were under sedation at the time, so I imagine that wasn't difficult."

"And the rest?" Falcone asked carefully.

"Are all various degrees of fucked," Michaels confirmed. "I won't plead innocence on any of their parts now, but we got suckered into this and trapped. We just didn't see a way out, either."

"I do," she told him. "Is forty-eight people enough to fly this ship, Commander?"

He waved a hand in the air.

"We could fly her with that. Probably even deploy the drones. That's it. We'd need more to man the weapons or even run half-assed damage control."

"But you could fly this ship up to your rendezvous with the incoming ship convoy and make them think you're aboveboard?" Falcone asked.

"Figured that was what you wanted," he agreed, and sighed. "Yeah, probably. You'd have to trust me with the coms and I'm guessing you'd have an entire damn platoon of guns watching us like hawks, but we could make it happen."

"If it goes wrong, you just said you can't run the ship's defenses," Brad said quietly. "You'd be sitting ducks."

Michaels shrugged.

"That's the game, Commodore. You put the right prize on the table and let me talk to them, and I think I can get you a skeleton crew for this ship."

"The prize is amnesty, Commander," Falcone said calmly. "If you fight for the Commonwealth, I'll take you at your word that you got trapped in this, and you all get sent home with your records expunged. Play nice, and we'll swing the whole lot of you into witness protection, with your families."

The Cadre officer studied his hands for a long time in silence.

"Yeah, okay," he said quietly. "Let me talk to my people? I'm in, to the end of the damn line, whatever it takes. But I can't speak for them."

"Are you prepared to give Commodore Madrid your parole?" Falcone asked.

He snorted.

"My parole? Everdarkened void, for a chance to get out of this room, save my people, and stick a knife in the Cadre's eye? I'd swear my undying allegiance."

CHAPTER TWENTY-NINE

BRAD GATHERED WITH DOARY, Saburo, and Falcone at the airlock. The shuttles were waiting to take most of his people back to their ships, along with their wounded and the half-dozen prisoners from *Longbow* who either Michaels didn't trust or had refused the offer.

"Do you trust Michaels?" Brad asked Falcone.

"Enough that I'm staying on this ship with him and, oh, thirty men and women with guns," the spy replied. "I'm a big girl, Brad; I can handle knives in the dark better than you can."

Saburo coughed.

"You have *seen* the boss fight, right?" the Colonel asked.

"He's a brilliant swordsman, but he's not a back-alley knife fighter," Falcone told him. "That's my field, and if Michaels tries to turn on us, he'll regret it."

"I don't see it," Brad admitted. "If there was a chance he could run and get away, sure, but we're in the middle of nowhere, heading for a convoy that no one is supposed to know exists. It's easy to give a man rope when you can see everywhere he can run with it."

"Exactly," Falcone agreed. "That's a man who *wants* to believe he has honor left but knows exactly what he became. But give him nowhere to run and the ability to screw over the people who screwed him, and he'll make them bleed."

"Speaking as the woman charged with making sure he doesn't knife us in the back, I like that idea," Doary noted. "I'd like to see my fiancée again when this is over!"

"That's the plan for everyone," Brad agreed. "Forty-eight hours, people. That's all. Stick that out and we can cut off the Cadre's supply line."

"Everlit, I don't care if they manage to get every damn ship in this convoy somehow," Falcone noted. "If we can pin the ships to somebody, I'm going to nail them to a wall."

"Let's hope," Saburo said grimly. "But let's remember—these guys managed to build *carriers* without being caught. They've got allies back home. That should never have happened, no matter what bribes they were paying."

"I know," Falcone said. "And *that*, ladies and gentlemen, is the string I intend to yank and see what unravels—wherever it leads."

Somehow, Brad wasn't sure they were going to like what they found if they yanked on that string. Every time he thought he had a handle on what the Cadre was and what their objectives were, something *else* came up.

He was wrestling a snake in the dark, and he was starting to be grimly certain the snake was actually an elephant's trunk.

———

Michelle was waiting for Brad and Saburo as soon as they stepped off the shuttle. She somewhat pointedly saluted them both first before wrapping Brad into a tight embrace and looking over his shoulder at the ground force commander.

"Someday, Colonel, you and I need to convince this man that the Commodore's place is not in the front lines of the boarding action," she told him.

Brad couldn't see his other subordinate, but he could imagine the shrug Saburo was giving her. He'd seen it before.

"You married him, ma'am," Saburo pointed out. "You've got the levers. I just work for the man."

Brad chuckled and shook his head as he and Michelle separated.

"I *do* try," he said plaintively. "But my job is to be at the turning point, wherever that is."

If the turning point was the command deck of *Oath of Vengeance*, that was where he belonged. If the turning point was a desperate boarding action across the decks of a carrier that shouldn't exist, well, that was where he belonged.

"We brought enough bodies home this time to make me worry," Michelle said quietly. "I know it's the job, but…"

"But it hurts, every time," Brad agreed. "Any updates on *Oath*?"

"She's fine," his wife told him. "We didn't even take a scratch. We can go over details in your office."

Saburo stepped around Brad and threw the Commodore a salute.

"I need to debrief my team leads," the Colonel noted. "The op went about as smoothly as we could hope after the landing went sideways, but there's always lessons to learn and things to do better next time."

"I would *love* to promise you that we will never attempt to board a Cadre carrier by crossing the refueling lines from a captured tanker again," Brad told him. "Sadly, I can't guarantee anything."

"Life would be *boring* if you could," Saburo replied. "And I'd hate for my troops to get bored. I'll fill you in on what we come up with. After you 'go over details in your office' with the XO, of course."

The wink he accompanied the last sentence with set both Brad and Michelle to blushing furiously. Brad was a mercenary flotilla comman-der, a reserve Fleet officer, a millionaire, and all that…but he was also under no illusions that the "briefing" with Michelle was probably going to end up exactly where Saburo was suggesting, either.

Rank hath its privileges, after all, and his office had a quite comfort-able couch that Michelle had already insisted on "testing" a few times.

––––––––

"All right, everyone," Brad told his people the next morning. "We are offi-cially committed to intercepting this convoy, so I hope everyone knows where to find their can of whoop-ass." He grinned. "Because unless I'm misreading Agent Falcone's face over there, we're going to need them."

"Ha. Ha," the spy replied from the screen linked to *Longbow*. "I've spent most of the time since you returned talking to Commander Michaels, and I am not liking anything I'm hearing. Most of that's general, though, not with regards to the convoy."

She shook her head.

"Michaels has a pretty solid idea of the strength of this so-called Independence Militia the Cadre are using for heavy muscle, and it isn't pretty. Sixty-five warships, people. Even with what they lost when we took *Longbow*, the Independence Militia has a *third of the strength of the Commonwealth Fleet.*"

Everyone on the video conference stopped. They hadn't run the numbers like that. Fleet was down to about a hundred and eighty hulls after the cutbacks, so…yeah. She was right, Brad realized.

The Cadre was unquestionably the second most powerful military force in the star system.

"Hulls don't tell you everything, though," Andre objected. *Law*'s Captain looked shaky. "Fleet has cruisers, lots of 'em. They've been downsizing the destroyer and corvette strength, but all thirty cruisers are still in commission."

Which was something the Cadre could never match. The Commonwealth had three battleships, eight carriers, and thirty cruisers as the core of that hundred and eighty ships. Brad exhaled a sigh of relief. Andre was right.

"Plus, if it came to a straight-up fight, the Guild and the Jovian flotillas would line up with Fleet," he pointed out. "None of the Guild companies have a lot of ships, but between us and the various authorized security squadrons, we match this Independence Militia's strength."

"And how many other ships does the Cadre have?" Falcone asked softly. "We know about *Lioness*. We're *pretty* sure that the Cadre doesn't have any other cruisers, but Michaels has no idea what operates under direct Cadre command. Add in the pirates and assume that they can bring in the Outer System ships?"

She shook her head.

"Fleet can beat them, yes. But nothing else can. They've been quiet for eighteen months, and then suddenly they have an Everdarkened *navy*."

"Where in Everdark did they come from?" Olhouser asked. "I guess…we know a chunk of that, between the Fleet drawdown and whatever yard is selling them ships—but where is the money coming from?"

"I don't know," Falcone replied. "Neither does Michaels. His salary cleared and no one blinked at any expense the ship needed, but the money flowed through the captain and XO, who were true-blood Cadre.

"So did a *lot* of navigation data," she continued. "And it was being wiped from the ship's computers on a regular basis. Unless we luck out and find someone's pilot data pad like we did on *Heart* way back… we have no idea where their bases are."

Brad snorted. That had been a fluke, and one that the Cadre associates they'd been dealing had moved Light and Dark to try and prevent. Of course, doing so had only drawn the Agency's attention to his ship.

"So, this convoy is our best shot at tracking down anything," he concluded aloud. "What do we know about it?"

"Quite a bit, thankfully," Falcone replied. "Michaels has been on hand for four of these pickups. He knows the procedures, and while he doesn't know most of the *names*, he's spoken with several of the recurring players."

A new screen lit up for the conference, showing a tactical plot with multiple icons.

"Generally, the Cadre or Independence Militia has arrived with four ships, one of them a carrier, to pick up eight ships," she noted. "Upon arrival, the supplier transfers all of their personnel to a liner, kept well inside the cordon of both escorts and convoy until the very end."

An icon on the screen flashed red.

"That transport is our primary target. We need it intact and we need prisoners. Secondary targets are these."

Two icons, flanking the entire convoy, flashed a darker shade of red.

"Escorts. Every time *Longbow* has had this duty, they've been the same ships. Michaels figures the transport is the same ship too, but they've kept it well away from the Cadre ships."

"If they're the same ships, do we have specs on them?" Brad asked.

"*Lancer*-class destroyers," she said. "It's not a type I'm familiar with, to be honest."

Brad leaned back in his chair, sharing a smile with his wife as everyone looked to him to see what he knew. His childhood obsession had become an extraordinarily useful adult skill that he kept up as best as he could.

"You wouldn't be," he noted. "Fleet never picked up the design. Like the *Bound* class"—he nodded to Andre—"they're specialized ships. In this case, escort destroyers. They have no torpedo launchers at all. No heavy guns, either. Just a *lot* of gatling drivers.

"Getting torpedoes through their guns to hit their charges or them is pretty damn hard. Fortunately, we have *Bound by Law*, so we don't need to get torps through their screen."

He shook his head.

"They're not common, but there's enough of them out there that no one is going to blink at them, either," he concluded. "Lots of corps have them for convoy security, and there's at least a dozen flying Guild company colors. They're about as common as any design Fleet never bought into."

"Makes sense, all told. They don't want to attract attention to this convoy—and it's pretty attention-grabbing as it is," Falcone told them. "Generally between six and eight warships each time. The supplier drops them off and the Cadre tows them to a second rendezvous point that *does* change each time, where another transport is waiting with crew.

"Michaels doesn't know where that rendezvous is this time, sadly. The Cadre is going to send *someone* to complete the handover ASAP, which means our time is limited."

"We come in fat, dumb, and happy," Brad told everyone. "*Oath* will be under stealth, sweeping in behind to make sure the transport doesn't get away. The rest of you will play *Longbow*'s escorts and try to get in as close as you can.

"We want them *off* those ships and onto the transport," he concluded. "If we can get them to complete the handover without blinking, that's our best-case scenario.

"Worst case, *Bound by Law* should be able to open the dance with the destroyers and either destroy them or take out enough of their guns to allow torpedo strikes from the corvettes. The convoy ships will only have passage crews, so they won't have the hands to fight.

"If we take out the escorts and capture the transport, the rest of them should fall into line under our guns—and then we can hand the damn *ships* over to the Commonwealth as proof of what's going on."

Saburo snorted.

"Can we keep some if we get that far?" he asked. "I mean, no one expects to get to keep the carrier, but hey! Free warships!"

"We'll talk to Fleet when the time comes," Brad hedged. He'd *love* to double his company's hulls at the Cadre's expense, but he wasn't going to assume the Commonwealth would let him keep what he "reclaimed" from the Cadre, either.

"Any questions, people?" he asked.

CHAPTER THIRTY

THE CLOCK CONTINUED to tick toward their rendezvous with the Cadre convoy. Part of Brad felt there should be something more dramatic than a simple timer, given just how important the operation could end up being.

But all they had was the timer showing they were sixteen hours away. According to their intelligence, the convoy should be arriving at the rendezvous point in the next eight hours, and Brad had made sure all of his people were going to get at least eight hours of rest before the penny dropped.

Oath was already vectoring away from the rest of the Vikings, the big destroyer's heat sinks online and radar baffling extended. They were venting her heat away from the convoy, into hopefully empty space. Combined with the heat sinks themselves, that should give them at least forty-eight hours of near-invisibility from their target.

"Still no sign of the convoy," he noted aloud. He was alone on *Oath*'s bridge, but he had a laser link to *Longbow*, where Falcone had taken over the captain's office. "Think Michaels is pulling a fast one?"

"Part of me is inclined to think so," the spy admitted. "He *is* a Cadre officer, after all, whatever his reasons or cause. But...no. I don't think so. I'm guessing we're looking at another of those damn heat umbrellas."

"Where did those even *come* from?" Brad asked. "I've never heard of anything like them."

"Take a guess," Falcone said with a sigh.

"Fleet R&D project killed just after prototyping?" he asked. That was where several pieces of illicit gear he'd acquired schematics for had come from, after all.

"Bingo. I'm starting to question if any of our R&D is actually for Fleet, or if it's all being done for the Everdarkened Cadre."

The mercenary winced.

"It can't be that bad, can it?" he asked.

"No, it's not," she conceded with a sigh. "*Invictuses* like the corvettes we keep running into are a Fleet design, with the latest and greatest in tech and gear. The fact that the Cadre seems to have as many of them as Fleet does, though…"

"You sound like that's taking you unpleasant places," Brad noted.

"I've pretty much drained Michaels's brain dry," Falcone said. "The Cadre has done a good job of keeping this Independence Militia of theirs in the dark and fed shit, but there's a limit to how much you can hide from the third officer of one of your major ships.

"Plus, well, they figured they had him pretty well trapped. His family under their thumb and they'd dragged him into enough crimes to guarantee his execution if captured? They trusted him as much as they trusted anyone who wasn't fully inside."

"I'm guessing we've got the answers to some of our age-old questions? Like where the hell does a pirate organization get dozens of ships and entire brigades of disposable shock troops?" Brad asked.

The attack on Blackhawk Station that had ended several of his officers' corporate careers, killed his old XO, and cost him his original arm had involved over ten thousand ground troops. Most of them hadn't made it aboard the station, but there'd been a lot of questions over where they had come from.

"None of those answers are pretty, Brad," she admitted. "The Cadre is recruiting from the Fleet and Marines as we draw down. They're buying ships from Fleet's own suppliers, and no one is even blinking.

"And, from some of Michaels's reading between the lines, they basically *own* a good chunk of the Outer System and are basically just conscripting ground troops as needed."

Brad winced.

"That doesn't *work* for modern troops," he noted.

"It doesn't work for commandos or ship crew," Falcone replied. "If all you need is warm bodies to fling at the defenses, like what they were bringing to Blackhawk?" She shook her head. "There's thousands of years of history of how to turn conscripts into mostly obedient killing machines. I imagine the Phoenix has access to all of it."

"I *really* hope I get to introduce him to the same fate as the Terror," Brad said grimly. One of the unpleasant discoveries of their last big victory over the Cadre had struck close enough to home that he hadn't even told Falcone. The Terror had been related to him. The man who'd killed the uncle who'd adopted him had, apparently, *also* been an uncle.

"You've more reason than you think," the spy said. Her face slid to one side of the monitor and a picture appeared on the other half. "Turns out the Phoenix has been aboard *Longbow* a few times. They did a good job of purging the visuals of him, but not a good-enough job.

"Michaels wouldn't have had a clue who he was, but *I* recognized him instantly."

Brad hissed as he recognized the Phoenix as well. The hair was shorter, more professional and in a military style now, and he wore an armored vac-suit with a gold-and-red phoenix blazon instead of the business suits he'd encountered the man in before, but it was unquestionably Jack Mader.

The man had once been an assistant to the Governor of Io. He'd also been a key component in the slaver organization Brad had ripped apart, and a major player in the Cadre's operations already.

Apparently, the Terror's death had earned him a promotion.

"Fuck," Brad finally said. "Mader."

"Yeah. He's a damned bad penny, keeps showing up. I'm glad I stopped at this picture to study it longer, though," Falcone told him.

"Why?"

The figure to Mader's right was suddenly surrounded in a golden aura that allowed Brad to make out the woman's face.

"Because while you and I know Mader, *I* know this woman," Falcone said quietly. "And she shouldn't be aboard a Cadre warship—not least because she's *dead*."

"And who is she?" Brad asked as he studied the stranger's face. She was an older woman, with sharp features but seemingly warm blue eyes.

"Ten years ago, before she died in a shuttle accident, *that* was Senator Jessica Andrews of Australia," the spy told him. "She was a senior member of the main opposition party of the Commonwealth Senate at the time and a key player in a number of committees on Fleet and the Agency.

"If she's alive and she's with the Cadre, then my biggest question is starting to look very, very terrifying."

"Which one's that?" the mercenary asked as he studied the supposedly dead woman.

"Where the money that funds the Cadre is coming from," Falcone told him. "And the answer is starting to look like it's coming from the Commonwealth itself...and I do *not* understand why."

Kate Falcone's words were still echoing in Brad's head when he returned to his and Michelle's quarters to get his own eight hours of sleep before everything. His wife was getting ready to head out herself, but something in his movements made her stop and study him.

"All right, love," she said briskly after a moment. "You look like you just found out your dog died, and we don't even *have* a dog."

Dogs were a bad idea on ships. They'd talked about a cat. Brad wasn't sure of the point of a pet—and wasn't entirely comfortable risking a helpless small animal aboard a warship, in any case—but he also knew he wasn't going to win the argument in the long run. He wasn't even fighting a particularly valiant rear-guard action anymore.

"Kate has been questioning Michaels since we left," he told her.

"And going through *Longbow*'s files. We now know who the Phoenix is."

"That's…good, right?" Michelle asked.

"It's Mader," he said flatly. "That son of the Everdark keeps turning up—and this time, he turned up with a supposedly dead Commonwealth ex-Senator in tow. I don't know what Kate thinks is going on, but I'm starting to think the Cadre aren't pirates."

"That makes no sense," she pointed out. "Just what *are* they, then?"

"I don't know," he admitted. "But I think that we're sending Kate back to Earth when this is over to dig it all up. Thankfully, that's outside our purview." He snorted. "Hell, that's even outside *my* Agency portfolio."

"Your 'Agency portfolio' is 'deniable combat asset,' love," his wife pointed out. "I don't think they need you on Earth, where they have access to national armies and the police."

"I bloody well hope not," he agreed. "That lines up too neatly, though. The whole thing is a mess."

"And what, exactly, do you think you can do about it?" Michelle asked.

Brad laughed.

"Fair," he conceded. "Capture this convoy and find the evidence so Kate can prove someone is providing the Cadre warships—that's what I can do."

"And we have a plan. So, go sleep, love," Michelle told him with a kiss. "Everything will go to hell in about twelve hours. We need you at your best and your sneakiest."

He laughed again.

"Sneaky, my dear, is what I hired you lot for," he told her. "My sneakiest is trying to get them to look at my right hand while I draw a gun with my left."

"That is, basically, our plan," she pointed out. "So, I guess it's got to be yours, huh?"

He threw a cushion at her.

CHAPTER THIRTY-ONE

"Are we seeing anything at the target waypoint?" Brad asked Bogdanov as *Oath of Vengeance* continued her stealthy approach, growing farther and farther away from her compatriots.

The rest of the Vikings were locked in a tight formation around *Longbow*, both fulfilling the plan of pretending to be the carrier's escorts and provided a pointed reminder to the carrier's current "captain" of the reasons to behave.

"Negative," *Oath*'s tactical officer replied. "I mean, I'm seeing a few hazy blots that might be something, but I'm looking for them. These aren't even sensor ghosts, Commodore. They could easily be in my head."

Brad tapped a command and opened up a laser link to *Longbow*. They were far enough away from the drone carrier for the time delay to be noticeable, though not far enough for it be a problem.

"Michaels, Falcone," he greeted the ex-Cadre officer and his current watchdog. "Are we sure they'll be there? So far as the Cadre knows, we wiped out *Longbow*'s group."

"You overestimate how much communication there is with the supplier at this point," Michaels told him. "There's an abort signal, and that's *it*. In the absence of that signal, they'll hold at the waypoint for seventy-two hours. I assume the Cadre has a secondary team heading in for the pickup, since the abort signal hasn't been sent."

"You can tell?" Brad demanded.

"This close to the rendezvous point? Yes," the redheaded officer replied. "If they'd sent it, it would be pulsing through this area every fifteen minutes for at least the next six hours. In the absence of the abort, the convoy probably reached the waypoint an hour ago."

"And unless they've grown less competent in the last two months, they're watching *Longbow* approach, behind one of the big heat shields."

"Any idea how to tell if one of those is there?" Brad asked.

"At this distance, the best we'd pick up would be a faint haze of heat too low for the sensors to even register as a ghost." Michaels shrugged. "I *think* they're there, but they won't fold up the heat shield until we're a lot closer."

"So, we still have no idea what heavy warship they're delivering, huh?"

"No," Michaels admitted. "Captain Vong might have known, but he hadn't briefed me."

The degree of information control the Cadre exerted boggled Brad's mind. It made sense—clearly, Michaels hadn't been fully trusted—yet they'd still kept the man as third officer on a carrier while keeping him in the dark on almost everything.

"What's our ETA?" Brad asked Michelle.

"*Longbow* and escorts will reach a zero-vee rendezvous in four hours, twenty-six minutes," she told him. "*Oath* will pass by ten thousand kilometers in-system of the waypoint eleven minutes after that at a relative velocity of about fifteen kilometers a second."

"We couldn't avoid the rendezvous waypoint if we wanted to now," Michaels pointed out. "We're all committed, Commodore. Let's hope your plan works."

"Any second thoughts, Commander?" Brad asked.

"None," Michaels said firmly. "These bastards owe me my honor and my soul, and I intend to take payment in full."

"That's the spirit," Brad said. "Let's go steal ourselves a convoy."

———

Minutes ticked away into hours as the flotilla approached their target, and the faint haze on their scanners slowly resolved into a wide splotch of slightly-warmer-than-background space several kilometers across.

Optical scanners confirmed what the thermals suggested: there was another of the strange heat-shield stealth umbrellas guarding their target from detection. As they drew closer, the umbrella began to move, the convoy adjusting their invisibility cloak to hide them from the rest of the system and no longer worrying as much about *Longbow*'s approach.

As it shifted, Brad and his people got their first good look at their prey. It was a slow process. They were still over two hours away from rendezvous and they could take their time.

"All right, there's escort number one," Bogdanov noted. "Exactly as Michaels said. Looks like one *Lancer*-class destroyer. Couple of shadows look like the escortees, destroyers running cold."

"Any idea what we're looking at?" Michelle asked.

"Hard to say with a hundred percent certainty," the tactical officer replied. "Looks like a *Bound* and a couple of *Warriors*."

"Because of *course* they've got *Warriors*," Brad said with a sigh. The *Warrior*-class destroyer was the big brother to the *Invictus*-class corvette, Fleet's newest and shiniest toy. The drawdown meant Fleet had only half a dozen *Warriors* in commission.

If even two of the ships out there were *Warriors*, the Cadre probably had as many of them as Fleet did. Something was bloody *wrong* with Fleet's procurement system.

"All right…I'm making another *Warrior*," Bogdanov noted as the shield continued to rotate away from them. "That makes four destroyers, one *Bound*, and three *Warriors*. Second *Lancer* just came into view, too. Nice and warm, all systems online, unlike the escortees."

"Where's the heavy?" Brad asked. "Michaels said six ships, one a heavy. Four destroyers is an ugly addition to the Cadre, but it's not…"

The shield turned further and a chunk of the fifth ship in the convoy became visible. The lines were similar to the *Warriors*…except they were drawn on nearly three times the scale. A *Warrior* was a big, heavy destroyer, clocking in at just over twenty thousand tons unfueled and just over a hundred and fifty meters long.

He could already see a hundred meters of the new ship and he wasn't seeing even half. Brad couldn't help holding his breath as the shield rotated to reveal his worst nightmare.

At eighty-two thousand tons unfueled and three hundred and fifteen meters from prow to stern, Fleet's *Tremendous*-class cruisers were the final word in modern warships. There was no way the Cadre's suppliers could have acquired a cruiser. It wasn't *possible*.

And then the shield fully rotated away from them and Brad realized his worst nightmares hadn't been imaginative enough—as a *second Tremendous*-class cruiser swam into view, the personnel transport for the passage crews drifting innocently between the two immense warships.

"Breathe, people," Brad snapped, once he'd swallowed hard in shock himself and forced himself to inhale. Directed laser-coms still linked him to his ships, though even the fraction of a second of time delay was enough that he could only see and hear the consternation on his own bridge so far.

"We knew there was a heavy unit and there was no way we were going to be able to fight even a fully crewed and operational drone carrier," he reminded them. "There's no real difference between our ability to fight a carrier and our ability to fight two cruisers. We proceed with the plan—which isn't to fight the 'cargo' ships at all!"

If everything went right, the two cruisers would provide unquestionable proof of both the yard's treason and the Cadre's resources. The data they already had was probably enough—but no one could argue with the ships themselves.

The acquisition of two cruisers by the Cadre when Brad was a child had changed the balance of power in the Solar System. The Mercenary Guild had wrecked one of the ships, and the Cadre had proceeded to be *very* careful with *Lioness* after that. The addition of two brand-new cruisers…

Brad couldn't let that happen. Which meant he was lying to his people. If everything went according to plan, yes, they'd take the convoy without having to fight the cruisers.

But while their odds against a fully operational carrier were crap, they could potentially win that fight. Against two cruisers? Even with just passage crews and automated systems, the two *Tremendouses* could fight off his entire fleet.

"We proceed with the plan," he repeated, meeting Michaels's gaze through the link to *Longbow*. "It's all on you, Commander Michaels."

The ex-Cadre officer smiled grimly.

"It always was, Commodore Madrid. It's time to see how those acting classes paid off."

With a shake of his head, he tossed off his grim expression and appeared to relax in the command chair of *Longbow*'s bridge.

"I'm muting all of the laser links," he announced calmly. "But we'll keep transmitting so you can keep an eye on me for the satisfaction of everyone's paranoia. Agent Falcone, I'll need you to step clear of the pickups."

Falcone did so, but her voice drifted over the audio pickups from out of view.

"Just as a *small* reminder, I set up a dead man's switch on the reactor core," she told Michaels sweetly. "If my heart stops beating, this entire ship blows up."

The redheaded Commander seemed completely unsurprised.

"If you could manage not to have a heart attack until we're close enough to ram them with the giant flying bomb, I'd appreciate it," he told her cheerfully. "Now, connecting with the convoy. Peanut gallery, fall in line, please."

———

"Convoy Mu, this is *Longbow*," Michaels said brightly. "We are inbound on your position from vector three-twenty-five by one-twenty-seven. Please identify and confirm link."

A few seconds passed and Brad had a sudden moment of panic, and then a new image appeared on his screen as *Longbow* relayed a copy of their incoming transmission.

"*Longbow*, this is *Cataphract*," an older-looking man in a plain business suit with a lapel pin of a pair of gold pips greeted Michaels. "We confirm laser link and your approach vector. Convoy is in stable orbit relative to Sol and we make one hundred seven minutes to rendezvous."

"I have the same," Michaels confirmed. "How's Victoria?"

"My executive officer says you owe her a rematch," the stranger told him. "Does your wife know about your regular 'chess matches,' Commander?"

The ex-Cadre man chuckled.

"My wife trusts me to be a big boy and keep my hands to myself, no matter how drop-dead gorgeous my chess opponent is," he told the other man. "We're running late; I don't think I'll have time to let Victoria try and even the score this time around."

"We were starting to get nervous," *Cataphract*'s commander admitted. "What happened?"

"Bunch of mercs jumped us at our refueling stop," Michaels said. "It went about as well as you'd think for them, but our corvettes got handled pretty roughly and we had to hold up for some field repairs.

"And you, Captain, should have asked us for our authentication codes since we're late," the turncoat continued. "Am I right?"

The convoy commander snorted.

"Five times we've done this dance, Michaels. Your captain hasn't bothered to be on the coms in three. I know who you are," he told the Commander. "But, if you insist, convoy authentication is *ultima ratio regum*. And yours?"

"*Deus vult*," Michaels replied. "Protocols exist for a reason, Captain. This isn't a game."

The older man sighed.

"Believe me, kid, I know," he admitted. "We'll have the destroyers and cruisers set up for your tow by the time you get here. *Protocol*," he said with a smile, "says the escorts remain with the ships until you've taken full possession."

"And protocol is reasonable in this case," Michaels agreed. "Though we'll want to make sure everything goes quickly. Captain Vong will be grouchy if we're late with *this* delivery."

"That's your problem, not mine," the corporate officer replied. "He knows better to be grouchy at me. He knows who I work for."

The whole conversation was dancing across Brad's strained nerves like a drunken elephant, but Michaels was playing things right so far.

"Oh, I know, I know," the ex-Cadre man told the corporate security officer. "We'll have our towlines ready when we arrive. If we're late, I'll just blame how much bloody extra mass we're hauling."

The other man chuckled.

"And I imagine the complaints will stop pretty quickly when they see their new 'argument,'" he told Michaels. "We'll see you at the rendezvous."

CHAPTER THIRTY-TWO

*O*ATH *OF* *V*ENGEANCE drifted through space toward her targets, and Brad watched his plan unfold like clockwork.

The convoy had accepted *Longbow*'s identity and the escorts had grown slightly but noticeably more relaxed in their station-keeping, drifting back toward the rear of the convoy and the transport belonging to their corporation.

"We're going to have to drop communications in sixty seconds, boss," Xan Wong told him as they closed. "If there's anything you have left to say to anyone, now is the time."

Brad nodded to her and looked at the pickups.

"This is it, people," he told them, meeting each of his captains' gazes levelly. He was almost starting to get used to sending Jason Finley into harm's way by now, but he trusted *Heart of Vengeance*'s captain completely.

Brenda Andre hadn't worked for him nearly as long, but *Bound by Law*'s CO had earned her place in his company long before she'd actually found herself looking for work.

He hadn't known Jace Olhouser as well, but the calmly competent man commanding *Alan-a-dale* had proven worth every penny of his salary.

They were all not merely his captains, but his friends.

Michaels, on the other hand, hadn't made that jump yet—but at some point had ended up in the "captains" category in Brad's head. Falcone was back in that pickup, and she gave Brad a serious nod.

This really was it.

"We'll see you all on the other side," he told them. "Everything's going smoothly so far, so let's watch for the wheels to come off."

"They always do, boss," Finley replied. "We've got *Longbow*'s back. We'll bring everyone home."

Brad threw them all a salute…and then the channels died, *Oath* now at an angle where even laser coms to the rest of the flotilla would put the whole operation at risk.

"We are on course and vector," Michelle reported instantly, her calm tones soothing his immediate nerves. His wife knew him *very* well.

"Based off their current position change, even if they don't break from the convoy before we arrive, we'll have a clean shot at the escorts and a straight path for Saburo's assault shuttles," Bogdanov reported. "Those *Lancers* are good ships, but between surprise and the dazzler torpedoes, we'll punch them out in one pass."

"Any chance of taking one of them intact-ish?" Brad asked. "I'd love to have a conversation with this Captain about who he works for."

The tactical officer shrugged.

"If they're lucky," he told the Commodore. "But the odds aren't good. We need to hammer them hard if we want them out of the fight."

"Miracles would be nice, but I'll take *mission accomplished*," Brad replied. "Don't risk us to save them."

Bogdanov didn't *quite* visibly sigh in relief. But he was clearly glad Brad wasn't going to ask for those miracles.

"I can answer at least one of those questions, boss," Xan Wong told him softly, and he glanced over at his communications officer.

"Xan?"

"Who they work for," she said. "Their IFF beacons are disabled to cover their tracks, but…well, there's only so many *Lancer*-class destroyers in the corporate security forces, and they have to register their ships and COs with the Commonwealth Fleet if they're going within a billion kilometers of Earth."

"And?" Brad asked.

"And I just found him in the database Fleet gave us. Captain Jordan Noah," Xan replied softly, flipping a file picture of a man that was definitely the Captain they'd seen on the link from *Longbow*. "He's bullshitting on the name; his ship is *Belisarius* and her cohort is *Galahad*. They're the only two *Lancers* registered to Transplanetary Macro Fabrication."

She brought up a second image of Noah from his brief conversation with Michaels.

"They did a good job of hiding identifiable characteristics on the bridge, but someone's coffee cup was turned the wrong way," she noted, zooming in on the offending container. It had a stylized dragon holding a hammer above the letters TMF.

"Record *all* of that and pulse it to home base with the scan data," Brad ordered. "No matter what happens, I want someone to know that TMF is dirty."

He shivered.

"They're, what, the second-largest spaceship manufacturer inside the Belt?" he asked.

"One of only three in the star system with the yards to build cruisers," Michelle confirmed. "Hell, TMF basically mass-produces the gas divers for Saturn and Jupiter. They run multiple facilities and basically *own* Earth-Sol Lagrange Three."

"Well, that does answer one of our questions," Brad agreed. "Well done, Xan. Well done indeed.

"Now all we need is to capture some of these ships so we have some physical evidence to give the Agency. A corp that big, that rich? Falcone is going to need every scrap of ammo we can give her to bring them down."

He smiled.

"Fortunately, the Everlit has delivered us the opportunity to do just that."

———

They drifted closer, distances shrinking as the two flotillas approached each other and *Oath of Vengeance* continued to move stealthily behind the convoy. More details emerged on their targets as they got closer, confirming their long-range assessment as correct.

Three of the most modern destroyers and two of the most modern cruisers built in the star system, plus a fourth destroyer that was a specialized ship-killer. With the cruisers, the convoy alone outgunned any of the Jovian flotillas.

"That's strange," Bogdanov said slowly as he studied the data on the destroyers.

"Those are dangerous words right now, Commander," Brad pointed out. "What's strange?"

"The destroyers are colder than they should be," the tactical officer said. "Fusion plants are on minimum; life support has to be shut down."

"They're rigged for tow," Michelle replied. "That would be the status we'd expect."

"Yeah…but they're too cold."

A chill ran down Brad's spine as he pulled the data to the repeater screens.

"It takes time for a ship to cool down," Bogdanov continued. "Even with heat sinks and radiators running, ships only cool so quickly. Those weren't shut down in the last few hours as they rigged for tow."

"They've been shut down for at least twelve hours," Brad concluded aloud. "And *uninhabitable* for at least six. Where did the crews go?"

He was already running the numbers.

A cruiser could run with a passage crew of about fifty, ten percent of its full complement. A destroyer needed a larger percentage, fifteen to twenty crew versus a regular crew of sixty to eighty.

Four destroyers' passage crew was probably eighty people. Maybe a hundred.

"What about the cruisers?" he snapped. An extra hundred people would take one of the cruisers from "passage crew" to "skeleton crew" —and the distinction between those two was that a skeleton crew could *fight* the ship.

"They're both live…no, *fuck*."

"They're too hot," Brad agreed. "They're not just live; they're at *battle stations*." He spun in his seat.

"Xan! Emergency transmission to the flotilla—*it's a trap*."

It was too late. With the time delay, the TMF crews had acted as he was speaking.

The closer *Tremendous*-class cruiser rolled to present an entire broadside of her turrets. Four of her eight immense weapons plat-forms, each a match for *Bound by Law*'s dorsal or ventral turrets, trained on Brad's people with deadly precision—and fired.

Even the fifteen-centimeter guns only fired their projectiles so quickly. The three mercenary ships and their stolen carrier had enough time to begin to maneuver—but their base velocities were already low.

Massive slugs, each with the power of a kiloton-range nuclear warhead, hammered home on Brad's ships. Reactive armor lit up, explosions driving the slugs away…but Brad's corvettes had already lost much of their armor.

They'd expected more warning, and Brad watched in silent horror as *Alan-a-dale* and *Heart of Vengeance* ceased to exist in glittering balls of fire and debris.

CHAPTER THIRTY-THREE

"Broadband transmission from Captain Noah," Xan said quietly into the silence. She didn't even ask before playing it.

"I'm insulted, Michaels," Noah said flatly. "Even if your bosses *hadn't* told us *Longbow* had been destroyed, even a blind man can tell an *Invictus* from a *Bard* or a *Fidelis* at twenty thousand kilometers.

"Everyone will be happier if we reclaim *Longbow*, though, so I give you this one chance to surrender."

The transmission cut off.

"*Longbow* is firing!" Bogdanov snapped. "I have torpedoes and gatling rounds in space. She's taken hits, but she's still in the fight."

"Andre?" Brad asked.

"*Bound by Law* is maneuvering and…*Everdark!*"

Captain Noah wasn't going to be sending any more surrender demands. Whether his flagship was *Belisarius* or *Cataphract* was irrele-vant, as Brenda Andre's ship fired both of her turrets into the ship.

The *Lancer*s were well defended against torpedoes, but nothing could stop a fifteen-centimeter mass driver. The same crushing force that had battered the Vikings hammered into Noah's flagship—and Andre wasn't planning to ask for surrenders. Three full salvos of heavy rounds struck home, accompanied by a spray of smaller projectiles from *Law*'s secondary guns.

The secondary guns were wasted ammunition. The *Lancer*'s reactive armor was an older, less capable model. *Bound by Law* had survived direct hits from two of the cruiser's guns, barely. Captain Noah's ship simply disintegrated—and Andre turned her fire to the other escort destroyer.

Meanwhile, *Longbow*'s torpedoes and drones flashed toward the cruisers. Both of the *Tremendouses* were moving now, and a chill ran down Brad's spine.

The convoy had only had enough crew to man one of those ships. Everdark, they only had enough crew to man half of the turrets on one of the ships…but they clearly also had the torpedoes running, at least in automatic mode for one shot as thirty-six weapons blasted free.

"Where's the transport?" Brad asked quietly.

"What do you mean?" Bogdanov demanded. "We have to interv—"

"Either Michaels can disable two half-manned cruisers with *Longbow*…or *Oath*'s intervention won't change anything," Brad said harshly, hating his own words. "We need to complete the Everlit mission."

His tac officer swallowed and checked his data.

"The transport is burning hard for the Inner System," he reported. "She's well out of everyone's range that she knows of, with the cruisers between her and our people."

"But not out of our range," Brad noted.

"No, sir."

"Saburo, prepare to launch the assault shuttles," Brad ordered. "Michelle, I want us to go after the transport for long enough to match velocities for the shuttle launch. Bogdanov—that transport is armed. Cripple the gatlings before we launch the shuttles.

"Then—and *only* then—can we go after the cruisers."

And pray that he still had friends left by then.

———

For a few seconds, it looked like the cruiser crews had made a mistake. *Longbow*'s handful of torpedoes traveled most of the distance to their target unopposed, and none of the *Tremendouse*s' secondary guns were firing at all.

Then the torpedoes flashed into terminal mode at a thousand kilometers...and disappeared as a net of laser fire swept out from their target.

"Wait, they have *lasers*?" Michelle asked. "I thought the focusing issues meant no one was using them as long-range weapons."

"They're not," Brad said, studying the data. "They can get a useful focus at a thousand klicks, so they're using it as an anti-torpedo system. *Longbow* isn't going to get birds through."

"Well, they might if Michaels does that," Bogdanov noted, gesturing to the screen where the drones were adjusting course. Instead of sending fifteen of them at each ship, they were now all charging the ship that had killed Brad's corvettes.

And they launched as one, thirty torpedoes unleashing into space even as their mass drivers started to target the torpedoes swarming toward *Longbow*.

It still wasn't an even fight, though the lack of secondary guns and follow-up torpedo salvos from the cruiser was helping level the playing field.

"Heat sinks or not, everyone is going to pick us up in about sixty seconds," Michelle announced. "Are we ready to disable the transport?"

"Standing by for your call," Bogdanov confirmed, tearing his attention away from the battle occurring behind them. "I should be able to do it in sixty seconds...but the closer we can get, the better."

"And the longer we wait to intervene in the main fight, the less likely we are to have friends left," Brad snapped. "As soon as we drop stealth, disable the transport and launch Saburo's shuttles."

The second *Lancer* blew apart as he looked back to the main battle, but it didn't go alone. The destroyer had cut through the Javelin drones from *Longbow*, wiping out over a third of the robotic ships.

It came too close to *Bound by Law* in doing so, and Captain Andre exacted a terminal price from the destroyer. The numbers were now even, but a carrier and a destroyer versus two cruisers wasn't a fair fight at all.

"Dropping stealth…*now!*" Michelle barked as she twisted *Oath* into a parallel course with the TMF transport. They were only aligned for a few seconds, but it was enough.

Oath's gatling mass drivers fired carefully, neatly targeted bursts that walked their way along the length of the fleeing transports. The ship's engines flickered and died as Bogdanov's fire shattered their thruster nozzles, and the transport's six defensive mass drivers didn't even start warming up before they died.

"Go! Go! Go!" Michelle chanted as *Oath*'s three assault shuttles broke free. Five seconds passed. Ten. Fifteen.

And then the parasite craft were far enough away to clear the safety radius, and *Oath of Vengeance* flipped in space and brought her drives up to maximum.

Brad's ship had been born for battle with the Cadre—and that battle was waiting.

That battle wasn't going well. *Bound by Law* was exchanging fire with the second cruiser, and even though the destroyer's continued survival was a sign of how undermanned the other ship was, it wasn't a battle she was winning.

Longbow's drones were spent, their torpedoes dying as helplessly against the cruiser's automated defenses as their motherships, and as *Oath* turned back toward the battle, Brad watched as the drones flung themselves suicidally into the stolen warship.

The lasers tried, but the drones were big enough that they made it through—and Michaels had clearly aimed his suicidal robotic friends carefully. Half of the cruiser's engines and three of the four turrets currently facing *Longbow* shattered under the impacts, clearing a path for…what?

"What is he *doing*?" Bogdanov asked. "I have multiple parasites breaking clear of *Longbow*. Shuttles? Life pods?"

Brad's own systems projected *Longbow*'s new course as the ex-

Cadre ship brought her engines back up to full, giving the same answer Bogdanov had just reached. *Longbow* was on a ramming course—and the engine damage meant there was no way the *Tremendous* could avoid her.

From the spray of mass-driver fire, torpedoes, and laser fire, however, her crew was hoping they could kill her.

"Incoming from *Longbow*," Xan reported. Michaels's face appeared on Brad's screen, and the ex-Cadre officer looked…drained.

Smoke filled the bridge, but Brad could still see that the redheaded man was alone.

"Life support is fucked," he said calmly. "Weapons are fucked. Armor is fucked. I've got engines and navigation, and you guys can't kill two cruisers, however shittily manned."

Michaels shook his head and coughed against the smoke, a timer over his shoulder counting down seconds.

"Tell Falcone I'm sorry," he continued. "I never did warn her that I had the ability to drop the bridge crew into escape pods from my command seat. She'll live." He paused, coughing again.

Brad wasn't sure if the tears on his face were from the smoke or from what the man had decided to do.

"Tell my wife…tell her I'm so—"

The transmission cut out.

"Direct hit on *Longbow*'s com center," Bogdanov reported quietly. "Probably took out the bridge, too." The tac officer shook his head.

"He's gone, sir."

"No, he's not," Brad murmured. "Not really…not until…"

Longbow slammed into the stolen cruiser. Even if they *had* killed Michaels, it hadn't been soon enough to save them—and moments after the impact, the nuclear warheads he'd warned Brad rested in the carrier's magazines detonated.

"Bogdanov, full dazzler salvo on the other cruiser," Brad snapped. "Clear the path for Andre's guns!"

One cruiser against two destroyers was still a winning combination for the Cadre, but the cruiser was badly undermanned. The chaff torpedoes were easily handled by a fully functional cruiser…but the *Tremendous* they were fighting wasn't fully functional.

The dazzlers detonated, throwing the entire defensive fire out of alignment as *Oath* dove into her own gatling range and *Bound by Law* targeted the cruiser's turrets with her own mass drivers.

"She's ceased fire," Michelle reported softly. "Most of her turrets are gone. Brad…what do we do?"

"Transmit a surrender order," he told them. "Get Andre on the line. We'll need Major Doary's people to take—"

The cruiser detonated. They hadn't hit her that hard. Brad closed his eyes.

"That's what I think it was, isn't it?"

"Fusion core overload," Bogdanov agreed, his voice slightly sick. "Unless I'm badly mistaken…initiated by remote. Someone just blew those people up to make sure they didn't surrender."

A horrified thought hit Brad as he studied the dispersing wreckage of the cruiser.

"Is the transport still with us?" he demanded.

Bogdanov checked.

"Yes," he confirmed. "They're dead in the water, but they're still with us."

"I want those last jammers of Falcone's on her *now*," Brad snapped. "Nobody is sending a message to that ship until *I* say so; are we clear?"

The destroyer trembled as the refitted torpedoes launched into space a few moments later, and he surveyed the battlefield and swallowed hard. He wished he'd thought to send the jammers sooner, but he hadn't been expecting anyone to be bouncing around suicide signals.

He should have known better. The Cadre was far too willing to sacrifice patsies and even commit suicide themselves for them to truly be "merely" pirates.

"Then let's coordinate search-and-rescue with Andre," he said quietly. "It's time to see just what this mess cost."

CHAPTER THIRTY-FOUR

Seven ships floated in deep space, shuttles circling around them as they picked up the escape pods and survivors.

Somehow, Brad was unsurprised that there were no survivors from the two cruisers. If there was one glaring sign that the Cadre was not what it pretended to be, it was the repeated willingness to fight to the death on the part of what he would have thought were ordinary pirates.

Escape pods had managed to launch clear of the two *Lancer*s. They weren't his people's priority, but they were there, and his people were keeping a careful eye on them to make sure they didn't lose anyone who'd made it this far.

The first priority was the wreckage of the corvettes and the pods from *Longbow*. Brad was waiting in the bay as the shuttle delivered the pod from the carrier's bridge. He was, quite correctly as it turned out, expecting Kate Falcone to be spitting nails.

"That fucking bastard," she snapped. "The whole trip, he's sitting there with a button that could launch me into space, just *smiling at me*. Where is he?"

"He's gone," Brad said quietly. "He rammed *Longbow* into one of the cruisers and detonated the nukes in her magazines. Which"—he sighed—"means we almost certainly have a Fleet patrol headed our way already.

"I plan on staying right here and waiting for them," he continued. "That'll give us time to make sure we don't miss anyone."

"The corvettes?" Falcone asked after swallowing an angry breath.

Brad shook his head.

"We're still looking, but our only chance is loose dutchmen," he admitted. "There were no pods launched, nothing. There wasn't enough warning."

"Any survivors from the cruisers?"

"None. I don't think Michaels's target expected him to detonate twenty-four nuclear bombs in their face…and the other was self-destructed by a remote instruction."

The Agent hissed.

"From where?"

"We don't know," Brad said. "I'm guessing the TMF transport…but I don't know."

"And the transport?"

He shook his head.

"They're crippled and jammed," he told her. "Saburo is aboard, but they're refusing to surrender. Last I heard, he'd killed the helium feeds to stop them blowing themselves up with the fusion core and was about to storm Engineering."

A task that would come with yet another price tag to add to this already expensive day. Jason was gone. Shelly was gone. Jace was gone. What a mess this all was.

"This better be worth it, Kate," Brad continued. "I lost too many people—too many *friends* today."

"You took the convoy intact?"

"Four destroyers, as much use as they'll be to anyone," he told her. "The transport…well, I suspect they've already blown their computers."

"We'll break all five of them down, find *everything*," she promised him. "Plus what we learned from *Longbow* and Michaels, I should have a case against Transplanetary. They're going to regret this Everdark-ened game they chose to play."

"I hope so."

"I know it doesn't help, but the Agency will pay you handsomely for this op," Falcone told him. "If I can swing it, you'll get the ships once we're done with them—or equivalents."

"*Warriors* aren't cleared for non-Fleet use, even for the Guild."

"Yes, but you're a Fleet reserve officer," she said. "And believe me when I say the Agency will make that enough."

"Sir!" another voice barked, and Brad looked up to see Jim Shoulter, *Oath*'s assistant engineer, waving at him. The younger man was helping coordinate the search-and-rescue effort; what did he need Brad for?

"We got a dutchman!" Shoulter told him. "Vectoring a shuttle in now, but we've got at least one dutchman off *Heart of Vengeance*!"

———

Brad didn't leave the shuttle bay. Falcone escorted her no-longer-quite-prisoners to new quarters aboard *Oath*, but the Commodore was going to be waiting in the bay until everything was done, one way or another.

"Boss, it's Saburo," his Colonel's voice echoed in his ear. "We…now control *Anchorage Dream*. Prisoners are…still being counted, but we've got more wounded than upright."

"What's your status?" Brad asked.

"Well, *I've* been shot," Saburo said dryly. "Fortunately, we have some very nice painkillers. We seized Engineering and evacuated the oxygen from the remaining holdouts."

Brad could *hear* the ground trooper's wince.

"I…figured more of them would have made it to vac-suits," he concluded quietly. "We've got a lot of cases of hypoxia. We're triaging as fast as we can, but we're going to lose some of the prisoners."

"Damn. That's not your fault, Colonel," Brad told Saburo. "You had a job to do. You did it. Our people?"

"Eight more dead, same wounded, including me." Saburo exhaled. "I could use Doary's people. Extra hands for triage and emergency first aid won't go amiss."

"The shuttles are currently doing search-and-rescue," Brad admitted. "How badly do you need them?"

"Not...that badly," the other man admitted. "We..." He sighed. "We're going to lose the ones in real bad shape in the next twenty minutes anyway. What about our people?"

"*Alan-a-dale* is a complete loss," Brad said levelly. "*Heart*... We may have a couple of survivors. No promises. *Law* lost about the same as you did in dead and wounded."

He shook his head.

"Lotta funerals and medical bills coming up."

There was silence on the channel.

"Was it worth it?" Saburo asked finally.

"Ask me after the funerals," Brad told him. "But...we stopped the Cadre tripling their cruiser strength. That's worth...something."

"Something," his subordinate echoed. "Yeah, that's something." He paused again. "Kyoko didn't make it. Took a burst of rifle fire when we stormed Engineering. I'm going to need some new lieutenants."

"We're going to need a lot of new people," Brad agreed. "We'll talk to the Guild when we get home. I think the Vikings need one *hell* of a vacation."

"You can say that again," Saburo replied.

Before Brad could say anything more, a shuttle tore through the bay doors at what had to be nearly double the recommended safe velocity. Engines flared to halt the small craft with *far* too much power—but carefully aimed so only hull metal got slagged as the shuttle ground to a halt and the ramp slammed down.

"I've got three dutchmen here," the medic barked as she pulled a wheeled stretcher out of the shuttlecraft. "I need hands, people; every second counts!"

———

Jason Finley died on the operating table. Luck had brought him through the destruction of his ship and back aboard the shuttle, but he'd taken shrapnel as *Heart of Vengeance* came apart around him.

The other two survivors from *Heart*'s bridge had been on reduced oxygen as their suits tried to draw out their survival time, but he'd been short on O_2 and bleeding out. It was a miracle he'd survived to pickup.

Heart's tactical officer, Erasmo Poulos, was luckier. He'd live. He'd need a new leg, but the piece of superheated metal that had sheared off his left leg above the knee had cauterized the wound and melted his vac-suit to his skin.

Shelly Weldon, Jason's wife, was uninjured. Physically, at least, but Brad was watching her carefully as the medics brought her back to consciousness. She gasped hard and sat bolt upright—only for him to clamp his hand on her shoulder.

"You're on *Oath*," he told her. "You're alive. You're okay."

Shelly breathed rapidly for several seconds, hitting the edge of hyperventilation before slowly calming down as Michelle stepped up to hold her other shoulder.

"Jason?" she asked softly.

"He took shrapnel as the ship came apart," Brad told her as gently as he could. "He…didn't make it."

Shelly closed her eyes.

"*Fuck*. Why? Why him? Why us?"

He squeezed her shoulder.

"Because we screwed up and assumed that because the man we knew was kept in the dark didn't know of a coms channel, there wasn't one," he said quietly. "Because *I* screwed up, Shelly. I'm sorry."

"Bullshit," Michelle snapped. "This was the job, Shelly. You knew that. Jason knew that. It was the risk—the ships we stopped making it to the Cadre today would have been responsible for hundreds of deaths. Thousands. Jason knew the risks."

It was funny, Brad reflected. His wife had been the least okay with what they did for a living at one point, but now she was the one pulling the two long-term mercenaries back from the brink.

Brad sat there in silence with Shelly and Michelle for at least a minute, expecting Shelly to break down in tears. Instead, she eventually swallowed and looked up to face him with a forced brave face.

"What happens now?" she asked.

"We go home," Brad told her. "You rest. Everything's in hand."

Which was true enough, as it went. Everything was as in-hand as it was going to get for quite some time.

CHAPTER THIRTY-FIVE

"Well, either we are about to get utterly screwed…or that's Task Group *Tremendous* heading our way," Bogdanov told Brad as their sensors picked up the incoming Fleet units. "*Tremendous* herself is the only one of those cruisers Fleet has in commission."

The sensors were picking up what looked like a standard cruiser task group—a single cruiser, three destroyers, and five corvettes. There were fifteen of those task groups patrolling around the star system, occupying just under half of the Fleet's cruisers.

And Brad's tactical officer was correct. The lead ship of the group was definitely a *Tremendous*-class cruiser, which meant that either it was TG *Tremendous* on its way to them or the Cadre had a *third* cruiser they weren't supposed to.

Forty-eight hours earlier, he would have assumed that it was Fleet arriving to investigate the aftermath of multiple nuclear detonations. Now, however, he wasn't so certain.

"Well, let's hope it's *Tremendous*," Brad finally said aloud. "Because if that's a *Cadre* task group, we can't fight it."

Oath of Vengeance might be undamaged, but she was outmatched by the cruiser. The destroyers could be of any of a half-dozen classes, most of which *Oath* could take one-on-one, but three of them could take her.

Bound by Law was…intact. Both of her turrets were even online, though having seen Captain Andre's damage reports, Brad wasn't entirely sure *how*.

"Xan, get me a channel," he instructed his com officer. "Let's see what we're dealing with."

"You're on, boss."

"Fleet cruiser group, this is Commodore Brad Madrid of the Vikings company of the Mercenary Guild, aboard the destroyer *Oath of Vengeance*," he said calmly. "We have been engaged in counter-Cadre operations under contract to the Commonwealth Investigative Agency. I presume you are investigating the nuclear detonations that occurred roughly twenty-six hours ago?

"We can provide the sensor readings from our surviving ships, but I assure you, we did not fire those weapons ourselves," Brad continued. He forced a pained smile. "I know my history, officers, but it really wasn't me this time."

A few seconds' wait passed, and then the channel linked up and the image of a broad-shouldered heavyset woman with piercing green eyes and black hair appeared on his screens.

"Commodore Madrid," she said slowly, as if the words were dirty. "I am Commodore Iris Nuremberg. I am investigating a series of nuclear explosions, yes, but I am *also* investigating an emergency pulse from the Transplanetary Macro Fabrications transport *Anchorage Dream*. Captain Marley's pulse stated they were under attack by ships transmitting Guild IFFs…and my scanner crews report that you appear to have *Anchorage Dream* under tow.

"My current evidence, *Commodore*, suggests that you are guilty of a pirate attack on an Earth-registry freighter. You will stand down your ships and prepare to be boarded while *my* people work out the details of what happened here!"

Brad could argue with the woman. He could give in to her demands. He had half a dozen ways to sort this mess out, but he didn't have the time or patience for her Everdarkened hydroponics fertilizer.

"Commodore, shut up," he said quietly. "I am overriding your orders. Your group will move into escort formation around the captured convoy and stand by for transfer of prisoners and Commonwealth Agent Kate Falcone. Once complete, you will take the TMF ships under escort to Jupiter under Agent Falcone's command.

"Authentication for my authority is Kappa Lambda Victory Niner Niner Seven Three Capital Lambda. I can connect you to Agent Falcone for additional authentication if you wish."

He'd never heard the bridges of two connected starships be *quite* so silent before. Nuremberg, to her credit, rotated a screen on her command chair and typed in the code.

"That is a valid code," she said slowly, "but one that requires a secondary authenticate. Commodore?"

"Secondary authenticate is 'Angel rising,'" Brad told her. "Do you confirm?"

"I confirm," she said. "Your 'orders' *are* outside your authority, you know," she pointed out.

Brad snorted. That was arguable. He'd just given her a Commonwealth Intelligence Agency authentication code that her system would tell her meant "provide all possible assistance."

"Consider them suggestions, then, Commodore," he said quietly. "But trust me when I say that *Anchorage Dream* is far from innocent. If you doubt me, scan the debris fields. We were just forced to destroy two *Tremendous*-class cruisers to prevent them being turned over to the Cadre."

Nuremberg studied him for a long moment.

"*Tremendous* is the only ship of her class in commission," she pointed out. "*Awestruck* is currently undergoing space trials. There aren't two other *Tremendous*-class ships in the star system."

"How classified is your anti-torpedo laser system?" Brad asked.

She winced.

"Your authentication is valid," she admitted. "I think I need to see that scan data, though, if you don't mind, Commodore. Once I have, may I impose on you and Agent Falcone for a videoconference?

"It seems that I have some work to do…and I'd like to make sure I don't get yanked up short by override codes again, if you don't mind."

———

By the time *Tremendous* and her escorts reached the collection of mercenary ships and their captives, it was clear that Commodore Nuremberg had made up her mind. The big cruiser positioned herself above and to the side of *Anchorage Dream*, neatly putting the transport under her guns while not impeding *Oath* or *Law*'s line of fire.

"You know, you could have just sent her the data," Falcone noted as she lounged in one of the chairs in his office. "Between that and my own authority, we would have avoided trouble."

"How quickly, Kate?" Brad asked, exchanging a look with Michelle who occupied the other chair. "Neither of our ships is ready to fight, even if we were anything resembling a match for Nuremberg's task group. *Anchorage Dream* pulled all the right levers to make her suspicious when she showed up; yanking our levers in turn was the only option we had."

Falcone made a throwaway gesture.

"You're not wrong," she admitted. "But even most of *your* bridge crew didn't know you were an Agent until today. And now Nuremberg and her staff know too."

"So, keep an eye on them. That's what the Agency is for, isn't it?" Brad asked. "My patience for games is pretty shot right now. There's too many bodies in my morgue for that, and too many empty coffins we're going to be mourning to go with them."

"I know," she allowed. "We'll watch the Commodore and her people. She *shouldn't* be in command of that task group if she isn't clean, but..."

"But we just discovered that one of Fleet's biggest suppliers is dirty," Michelle noted. "That suggests there's more games playing than we know of."

"And there aren't *supposed* to be games that the Agency doesn't know of," Falcone agreed. "Is our new friend calling in?"

"Xan should be setting up a conference as we speak," Brad confirmed. "Our new friend is your ride, after all."

"Do I get a say in this?" the Agent asked.

"Only if you want to go straight back to Io," Brad told her. "We finished the job, Kate. From here...we're going right home while I still have people *left*."

A chime announced that Xan had connected Nuremberg to them, and they left it there as Brad brought Nuremberg's image up on his screen.

She was in her own office now, the camera drawn back far enough to show that someone had spent a great deal of effort trying to hide the Commodore's bulk by modifying the standard Fleet uniform.

They'd *failed*, but they'd tried. Sitting down did her no favors, but Brad wasn't enough of a fool to let her weight distract him from the deadly-sharp focus in her eyes.

"I would very much like to have a long conversation with Captain Marley in a dark room," Nuremberg told them. "Unfortunately, from what your people said, an innocent-seeming Transplanetary freighter captain had a poison tooth and suicided when you took his ship."

She shook her head.

"Even looking at your data, I find it all hard to believe." She held up a hand. "I *do* believe it, to be clear; it's just terrifying. TMF just nearly delivered enough firepower to take out my entire task group to the Cadre…and we apparently *missed* them building it."

"That's on the Agency," Falcone admitted.

"Bullshit," Nuremberg told her. "The Agency is supposed to be watching our enemies, not our suppliers. That's on Fleet and Commonwealth Internal Audit. And between us, I think we can make damn sure that the IA teams who should have found this get checked out."

"I'm glad to hear you're on our side," Falcone replied. "We had some concerns when you first showed up."

"Marley set me up," she said grimly. "What pisses me off is that I *knew* Donald Marley. His daughter was dating my son. He knew I'd trust him. If you *hadn't* had an authentication code I couldn't argue with, I'd have come in looking for blood.

"And the man was Cadre. *Fuck*."

"That's the problem with all of this," Falcone told her. "We don't know who we can trust anymore. People who should be above question are neck-deep in the muck. What data we have suggests the Cadre now has a third of the strength of the entire Commonwealth Fleet—that didn't come from nowhere, and it sure as hell hasn't been built in just the last eighteen months since the Terror got shortened by a head."

"You need to go back to Earth," Brad told Falcone quietly. "Take the ships, the transport, the data…everything. Get back to your offices on Luna and point the Agency at this whole mess. Safest way for you to do that is aboard *Tremendous*."

"We can haul that whole convoy, yeah," Nuremberg agreed. "This whole mess is out of my scope; I'll admit that. I'm no innocent—you don't get the fanciest cruiser in the Fleet as your flagship without kissing ass—but this kind of twisted mess…"

She shook her head.

"I'm a soldier. Give me an enemy, I'll kick their head in…but reading between the lines of what you're saying, that's exactly what someone *wants* us to do."

Brad sighed.

"And that's why we need Falcone on Earth," he told the women. "Someone with all of the data and the authority to start turning over rocks. That's her. It sure as Everdark isn't me. I have ships to repair, friends to bury, and a mercenary company to rebuild from the wreck this op left it in."

"You're right," Falcone admitted. "Got room for supercargo and a few confiscated spaceships, Commodore?"

"Anywhere you need us to take you, Agent," she said. "We'll make it happen."

"Soon," Brad told them. "We've all got places to be now."

"I won't forget what I said, Brad," Falcone told him. "When we're done with these ships, you get them. I don't care what levers we've got to pull. You've earned them."

He shook his head.

"Won't turn them down. I just can't say I like the price, either."

CHAPTER THIRTY-SIX

"PRESENT ARMS!"

Saburo's bellow echoed across *Oath of Vengeance*'s shuttle bay. Fifteen men and women, the survivors of the destroyer's landing contingent, presented their carbines in salute over the rows and rows of plain black coffins and the accompanying boxes of personal effects.

"Company, salute!"

The rest of the destroyer's company stepped up, hands snapping into crisp salutes as they walked by their friends.

Brad himself stood stonily at one end of the bay, watching his people shuffle by the plain boxes that contained the last remains of their colleagues. All of the personal-effects boxes were full, but only about two-thirds of the coffins actually contained bodies.

Mercenaries didn't wrap their dead in flags or patriotism. Each coffin simply had a name and the armored Viking of the company logo carved into the top. Tradition said that the empty coffin would be delivered to the families, same as the full ones.

It gave them something to bury of the family member who'd died for money.

The Vikings might have bled for honor and freedom this time, but their traditions were the traditions of a profession that fought for money. Two ships, gone with almost all of their crews. When the dust settled, Brad had lost over a third of his ground troops, as well.

Those weren't casualties that a mercenary company could walk away from without impact. He'd already put the entire company on furlough, bringing in trusted people from Saburo's father's shipyard and the Mercenary Guild itself to take care of the ships while his people rested.

This was the last duty they all had, and they fulfilled it willingly. Each coffin was picked up by a set of four, always people who'd known and been friends with the occupant, and carried out of the bay onto the space station.

One by one. Again and again.

And Brad stood by, watching stiffly. Michelle was next to him, but she knew better than to say anything. No one spoke at all.

This was a moment for silence and remembrance.

———

"L'chaim!" Michelle barked, slamming back the shot of whisky as the Vikings' officers gathered. The bar was a long way from their ships, but everyone was here. Even Shelly Weldon, looking just as shattered and exhausted as ever.

"To absent friends," Saburo replied with his own toast. "To the ones who never make it home."

Brad drank in silence, watching his wife half-sneak up on Shelly to wrap her old friend in an embrace. He wasn't sure if it was the timing or the alcohol, but it was…enough. For the first time since he'd told her Jason hadn't made it, Shelly finally broke, collapsing into Michelle's shoulder with heaving sobs.

A pile of money had made sure they had the bar to themselves. The rest of the officers gave the two women space, and Saburo stepped up to join Brad in studying the rest.

"You doing okay, boss?" he asked.

"Better than the friends we've buried," he replied. "But no. Not really."

"You know it wasn't your fault, right?" Saburo asked. "This is on the Cadre."

"It's all on the bloody Cadre. Everyone I've watched die in the last few years," Brad snapped. "Sooner or later, there has to be an end to it —but I swear, every time I turn around, they're just stronger."

"What was that old myth? The beast where you cut off one head and three more grew to take its place?"

"The hydra," Saburo replied. "You had to burn off the stumps, I think?" He shrugged. "Or that might have been the D&D rules. I'll admit, I never read the original myth."

Brad shook his head and stepped over to a "window" that was actually a screen showing the outside of the station. Io filled the bottom third of the screen, and Jupiter blocked most of the rest.

"What an Everdarkened mess," he whispered.

"You said to ask you if it was worth it after the funerals," Saburo reminded him. "We've buried those without families and sent the rest home. Was it worth it?"

Brad snorted.

"The check cleared. That's enough for a damn warship all on its own. And I got confirmation yesterday—Fleet is honoring Falcone's promise. I'm not sure we're getting the *exact* ships we captured, but there's a *Bound* and three *Warriors* on their way to Io under my name."

Saburo whistled silently.

"That's a pretty nice payday, but it doesn't answer my question," he pointed out. "Was it worth it?"

"No," Brad said very quietly. "It wasn't worth it. It wasn't worth it at all.

"It was just necessary."

"It's not over, though," Saburo replied, equally quietly.

"No. It's not. And we *will* finish it."

ABOUT THE AUTHORS

#1 Bestselling Military Science Fiction author **Terry Mixon** served as a non-commissioned officer in the United States Army 101st Airborne Division. He later worked alongside the flight controllers in the Mission Control Center at the NASA Johnson Space Center supporting the Space Shuttle, the International Space Station, and other human spaceflight projects.

He now writes full time while living in Texas with his lovely wife and a pounce of cats.

———

Glynn Stewart is the author of *Starship's Mage*, a bestselling science fiction and fantasy series where faster-than-light travel is possible–but only because of magic. His other works include science fiction series *Duchy of Terra*, *Castle Federation* and *Vigilante*, as well as the urban fantasy series *ONSET* and *Changeling Blood*.

Writing managed to liberate Glynn from a bleak future as an accountant. With his personality and hope for a high-tech future intact, he lives in Kitchener, Ontario with his partner, their cats, and an unstoppable writing habit.

OTHER BOOKS BY TERRY MIXON

You can always find the most up to date listing of Terry's titles on Amazon at
author.to/terrymixon

The Empire of Bones Saga

Empire of Bones

Veil of Shadows

Command Decisions

Ghosts of Empire

Paying the Price

Reconnaissance in Force

Behind Enemy Lines

The Terra Gambit

Hidden Enemies

Race to Terra

The Empire of Bones Saga Volume 1

The Humanity Unlimited Saga

Liberty Station

Freedom Express

Tree of Liberty

The Fractured Republic Saga

Storm Divers

The Scorched Earth Saga

Want Terry to email you when he publishes a new book in any format or when one goes on sale? Go to <u>TerryMixon.com/Mailing-List</u> and sign up. Those are the only times he'll contact you. No spam.

OTHER BOOKS BY GLYNN STEWART

For release announcements join the
mailing list or visit **GlynnStewart.com**

STARSHIP'S MAGE

Starship's Mage
Hand of Mars
Voice of Mars
Alien Arcana
Judgment of Mars
UnArcana Stars
Sword of Mars
Mountain of Mars
The Service of Mars
A Darker Magic
Mage-Commander (upcoming)

Starship's Mage: Red Falcon
Interstellar Mage
Mage-Provocateur
Agents of Mars

Pulsar Race: A Starship's Mage Universe Novella

DUCHY OF TERRA

The Terran Privateer
Duchess of Terra
Terra and Imperium
Darkness Beyond
Shield of Terra
Imperium Defiant
Relics of Eternity
Shadows of the Fall
Eyes of Tomorrow

SCATTERED STARS

Scattered Stars: Conviction
Conviction
Deception
Equilibrium
Fortitude (upcoming)

PEACEKEEPERS OF SOL

Raven's Peace
The Peacekeeper Initiative
Raven's Course
Drifter's Folly (upcoming)

EXILE

Exile
Refuge
Crusade
Ashen Stars: An Exile Novella

CASTLE FEDERATION

Space Carrier Avalon
Stellar Fox
Battle Group Avalon
Q-Ship Chameleon
Rimward Stars
Operation Medusa
A Question of Faith: A Castle Federation Novella

SCIENCE FICTION STAND ALONE NOVELLA

Excalibur Lost

VIGILANTE
(WITH TERRY MIXON)

Heart of Vengeance
Oath of Vengeance

**Bound By Stars: A Vigilante Series
(With Terry Mixon)**
Bound By Law
Bound by Honor
Bound by Blood

TEER AND KARD

Wardtown
Blood Ward

CHANGELING BLOOD

Changeling's Fealty
Hunter's Oath
Noble's Honor
Fae, Flames & Fedoras: A Changeling Blood Novella

ONSET

ONSET: To Serve and Protect
ONSET: My Enemy's Enemy
ONSET: Blood of the Innocent
ONSET: Stay of Execution
Murder by Magic: An ONSET Novella

FANTASY STAND ALONE NOVELS

Children of Prophecy
City in the Sky

www.ingramcontent.com/pod-product-compliance
Lightning Source LLC
Chambersburg PA
CBHW021304190726
48288CB00003B/687